OF COURSE I'M CRAZY
I JUST GOT BACK FROM
FIGHTING A WAR

MARY BARRETT

Of Course I'm Crazy I Just Got Back From Fighting A War

Cover illustration by Kathy Campbell
Cover Picture by Hector Cuyar

First Printed in the United States

Library of Congress Control Number: 2011912571

ISBN 978-0-615-51436-9

To God I give the glory

To Kate and her trip to a former war torn country and Kyle and his purple smelly soap.

You were both the inspiration for this endeavor.

With special thanks and gratitude to our men and women of the Armed Forces and to the staffs of medical facilities everywhere.

1500 hrs
MAY 14th

"How's that leg feeling, boy?"

"My leg's gone, Sir."

The Sergeant made a closer inspection.

"So it is, boy. So it is."

Continuing on through the hallway with men lined up on beds and in chairs against the wall, the Sergeant, with duffle slung over his shoulder, came closer to the two doors that led to the end of his existence as a cog in the military machine.

If he could only get past the guards.

The Sergeant's first thought was to grab the pretty nurse who was coming his way, but he had a strict moral code and the feeling that he'd attract the unwanted attention of the two guards at the door.

As he neared the pretty nurse who was holding a tray of medical paraphernalia, he fought the urge to kiss her, and instead, as their paths crossed, he quickly put his hand out and upset her tray.

The sharps went flying, landing on the soldiers who were lined up on beds and in chairs against the wall. The metal pan flew into the air and landed with a clang upon the ground.

The pretty nurse, though flustered, quickly rallied as she knew the men who were in her care were now in grave danger. She called out to the guards.

"Help me, before they hurt themselves!"

They immediately left their posts and came to her rescue.

One guard managed to save the life of a dozing private, who after having the needle fall into his lap, thinking it was part of a dream and totally unconcerned whether there was drugs in the needle, was about to shoot air into his bloodstream.

With the two guards and the pretty nurse concerned about the welfare of the soldiers, the Sergeant walked through the doors un-accosted, and after years of service, he was a free man.

***

It was hours later, long after the pretty nurse went off duty and could be found dancing with the two guards at the nearby Rustic Lodge, that the soldier patients were returned to their rooms and an inventory of beds was taken.

On the fourth floor, the male nurse, who had served in a former war which we will leave unnamed, while making rounds discovered the lack of a soldier patient in Bed No. 42.

Much to his credit, training, and years of experience with wayward patients, he chose not to become alarmed. His job in the psyche ward was a piece of cake as it was the only floor in the facility that came equipped with metal bars on all the windows and a main door that needed a key to get in and out of.

Knowing that copies of the aforesaid key were chained to the belts of qualified staff; the male nurse was unperturbed as he started a search for the patient who belonged in Bed No. 42.

Soldiers, especially those who had not been given desk duty but found themselves going into foreign lands which did not have the accoutrements of home, had no choice but to get over their acute shyness put into them by their potty training mothers with their antiseptic toilets.

Many of these soldiers, no, make that all soldiers in training found themselves reliving the nightmare of their youth in the guise of their rifle range teachers, who much like their mothers before, stood by their side which made them afraid of missing the mark.

Potty training mothers and rifle range teachers knew the same lingo and accompanied their training expertise with angry shouts to "aim straighter."

After spending months, and in some cases years, of hiding in jungles containing vegetation, some poisonous, or finding themselves surrounded by sand dunes in the desert, those in service to their country could make do with relieving themselves just about anywhere.

And it made no bit of difference to a particular breed of soldier, when they came back to civilization if they felt the urge they just sat by the side of their beds and let it go.

Even so, the male nurse chose to first search the bathrooms. Looking back at his own experience, he thought soldier patient Bed No. 42 could be a man who finding himself stateside would automatically recall the training of his youth and go back to using the facilities.

All in all the search of bathrooms took a mere five minutes with no positive results. It was then the male nurse decided the next plan of action was to do a double body bed check.

It was not unusual for some of the patients to get into the wrong bed as all rooms looked very much the same. As such it was a routine part of the job to take a bed inventory each night and part of this was locating patients with a notion to roam, which was a regular happening. Like a few years back when the male nurse was making rounds and found a patient bed to be empty.

This was way back when the male nurse worked the surgery ward. It wasn't long after starting the search that he found soldier patient from Bed No. 8 cuddling, and that's using the term lightly, with the soldier patient in Bed No. 10.

The male nurse being a lanky fellow who came from a small town somewhere in the Midwest, which we will leave unnamed, quickly identified what he was seeing. After all he may have been a small town boy, but there were plenty of stories passed around at the local bar to give him a thorough knowledge of what might be going on in Bed No. 10.

When he heard one of the cuddling men whisper "I love you, Maggie" he swiftly came to the conclusion that the actions of soldier patients Bed No. 8 and 10 were a case of mistaken identity and/or the results of post-surgery anesthetic wearing off.

He quickly separated the cuddling soldiers and took them to task for upsetting the morale of the just operated on patients who themselves were yearning to be back among the civilians and in the arms of the female sex.

To be sure this never happened again on his watch, the male nurse reported the evening's happenings to the doctor in charge and soldier patient Bed No. 8, by reason of the fact he was not found in his own bed but had wandered to another soldier's bed, was the next day dispatched to the psyche ward and Bed No. 50.

The male nurse did his utmost in the way of duty to find soldier patient Bed No. 42. Included was the bathroom check and the double bedding check, which he followed up with the under the bed check, the closet check and the behind the nurse's station check.

Two hours of searching, he thought the ordeal had finally ended while making the common room check.

The TV was on with the latest hot shot late night host making fun of whatever was happening in society at the moment, which if you were a purveyor of late night always went something like this - Guess what movie star left her husband for what movie star who left his wife?

Known for being fastidious in his job duties, the male nurse had bigger fish to fry than to pay attention to such trivia. Besides he'd catch it at home on the morning show as he was eating his dinner.

He came into the common room to see sitting against the slightly open window a wheelchair and in that wheelchair was for all appearances a soldier.

The soldier was smoking a cigar the size of Panama. This appendage that was the size of Panama was without question snuck in by a friend or relative who thought they were doing a good deed as it was not the hospital's policy to give cigars out in their non-smoking facility.

The breaker of facility rules was facing the window in order to let the smoke escape. The male nurse couldn't tell who was in the chair, not that he would have recognized soldier patient Bed No. 42, as he was a new patient who came in just hours after the male nurse left duty the morning before.

With great relief that his hunt was finally over and that he could still make his rendezvous in the employee break room with the single nurse who had been giving him the eye for some time, the male nurse charged across the room.

"I found you!"

He pulled the wheelchair around, Doctor Sorenson looked up at him.

"Patient missing?"

5

"No. No. I knew it was you, Doc. Just having a bit of fun."

Doctor Sorenson took a long drag on his cigar, "What's your name? Hold your badge closer."

The male nurse went right into job survival mode. He covered the nameplate on his chest and with an abrupt twist and turn shouted, "Did you hear that?"

"Hear what?" questioned the astute doctor.

"One of the men just fell out of bed. I'd better see to him."

"Yes, you'd better."

Doctor Sorenson turned the wheelchair back toward the window and continued on with his smoking.

It didn't take long for the male nurse to finish his search and come to the conclusion that soldier patient Bed No. 42 was no longer an inhabitant of the ward.

Now he had one of two choices where to go from here.

Choice No. One - let his co-workers know that soldier patient Bed No. 42 was missing.

This would set off another search of the floor, which in his eyes would be a major waste of time as he prided himself on his thoroughness. Then there would be the miscellaneous finger pointing and mudslinging that goes along with incidences of this nature.

The chain of command, doctors being first, would see to it that the nurses were taken to task. The nurses would see to it that the aides were taken to task. The aides would then take their misery out on the patients.

Being sympathetic to the men in his ward he would not make them the folly of soldier patient Bed No. 42 and his lack of long range thinking about what would take place if he were to leave the facility without permission.

By the time an overall search of the building was begun the morning shift would be clocking in. After more finger pointing and mudslinging, the evening shift would be forced to stay by the morning shift and they would not be able to go home until the patient was found.

This to the male nurse's thinking would be never. Even though the closest he had been to the frontline was a double feature at the Milago Theatre where they had afternoon back-to-back showings of the award winning comedy - Have You Seen My Platoon? - he knew without a doubt if he was a soldier just come back from war like soldier patient Bed No. 42, as soon as he had the chance he'd leave the facility for greener pastures.

Or

Choice No. Two - he could keep the knowledge of the missing soldier to himself and leave it to the morning staff to deal with.

With the night shift ending in less than an hour, he spent these minutes weighing the pros and cons. The deciding factor came to him when he remembered he had a crock pot with a stew made from his mother's family recipe waiting for him at home.

And taking into account he didn't want to miss the morning show to see which movie star left her husband for what movie star who left his wife, he let the whereabouts of soldier patient Bed No. 42 go.

***

With no guards chasing him, the Sergeant, soldier patient Bed No. 42, had walked calmly out of the facility straight into the emergency entrance parking lot.

Ambulance drivers were unloading the latest attendee, who would upon entering the facility be known as soldier patient Bed No. 65. The Sergeant seeing the soldier was awake wanted to do his best to assure the young man that he was in good hands.

To the surprise of the drivers he ripped off the sheets that were covering the soldier and inspected his wounds as closely as he would inspect a marbled piece of beef he was about to put on the barbeque.

Lowering the sheets again the Sergeant stood over the patient and asked, "Are you worried, boy?"

"No, Sir," the young soldier grimaced.

"You'll find the facility is a numero uno."

"Thank you, Sir. That's good to know."

"You're welcome, boy."

And with that the Sergeant turned to go. In a split second, he turned back.

"Just don't let none of those nurses handle your pecker, they all have the clap."

The soldier lifted his head and the drivers turned around to get a better look.

"Just kidding. Get going now, else you're gonna let that boy bleed out here in the parking lot."

"He's not bleeding," stated one driver.

"This day just keeps on getting better and better," replied the Sergeant.

They wheeled the young man inside. The escaping soldier walked away proud as punch as he had just fulfilled a secret pact he made with himself to make one person a day laugh at the absurdity of life. This was a life goal he set when being fired upon by the enemy as he was squatting in some of the poisonous vegetation spoken about earlier.

The Sergeant, before being waylaid with the concerns of the wounded soldier, had been in the process of making his first civilian decision after exiting the doors of the medical facility and that was which direction to take.

Across and beyond the parking lot was a wooded field. To the left was the Witchitauki Highway and to the right was the Rustic Lodge.

In need of a drink to quench a thirst that came upon him while flying onto the landing field midnight of the previous day, the Sergeant thought it important enough to get that out of the way before he made any more decisions. He proceeded to walk to the right of the facility with the Rustic Lodge as his destination.

Upon arrival at the medical facility the Sergeant had made it his business, as had become a habit that the army instilled in him, to be made aware of his surroundings.

He had spent the hours between 0300 and 0700 being poked and prodded. It wasn't until he was being x-rayed by a lone technician that he had the opportunity to ask about the local points of interest.

The x-ray technician knew his job, but little more. A young man of Indian heritage, he conversed about how he was married, and even with his broken English, the Sergeant understood this was a fellow that went straight home after work with no thought of ever delaying the process and thereby upsetting the better half.

Forced to find another constituent of the facility to give him the lowdown on the surrounding terra firma, he found what he needed in the server of his morning meal.

This was the attendant, Salvatore Krishnecki. Sally, as his friends called him, spilled the beans to the Sergeant that he was the guy who knew all and when asked would never admit to seeing anything.

With an outstanding knowledge of the surroundings, Sally gave the local logistics on the terrain and its occupants to the recently admitted patient.

According to Sally, the owner of the Rustic Lodge was Russ Longstrong. He himself was a patient at the medical facility many years before after a brief stint in the service where he suffered a wound to his lower extremities.

Russ was wounded in a foreign country, we will leave unnamed, and transferred back to the states after first making the propriety pit stop. And even though the medical doctors in Germany performed the seven operations necessary, the wounded soldier felt slighted as the American nurses were mostly married to soldiers stationed in Germany and they were actually too busy doing their jobs to see that a man got the right amount of flirting time justified by his wounds.

Further frustration was felt by Russ as the German nurses had consisted mainly of the male sex. That didn't sit well with his hopes for solace against the nestling breasts of female nurses that he envisioned as he lay in an open field, shot up and delirious.

Returning to the good old US of A, seeing the sweet, concerned, unmarried nurses with their wide-eyed looks of pity took Russ' breath away. That he felt, and that alone, had given him the will to live.

Unable to continue his duties, as his lower extremities would take some time to heal, Russ was released with an honorable discharge. A senior officer looked into Russ receiving the Purple Heart, but upon investigation, the details of which we won't get into here, he decided it was best not to push the issue.

Wishing to stay close to the restorers of life, and as he was dating one Heidi Swenson, a newly recruited surgical nurse, Russ went to see his aging grandfather, a member of the First Battalion during World War I.

When Grandfather Longstrong was a little boy his mother was told by a reader of tarot cards that the Longstrong clan came from Viking stock, which explained the high content of iron in their blood that had baffled their family physician for years.

The former soldier, who wanted to be an entrepreneur, referred to the family curse that went back to the time of the Vikings as he spoke to the old man, emphasizing he could live another twenty years. At the time of this meeting his grandfather was six months from his ninety-third birthday. Russ used every tactic he could think of to get the hierarchal

10

member of the Longstrong clan to part with his money before he died.

It wasn't until he reminded the old man that there was no drinking in heaven, and that he should take advantage of his time here on earth by investing heavily in his idea, that the senior Longstrong saw the benefits of not waiting till he was dead to make his grandson happy.

Drawing up a written contract, signed and notarized by both parties, the patriarch of the Longstrong family released the inheritance with the promise that he'd be the first customer and have a table in the back that was wheelchair accessible for his exclusive use.

Russ bought the land next to the medical facility and put together a work crew of his soldier buddies, all men of considerable talent who found themselves unemployable due to their various drug and alcohol addictions. Together they built the Rustic Lodge.

It was those same men who stayed on and served Russ in the way of waiters, bartenders, bouncers and cleaners of toilets among other duties.

They were a happy crew who made it their business to give something back and that was in the form of showing the staff of the medical facility a place to let off a little steam.

Louie Dombrowski, Jr. was the first of Russ' friends the Sergeant would make the acquaintance of. He stood guard at the Rustic Lodge entrance smoking his RYO cigarettes, a habit he picked up from his daddy who was a World War II veteran.

The senior Dombrowski enjoyed the pleasure he got out of each and every hand-rolled cigarette as they always brought back the memory of him and his buddies and the moments under fire that bonded them.

Louie, Sr. had lived through the big one, but in the end it was the cigarettes that got him.

"Whatcha got in that duffle, soldier?" Louie Jr. asked between puffs.

"Dirty underwear. Are those RYO's you're smoking?"

"Yeah."

"My daddy was a roll-your-own man in the big one."

Louie's left eyebrow cocked higher than his right. He walked around the Sergeant giving him the once over.

"Is your daddy still alive?"

"Yup, got half a lung but he's holding on."

Impressed, Louie opened the door for the Sergeant and after he walked through, the chain-smoking ex-soldier closed the door, stamped out his cigarette and lit up another.

***

There were only two businesses in the whole of Buckerston County, the medical facility and the Rustic Lodge. Other than the town hall the rest of the county ran for miles in all directions with open fields and woods which contained an overabundance of spirited moose that would break into people's yards and ruin their yearly crop of begonias.

Russ and his soldier buddies were always ready to lend their hand to the local constituency by keeping the moose population to a suitable level. Each year on the first day of hunting season, they could be found at the local licensing department run by Martha Allacove. She took kindly to the former soldiers as she always won the annual county fair's Beautiful Begonia Contest.

Knowing they were respecters of the law and would report dutifully for updates on their hunting licenses, Martha was sure to have a pot of coffee brewing and homemade apple pie, which was Russ' favorite.

After the niceties of drinking, eating and polite conversation were over, Martha would stamp each license, and because she repeatedly beat Dorothy Twinston of

Nighthall Township, she made it known to the fellows that the $5.50 license fee was in the future being waived.

Accept for the moose heads on the wall and assorted war memorabilia the soldiers donated for the decor, it appeared to the Sergeant upon entering the Rustic Lodge that he could have still been at the medical facility as every table contained a fair amount of doctors, nurses, technicians, administrative and reception personnel, cooks, food servers, cashiers, custodians and volunteers who worked the gift shop.

He could tell this by the way they were all still wearing identifying nametags.

Now if a wayward traveler who had gotten off the Witchitauki Highway by mistake happened to come in asking for directions, they'd have no choice, if Russ were behind the bar, but to stay long enough to try out the house special. As they would wait for him to fix the cocktail they could take a look around the place and make the snap judgment, as people often do, that the consorting of doctors and nurses was filled with impropriety.

Not so the Sergeant. He had grown up sitting at his World War II daddy's knee as he regaled him with stories of the assorted gritty and mind-boggling liaisons that took place, especially when both sides would take a break from fighting to observe holidays such as Christmas.

Besides the escaped soldier was a faithful watcher of a successful comedy sitcom that took place during a war we will leave unnamed. He had predicted by the first season that a certain male character would one-day lock lips with a certain female character. The Sergeant even went as far as to bet his motorcycle against Clyde Fresion's favorite hunting rifle.

Clyde's daddy was a cigar maker who never had the experience of handling a firearm. He had been born in a year that was fatefully timed so that when he came of age the country didn't need his services as it was between wars. So he never saw the need to get into the habit.

13

The rifle that he won sits in a closet, but the Sergeant always had the hope that if he someday made enough money to move into a house that had all the amenities, the first thing he would do was hang it over the fireplace.

Crossing the Rustic Lodge threshold, the Sergeant felt right at home and to further this feeling Russ, who stood duty behind the bar and never failed to observe a new customer walk through the door, shouted out to him to come and have a drink on the house.

It was Russ' philosophy if you buy a man the first drink, in the future when deciding between buying drinks at his place and Desire's House of Beautiful Ladies, he'll always come to the lodge first as a token of fidelity.

"C'mon over soldier, I've got your drink waiting for you right here."

"Why thank you…?"

"Russ. Russ Longstrong, owner and proprietor."

"Michael A. Delaquot."

"Mind if I call you Delaquot? I took a bullet back in '84 and if I have to memorize a fellow's first and last name I find it puts my brain into a quandary."

The medical facility escapee had no take about being called by his first or last name. Though knowing his own memory to be intact, he recalled with assurance that Sally told him it was Russ' lower extremities that were the cause of his seven operations. The Sergeant was not in that much of a rush that he couldn't ponder and debate a former soldier's lower extremity–brain connection. Not one to pry having just made the owner's acquaintance, he let it go for another time.

"What's this drink you got here waiting for me?"

"I like to think of it as the house special. Go on won't hurt you none."

The Sergeant put it down in one draw. With a cough and a check of the neck to be sure his head was still on his shoulders, he slapped the glass down and asked for another.

Without turning his head this way or that, the Sergeant used his highly developed peripheral vision to check out those next to him at the bar. There was a familiar face to his left. It was the woman who had tagged his wrist with identifying information when he first came through the doors of the medical facility.

He looked down at his hands that were on the bar. In plain site was his patient identification bracelet gleaming white against his tanned right wrist.

The lodge owner stepped before him on the other side of the bar holding the just made house special. The escaped soldier looked up and locked eyes with the former soldier.

Russ knew that look. It was the look of a man in trouble. His brain that went into a quandary when asked to remember a fellow's first and last name zipped into full gear. The hair's rose on the back of his neck.

Without moving his head, Russ looked down and spied the Sergeant's two hands on the bar. He saw those hands were attached to wrists and that the right one was encased in a patient identification bracelet.

Again without moving his head, Russ' eyes veered to the right to see who was standing next to his customer. It was Betty Lu Donahue, patient coordinator.

Having lost none of his tactical training even though he had left the service in '84, Russ in a split second came up with a plan. He placed the house special down on the bar with his left hand and reached down under the bar with his right.

The two men locked eyes. Russ' hand came up from below the bar holding a knife. Without a moment's hesitation he slipped it under the bracelet and with an upward sweep cut it in two.

With the same swiftness, when the Sergeant felt the tug of the knife on the bracelet, he pulled back from the bar allowing it to fall to the floor.

"What was that?" Betty Lu questioned.

"Damn cock-a-roach," Russ replied while wiping the knife with a cloth.

"I know a man who can take care of them. I'll give him a call for you."

"Why thank you, Betty Lu," said Russ. "You are a woman who's always on top of men."

With a wicked smile as she was already on her fourth house special, she replied, "I like to think so."

Russ turned away and signaled to one of his men. That man called the medical facility and within a minute Betty Lu's pager went off, so she went back to work. All the while, the Sergeant was making sure his hand was still attached to his wrist. He picked up the house special and downed it with fervor. Not one to be particularly afflicted with nerves of an agitated kind, he took this bonding moment to inquire of Russ the likelihood of borrowing a car.

"Where you headed, why are you headed there and how long will you be needing it for?"

"Tuscaloosa, family, back on the nineteenth give or take a day or two."

Russ scoured the landscape. All the tables were taken. The floor was crowded with folks dancing to the 50's tunes, the only available selection on the jukebox. A game of darts was in progress as the doctors had challenged the throwing expertise of the kitchen staff. He looked deeper. There was a table in the back, in the corner, in the dark, that was occupied by one Nathanial Seltingbaum, the medical facility's PR.

***

Several weeks in, Nathanial had come to the conclusion that holding the position of public relations for a facility that dealt exclusively with the medical conditions of men and women serving duty was much like being a bathroom attendant handing out paper towels while a full paper towel holder was attached to the wall.

It was a personal touch, but totally unnecessary

During the job application process, Nathanial met with Mr. Flack, the medical facility administrator, who told him the key reason he wanted a public relations person was in case something bad happened and the press got a hold of it.

During the interview it was made clear that the person holding the responsibility of public relations, no matter how dire the circumstances were, would be the one to take care of the matter using the utmost of discretion. This discretion could be achieved any which way the PR decided. They'd have free reign with regard to pay-offs, coercion, arm-twisting or any other device necessary to keep the members of the press quiet.

It should be explained that before Mr. Flack came onboard as the medical facility administrator he was vice-president of a lobster and shrimp shipping business, which we will leave unnamed. He had lost this position when the Double Daily Newsreport, a small town gossip rag, ran an article that the president of the lobster and shrimp shipping business had three wives in the same city.

The wives bumped into each other while attending a fundraiser for the erection of a statue in their town and were seated at the same table.

As they dished the dirt, the three women, over a luncheon of chicken salad on crackers, told the same story. Husband was never at home, never found time for the kids or for them, and was a cheapskate who believed the entire family can find everything they need at the local thrift store.

As you can well imagine, the thrift store angle was the key that opened the president's Pandora's Box.

Within minutes of learning they all had the same last name, the wives were on their way to the office of the daily rag.

As all the reporters were out covering a possible arson at the tractor trailer camp over on Route 73, it was up to Carol Baumgarten, secretary, to meet with the three wives when they came into the office of the Double Daily Newsreport.

Carol kept a new bottle of whiskey in her bottom draw for when the locals came in with unusual stories. She broke the bottle's seal, retrieved four paper cups and poured drinks for all before setting out to obtain every detail of this soon to be Double Daily Newsreport's all-time most copies sold story.

Not used to consuming good whiskey, as their husband was so cheap, the wives became blurry eyed rather quickly and were unable to see the numbers on their cell phones as they tried to call Tom Wilkinson, the local divorce attorney.

As the wives were dialing wrong numbers to various establishments and private residences in their calling areas, it dawned on Carol to ask one last question.

"How'd you all, in a small town like this, not know there were two other women and a passel of young'uns with the same last name as yours?"

The three wives looked up from their cell phones. They pondered and thought, thought and pondered. Carol knew they were concentrating with all their might as she could see the pulse lines in their foreheads looking like they were about to pop.

After several minutes of this, and the passing out of one wife who fell off her chair onto the floor, Carol put a halt to the questioning.

The story went to press the way it was. When the three wives sobered up and were beset by the entire community with questions, they still couldn't identify how they didn't know what their three-timing husband was up to.

And even to this day it remains such a mystery that every month the Double Daily Newsreport devotes a full front page to the headline -

"WHY DIDN'T THEY KNOW?"

At an emergency meeting of lobster and shrimp stock-holders, the president blamed Mr. Flack with lackadaisical job performance in not hiring a public relations person who had an in with the Double Daily Newsreport. Mr. Flack was promptly called on the carpet before the stockholders and they discharged him.

It didn't matter to the aforesaid stockholders that the head of the company had three wives. After all that was his private life.

Thus the reason Nathanial Seltingbaum received the position of PR man for the medical facility. Desperate to get the job he lied to Mr. Flack that he had a connection to a local newspaper via his fourth cousin twice removed who worked as a typesetter.

With not much to do and no one checking up on him, Nathanial spent much of his time at the Rustic Lodge. After downing more than his fill to help ease twangs of guilt for telling a lie and taking a weekly paycheck for a job that had no purpose, the PR could usually be found at a back table sleeping.

Russ went over, lifted the car keys from Nathanial's jacket pocket and came back to the bar dangling them before the Sergeant.

"Before I give you these keys, you have to give me twenty-five dollars to keep him liquored up so he won't know his car is gone. Deal?"

The Sergeant couldn't understand how Russ would keep a man liquored up for that sum of money. Not one to look a gift horse in the mouth, he laid out the twenty-five dollars and $3.50 for the second house special.

0600 hrs
MAY 15th

After too many drinks later, a brief nap in a booth, and helping himself to a pocketful of pigs in a blanket that Russ kept on the bar for his customers, the Sergeant got into PR, Nathanial Seltingbaum's, automobile and took the south-bound entrance ramp on the Witchitauki Highway.

When he set out, it was an hour before sunrise of a beautiful day and the freedom he felt being behind the wheel of a car that wasn't painted in army colors filled the soldier with love for the country he served. Almost any man who was born and raised in America after World War II finding themselves behind the wheel of a metallic red convertible would be hard pressed not to reminisce about one's youth.

In response to his youthful memories, the years in the service disappeared. Michael Delaquot felt seventeen again. He turned the radio to a favorite station, opened the driver's window all the way, let his left hand dangle as his right hand steered, and being the top was down, the wind blew his crew-cut hair any which way it wanted.

After a while, being thoroughly filled with the spirit, the radio was turned off, and as the car zoomed past trees, mountains, cornfields, filling stations and truck stops, he sang America the Beautiful in full voice.

Back at the medical facility the male nurse was not singing. Unhappy that the current state of affairs would cause him to lie, the male nurse had crossed his fingers behind his back when instructing his counterpart on the morning shift that all was well. The work day officially over, in lieu of taking the elevator down to the main floor, he took the stairs by twos and when crossing the lobby, thinking he heard his name being called by a volunteer who worked the main reception desk, he skedaddled out of the building.

Upon gaining the sunshine and cold fresh air of a day only beginning, the male nurse paused to take a deep breath. Thoughts about the whereabouts of soldier patient Bed No. 42 were replaced by the thought of the stew that was waiting at home. This nirvana lasted a mere moment.

He paused. Was he hearing things? He didn't want to, yet couldn't help himself, the off duty worker looked back, and there in the fourth floor window was the entire morning shift and the remnants of the night shift of the psyche ward banging on the windows.

It's a fact of human nature that when the good have done bad the news travels faster than when the bad do bad. Since the good aren't used to doing bad they also feel the guilt of their actions in direct proportion to their goodness.

Seeing the faces of his co-workers looking crazier than the patients they were paid to take care of, the male nurse had an intense stab of remorse rip through his guts. Agitation coursed through his bloodstream. He ran to his car, took the third exit off the Witchitauki Highway, parked the car in the driveway, entered the front door, pulled the phone cord out of the wall, put his cell phone in the freezer, got a bowl of stew out of the crock pot and turned on the morning show just as they were reporting on which movie star left her husband for what movie star who left his wife.

***

Salvatore Krishnecki, or Sally as his friends call him, was the attendant who had given soldier patient Bed. No. 42 a verbal map of the area surrounding the medical facility. Being in the know about pretty much everything concerning the facility, he had been unaware that the Sergeant slipped out and had

21

spent the night standing only a few feet away enjoying Russ' hospitality.

Sally's focus had been directed at a staff member of the medical facility who worked in the kitchen. Making his best effort to get to first base with Mildred Harrington, the only person he had been on the lookout for was her husband.

The night passed quickly with no incidents concerning jealous husbands. Sally's watch had an alarm that was set to ten minutes before he was to be on duty. When it went off, he took Mildred's hand and walked her over to the medical facility.

She went to work preparing meals for the patients; he took a rolling cart of breakfast trays, and headed for the fourth floor. Passing out meals to the soldiers in their beds, he was quick to observe Bed No. 42 was not slept in.

Spending the entire night trying to get to first base was exhausting and as he had until lunchtime to serve breakfast to the constituents, Sally took to the empty bed like a duck takes to water.

But his rest was not to be long. In the hands of Nurse Cheryl Chelswick was a list and on that list it said that the soldier patient in Bed No. 42 was among those due for an enema. The nurse hated this duty so profoundly she made a point of getting it out of the way first thing when coming on duty in the morning.

To Nurse Chelswick's way of thinking, a sleeping patient was an unaware patient, and an unaware patient was not going to give her any flak as they wouldn't see what was coming at them.

With no courtesies for the human condition, she determined where the backside of occupant Bed No. 42 was, lifted the sheet, gave the pants a tug and stuck the enema in.

Sally let out a roar of surprise.

As he had dated the nurse on an occasional basis, the fact that he was sleeping in a patient's bed was not the question.

Nurse Chelswick wanted to know where she could find the soldier so she could get this enema thing over with.

In his rush to get to the bathroom, the attendant gave no answer. The nurse sounded the alarm that there was a missing patient. This was at the same moment the male nurse was in the stairwell, sliding down the third floor banister to the second floor.

The news spread quickly and all morning shift members stopped what they were doing. Rallying quickly, some of the staff blocked the elevator and stairways to ensure the remainder of the night shift did not leave the floor while others quickly searched for the missing soldier.

Just starting her day was Nurse Holly Shipley. Fed up with being made the folly of the evening shift, she took it upon herself to sound the alarm to the other floors. She was on the phone with the volunteer at the reception desk at the very moment the male nurse was speeding by. The volunteer called out to him with no avail.

By the time the male nurse walked out of the building and into the parking lot, Nurse Shipley had both shifts banging on the windows to get the escaping man's attention.

They watched him drive away. As they turned from the windows there were several vows made by members of each shift to seek revenge the next time he appeared on duty.

The morning shift went back to their duties and the remains of the evening shift put their names in a hat to decide who was going to tell the hospital administrator.

Mr. Flack did not take the news of a missing patient with a grain of salt. As a matter of fact when the member of the night shift knocked on his door he was in the process of salting his breakfast of eggs and bacon.

The night shift member wanted to get home to his own dinner. With his low blood sugar rising he could barely emit the news to the administrator. Hearing about Bed No. 42's mysterious disappearance from a locked ward, Mr. Flack's mind flashbacked to his final days at the lobster and shrimp shipping company. He was unaware that he was over salting and spoiling his breakfast.

Asking if the missing soldier had been identified, he was given the name of one Michael A. Delaquot, sergeant. The night shift member was dismissed with the message that this was to be kept confidential and all night shift personnel could go home.

Mr. Flack took a deep breath and remembered that for such a time as this was why he had hired a PR person who had an in with the local paper.

Dumping his over-salted eggs and bacon into the trash, he took the elevator to the fourth floor to see the empty bed for himself. After being buzzed in, just to be thorough, he took the time to go to Room 423 and look under the bed to be sure the staff had not simply misplaced their patient.

Seeing no soldier under the bed, the administrator had no choice but to speak with Nurse Shipley. He went up to the nurse's station.

"How's it going?" questioned Mr. Flack with as much nonchalance as he could muster.

The nurse looked at him. The fourth floor staff had very little dealings with administration as they ran a tight ship and the door was always locked.

News traveled like wildfire and in the hopes of catching the stray patient, Nurse Shipley had fanned the flames, still she couldn't be quite sure of what he was getting at and felt it would be best to skirt the issue.

"Fine, how are things with you?"

"Fine," he answered.

"I'm glad."

"I have to get back to my office."

"I have patients to take care of."

"How many patients do you have on this ward?"

"Why do you ask?"

"Just curious."

"You know what they say about curiosity. It killed the cat."

The blood drained out of Mr. Flack's face. Pale and about to faint, he sat down. Something told him this was going to be worse than the business at the lobster and shrimp shipping company.

Nurse Shipley gave him a drink of water and sat by his side. "I don't think there's any reason to panic, do you?"

He couldn't answer.

"Look at me."

The administrator looked into the nurse's eyes. These were not the eyes of a woman upset that her husband was married to two other women. These eyes said, "I will protect the patients, my job, the jobs of those on my staff and the medical facility's reputation no matter what it cost."

He took courage and a deep breath.

"Feeling better?"

"Yes, much."

Nurse Shipley walked him to the elevator and pressed the down button. "I'm sure you'll take care of things on your end."

Mr. Flack nodded.

The elevator doors opened and he got on. As the doors closed the fourth floor nurse gave the facility's administrator a smile of confidence. That confidence spread throughout his body. He marched back to his office and called Ms. Betty Lu Donohue, patient coordinator, to bring him the file of one Michael A. Delaquot, soldier patient Bed. No. 42.

With file in hand, she entered his office. Not one to part with patient information without good cause, Betty Lu questioned why he was in need of it. The administrator tut tutted her. Feeling lion-like he added it was frankly none of her business.

The patient coordinator had all the appearances of being a sweetheart of a woman, but was famous throughout the facility for being sharp as a tack. Not used to being dismissed so abruptly, after leaving the office, she made it her business to pay a visit on soldier patient Bed No. 42.

Nurse Shipley was loaded with common sense and a bit of a psychic ability concerning approaching danger. She knew the moment the patient coordinator was on the way. Having served as a battlefront nurse, in a war we will leave unnamed, she quickly alerted the staff and began the subterfuge.

Betty Lu took the elevator to the fourth floor. Making her exit, she had to step out of the way of a soldier patient on a gurney as he was being wheeled in. The psyche ward's locked door was in the process of closing. She ran and stuck her foot out just as it was about to shut.

When they saw Betty Lu coming, soldier patients standing in the hallway were reminded of the enemy and quickly ran to their rooms. At the nurse's station, she demanded to speak to Michael A. Delaquot. Nurse Shipley calmly put down the file she was reading.

"You just missed him; he's on his way down to x-ray."

"So there's no problem with soldier patient Bed No. 42?" questioned Betty Lu.

"What gave you that idea?"

"Mr. Flack asked for his file."

"Mr. Flack?"

"Yes."

Nurse Shipley leaned in. "Do you have time for a cup of coffee?"

Men don't know it but 'time for a cup of coffee' is woman's office code to alert another member of their sex that they are the bearer of a juicy bit of gossip that needs telling. The equivalent words for men - time for a drink. Regardless of her work schedule, the patient coordinator always had time for gossip.

Eyeing her fellow staff members, Nurse Shipley took Betty Lu by the arm.

"Let's go down to the coffee shop, shall we?

As Betty Lu and Nurse Shipley made their way down to the coffee shop, the Sergeant found himself sitting in traffic.

Not in a rush of any kind and enjoying the wind blowing through his crew cut hair, the Sergeant had gotten off the Witchitauki Highway for Route 28 where just hours before a truck carrying logs to be used as telephone polls had unloaded its cargo.

Route 28 was a winding back road in hill country. The driver of the rig was Milton Azbur. He was trolling along at a moderate clip when a deer took a giant leap out of the woods into the pathway of his front bumper.

The young trucker had no problem keeping his rig steady as he killed miscellaneous wildlife that appeared in the range of his headlights. When starting out on his load-carrying career he was warned that this was a trucker's lot in life.

Milton was also an enthusiast of dirt bikes and when not driving his big rig could be found motoring in the backwoods in his home state. Just as the deer was deliberating to jump or not jump across the road, he was thinking that after delivering this load the first thing he was going to do was get on his dirt bike and do some riding.

It was with this mindset that he mistook the crossing deer for a biker.

As the creature made connection with his front bumper, Milton turned the steering wheel a hard left. The cab of his truck went one way, the flatbed another.

It being early morning, with scarcely anyone on the road, no one was hurt. Milton, who knew it was only a matter of time before his number was up, always wore protective gear and a helmet, which all truckers should think about doing. He came away without a scratch.

As the day progressed, Route 28 was backed up for miles with drivers who didn't see the morning traffic report that held valuable rerouting information. The Sergeant was taking it all on the chin.

Along with the breaking of the service men and women's addiction to using porcelain toilets to relieve themselves, the United States Army also had to break their members of the addiction to sleeping on comfortable beds.

Before studies were done and the Army began the systematic breaking of their member's need to sleep in comfort, it was known that service people out in the battlefield would not sleep at all, sometimes for days or weeks at a clip.

The idea of laying your body down in mud pits and foliage and then falling asleep went against everything a mattress-loving person knows. For those soldiers who had spent their formative years in the scouts or on farms where they had to spend nights in the barn with sick or birthing animals, where they slept was not a problem.

Soldiers used to their comfortable mattresses would eventually fall asleep, but it could be when they were firing their guns or having to trek to the next war-torn town. Non-sleeping soldiers made it dangerous for everyone.

The only solution was found to be in basic training. When newbie's arrived they were given bunk beds with only the barest of support. They were forced to rise early and retire late. Night maneuvers became the routine. The newly arrived soldiers thought the military was sadistic in their nature, but being scientifically proven these methods saved lives.

When he was growing up Michael Delaquot's parents gave him all the luxuries in life they could afford including a bed that had a mattress of some comfort. Over twenty years of active duty hardened the Sergeant. He could sleep just about anywhere the situation called for. Unperturbed by the delay, he took his cap out of his duffle, put it on so the visor covered his eyes and fell asleep behind the wheel.

As the escaped soldier from Bed No. 42 was sleeping on Rte 28, Mr. Flack was trying to make sure all hell didn't break out at the medical facility.

Looking over Michael A. Delaquot's file, he learned there was a wife and four kids in Tuscaloosa. This was a good thing. They were far enough away to not come barreling in on the facility with charges and threats about suing for the loss of their loved one.

It came to his mind that if no one telephoned the family, and the staff kept the news contained to the facility, there would be no one concerned about the recent disappearance. To be sure all details were covered Mr. Flack would touch base with PR person, Nathanial Seltingbaum. He closed the file and phoned the public relations office. The phone rang and rang.

Unable to reach out and touch Nathanial, the administrator first made a note to acquisition an answering machine and then decided a trip down to the PR office was called for. Having foregone his over-salted bacon and eggs he would stop first at the coffee shop which was on the way.

It was at the same coffee shop where the fourth floor nurse was making the transfer of gossip to the patient coordinator.

"I knew it!" stated Betty Lu firmly.

"I think everyone knew," said Nurse Shipley.

"Oh, his poor family, do you think his wife knows about his peccadillo?"

"He has a wife? I mean…I've never had the pleasure of meeting a Mrs. Flack," answered Nurse Shipley.

"There's a picture on his desk, they have children."

"Oh."

"Last year I asked why she never attended the annual picnic."

"What did he say?"

"She was always taking the kids to see her parents."

"Typical."

"I bet she doesn't even know about the annual picnic."

"The wife is always the last to know."

Betty Lu nodded in agreement. Just then the administrator came through the door. The nurse took up her coffee and looked away while the patient coordinator followed his every step to the espresso machine. She watched closely as he handled the coffee cup, looking for just the little bit of a raised pinky.

She noted how he knew the inner workings of making an espresso - milk first, then coffee. The men she knew didn't know that trick. Heck, they didn't even know what an espresso was.

Eyes wide open and staring, Betty Lu could see what she hadn't seen before. How could she have been so blind when all the signs were right in front of her?

Mr. Flack picked up a donut. He put it down and chose a whole grain muffin instead.

"Did you see that?"

Holly turned back, "See what?"

"He chose whole grain over white flour."

"Oh my."

As if on cue, before sitting down at a table, he took a napkin and wiped the chair. About to take a bite of his whole grain muffin, he placed a second napkin on his lap. That was it. Betty Lu was convinced. Mr. Flack was of a certain nature.

The administrator finished his whole grain muffin and espresso. He took the napkin wiped his mouth, stood, and unlike the other men who worked at the facility who thought some woman would be around to clean up their mess, he took his cup and placed it in the dirty cup bin and threw his trash in the garbage before leaving.

Betty Lu's mind was boggled. Nurse Shipley had to get back to her duties.

"I have to go."

"I'm going with you."

"Why?"

"I've got to see Sergeant Delaquot and be sure that he's okay," replied Betty Lu with urgency.

"You can take my word for it. He's fine."

Now Nurse Shipley didn't know that for sure, but in her eyes, seeing how he was able bodied enough to make his way out of the building, thereby causing her so much trouble, soldier patient Bed No. 42 had a lot more going for him than most of the soldiers in the facility.

"I won't rest until I see for myself," stated Betty Lu.

"Wait here a moment and I'll go up with you."

The fourth floor nurse went across the room where Nurse Happenstance was sitting. They spoke for a moment. The two nurses looked the patient coordinator's way. Betty Lu was fixing her lipstick. Nurse Happenstance nodded her head in agreement then left the room. Holly went back to the table.

"Shall we go?"

The two ladies put their coffee cups in the bin and threw away their trash. Leaving the coffee shop, they walked down the hallway to the elevator. An out-of-order sign hung from the buttons and two workmen were deliberating about its troubles.

"We'll have to take the stairs," said Nurse Shipley.

"All the way to the fourth floor?" questioned Betty Lu.

"I'm afraid so."

"Perhaps I'll wait till the elevator's fixed."

"We could go down to Wing Two and take that elevator," suggested Nurse Shipley.

"That's quite a walk and it's so early in the morning."

"True."

Just then Betty Lu's cell phone rang.

"This is Ms. Donohue. Oh hello, Nurse Happenstance. You're where? I'll be right there." She hung up the phone. "I have to get back to my office."

"I'll see you later then."

Nurse Shipley watched Betty Lu turn the corner before giving the all-clear. One of the workmen pulled the out-of-order sign and she got on the elevator.

***

Mr. Flack, operating with a full stomach thanks to the espresso and whole grain muffin, had left the coffee shop and made his way to the office of public relations which was on a lower level.

The architect for the medical facility had been one Major Daniel Tripington. In his lifetime, the Major saw war up close and personal while stationed in London during World War II. At the time he was there, the Germans were creating havoc that commonly came to be known as 'the blitz'.

With the Luftwaffe doing their best to obliterate the city, the Major found himself having to practically live in the London underground. It was this he kept in mind when designing the medical facility.

After World War II ended, he took the benefits offered to all servicemen and furthered his education. With an architectural degree framed behind glass, he rented an office, hung said degree on the wall, and began the next phase of his life, designing buildings that if a blitz took place the occupants would be well protected.

The Major received the position as architect of the medical facility due to his friendship with a Colonel Dodger who was a close friend of the President of the United States.

Called to a meeting in the oval office, the Major felt he had died and gone to heaven as he swapped war stories with the President over cigars and whiskey.

The President had served his country during the big one, so the Major didn't have to twist his arm with regard to the vision of having underground levels in all buildings in every metropolis throughout the States.

Even though the medical facility was going to be the only building for miles and was not located near a big city, the architect firmly expressed his opinion that a four-story building in the middle of cornfields was a sitting duck.

The President couldn't be happier with his legacy of spending tax dollars not only to care for injured service men and women, but also insuring their safety against a future enemy, whomever that may be. He personally gave the Major the job of designing the medical facility.

His only experience being the London underground, the Major designed the below ground floors with long tunnels and lots of rooms. He even thought of putting down railroad tracks with cars traveling through the long tunnels, but that idea was eventually dropped, as the tunnels didn't lead anywhere in particular.

Having seen firsthand that elevators could easily become useless with the loss of power, the Major didn't bother throwing them into the design either.

The public relations office was actually a type of bunker, which in case of emergency could hold up to fifty people. The walls were lined with shelves holding k-rations left over from the Korean War, which the Major acquisitioned upon learning from Colonel Dodger that they were available.

Mr. Flack made his way down the flight of stairs to the below ground level. Still feeling Nurse Shipley's confidence coursing through his veins, the administrator charged full steam ahead and didn't bother to knock on the PR door.

The room was in darkness. He found the switch and when the lights came on, he spied Sally and Mildred Harrington, the kitchen aide the attendant had walked to the facility only hours before, locked in an embrace on the public relations desk.

This was the administrator's first travail into a world he didn't know existed in the medical facility. Fully aware that nurses and doctors did from time to time consort with each other, which was due to the nervous tensions created by the care of their patients, he was unaware of any such high tensions developing in those who serve breakfast trays and the staff members who cook and put the breakfast onto those trays.

Mr. Flack reeled in his unbelief. He didn't know whether to go further into the room or to reverse his steps. He didn't know whether to ask their pardon for his intrusion or to take a stand with both parties for the desecration of the public relations desk.

While waiting to see which way he would go, Sally and Mildred were starting to get cold. In various stages of undress and with no heat afforded to the underground office, a slight chill came upon both parties as the heat of passion waned.

The attendant knew it could take awhile for the administrator to gain his equilibrium. So he made the first move. He gently lifted himself off Mildred, picked up his pants and zipped them.

Being a gentleman, Sally then took his shirt, came around the desk and blocked the view of Mr. Flack as Mildred came up off the table. Holding his shirt as a screen, she gathered her things and departed.

"Time for lunch trays to be readied," she off-handedly said to Mr. Flack as she passed him on her way out the door.

His eyes shut, the administrator nodded.

Sally buttoned his shirt.

I'd appreciate it, sir, if you didn't let this get out. Mildred is married you know."

"She's married?" retorted Mr. Flack with some dread.

"He's an awful brute, works in maintenance, Swedish, name of Stan Harrington. You may know him."

The administrator thought for a minute. He did know Stan Harrington. Big. Very big, guy. Former wrestler. Was known for setting traps in the below ground levels, and when he caught rats, twisted the heads off them barehanded.

Mr. Flack remembered him well. He also remembered his well paying job with great benefits and all he would do to keep them.

"I can see that being married to a man such as…the tension she must live under…you were only helping her…," the administrator sputtered.

"Yes, I was. The tension was killing her."

Mr. Flack recouped his equilibrium and was all business.

"Modern day living and tension will kill us all in the end. Well done. Now back to the item at hand. Have you seen Nathanial Seltingbaum? I have a bit of business to speak to him about."

Of course, Sally knew the medical facility's PR spent his days at the lodge.

"I have seen him. He was taking care of matters on the third floor. Should I get him for you?"

"Please do. Tell him I want to see him in my office as soon as possible."

"I'll have him there in a jiff. Shall we go? Bit cold down here."

"I never realized that before. When I get back to my office, I'll be writing a requisition for an answering machine, I'll add a heater to the list."

Sally nodded his appreciation of Mr. Flack's ideas for the improvement to his – Nathanial's office.

"It could use a couch, too. You know when PR has to meet with the press or families, etc. etc."

"Excellent idea," said Mr. Flack as they walked out the door. "I'll ask for leather, lasts longer."

The attendant put his arm around his boss' shoulder.

"You're a man who thinks on his feet."

The administrator took the compliment to heart.

"I like to think so," he said proudly.

***

As Mildred Harrington prepared lunch trays back at the medical facility, the Sergeant was coming out of a deep sleep in Nathanial's car. The smell of meat cooking roused his spirit. He lifted his cap, eyed his surroundings and seeing that traffic had not moved, he meandered into the woods and relieved himself.

With nature taken care of, he followed the drifting smoke. Twelve cars down was a large RV. Outside the RV was a group of people and in the middle was Fred Framer standing over a portable barbeque.

The soldier made his way over to a portable table set wide with the contributions of his fellow travelers. There were sodas, plenty of beers and an array of sandwiches wrapped in wax paper and plastic. Bags of chips, even a jar of guacamole had been donated.

The honoree of the party was trucker, Milton Azbur.

While the Sergeant was sleeping, a salesman, late for his meetings in Porchesky, went up and took Milton to task for his stupidity in creating the entanglement he found himself in.

With the loss of a sale pending, the salesman was more than a might miffed and it took six hearty fellows who were engineering the poles off the road to pull the salesman off Milton.

One of the hearty fellows handed the salesman the keys to his car. Deeply grateful, the salesman thanked the trucker and promised to be back with the car as soon as his meeting was over.

The majority of the salesman's fellow travelers seemed to be of the nature of taking all things in their stride. Fred Framer pulled out his barbeque and set to cooking while his wife, Pansy, went around inviting their neighbors for lunch. All donations gratefully accepted.

36

Fred had given Milton the first burger off the grill. Relieved that he wasn't going to be killed by a lynch mob, the trucker went into the details of how his rig and flat bed parted ways on Rte. 28.

The Sergeant hankering for a burger also wanted to do his part. Seeing an empty bowl, he dipped into his pocket and brought out Russ' pigs in a blanket. Pansy Framer had tears in her eyes when she saw the soldier's donation and alerted Fred to give him the next burger off the grill.

With beer and burger in hand, he took a seat on a log that was on the side of the road. Having told many an audience of killing many a species while driving an array of army vehicles, the Sergeant enjoyed Milton telling of his first encounter with a crossing deer and the fact he always drove prepared for his number being up by wearing protective gear and a helmet.

***

After redirecting Betty Lu from the concerns of the patient onto the cares of Nurse Happenstance, Nurse Shipley checked back with her staff with the hope there was a return of soldier patient Bed No. 42. The answer being no, she took the elevator down to the second floor.

Chief of surgery, Dr. Sorenson had an office on the second floor where he could meet with patients and nap as needed. It was at this office door Nurse Shipley knocked.

"I'm only sleeping."

"It's me, Bryan."

"Holly. Come on in. I'm sorry I was abrupt, spent the last eight reattaching the blood vessels of some kid who didn't have the fool sense to stay out of the way of some flying shrapnel. Thanks to me, the next generation will see a passel of Wallingtons."

"I'm sure he'll always be beholding to you."

Knowing Nurse Shipley would not leave her post unless it was soldier related; Dr. Sorenson got off the couch and sat at his desk.

"Please have a seat."

"Thank you, Bryan."

"Drink?"

Holly looked at her watch.

"It's past twelve," noted the doctor.

"I don't think I will."

He put the bottle back. "How can I help you?"

"I have a little problem."

Doctor Sorenson leaned back in his chair.

"Missing soldier?"

"You knew about it?"

"Let's just say I had my suspicions."

***

Conversing on their way up from the underground level, Sally had convinced Mr. Flack of the need for a small refrigerator and microwave in addition to the new couch for his - the PR office. Reaching the first floor, they parted ways. Sally pushed the up button on the elevator and watched as Mr. Flack turned the corner.

The elevator doors opened, Sally didn't get on. He ran the other way, went through the kitchen and out the back door to where the trash compactors were. Without breaking stride he ran the short distance to the Rustic Lodge.

Being more of a crowded at night and between shifts type of establishment, the place was pretty much empty as it always was at this time of the day.

Russ was stacking glasses behind the bar when the attendant rushed in.

"Where's the PR?"

"What's up?"

"Mr. Flack wants to see him."

"That's a first. Do you know why?"

Sally's radar went up.

"What's going on?"

Knowing he'd find out sooner or later Russ opened the cash register.

"May be something about a missing soldier, he said.

"What floor?"

Russ handed over the id bracelet.

"Michael A. Delaquot…fourth floor," read the attendant.

"I didn't know he was from the fourth until I read that. Otherwise, I wouldn't have…"

"I remember him," Sally cut in. "He asked me all kinds of questions. Thought that was kind of fishy for a crazy guy to do. Why I told him about…You wouldn't have what?"

The lodge's owner hung his head, poured himself a drink, then another.

"Russ?"

"I wouldn't have given him the keys to the PR's car," he stated flat out. "Damn."

Sally sat down on a stool. Russ poured the attendant a drink and another one for himself.

"Does anyone know besides you?"

"No," answered Russ.

"Let's keep it that way," stated Sally.

Russ put the identification bracelet back in the cash register draw.

***

Doctor Sorenson sent Nurse Shipley a substitute for her missing patient. She had explained why one was needed and promised that it was only for a couple of hours. Wanting to oblige, after she left his office, the doctor went to the nurse's station and helped himself to the files of all the patients on the second floor.

He already had it in his mind that Private Bobby Wallington, soldier patient Bed No. 65, was going to be the most likely candidate for the job of replacing soldier patient Bed No. 42, as he was the patient Dr. Sorenson had most recently operated on.

Bobby was in an induced coma.

Though his injuries were not life threatening they were in a delicate area. Usually operations involving a soldier's 'little soldier' were to be handled with delicacy, and if bandages were included someone strong had to be sitting by the bedside to explain why the patient's most important anatomy member was encased. Then if the patient became frantic about his 'little patient' he would promptly be given a shot of something to put him back to sleep.

Medical facility staff could not be spared to sit by a soldier's bedside for hours on end, so Dr. Sorenson always took the road of least resistance being the induced coma.

The doctor had learned all this from experience. As a first year intern, he had watched Dr. Basil Wilcox operate on a Private, who we will leave unnamed, which included his 'little private'.

When the Private woke up, he didn't care that both his arms were in casts. He saw his bandaged 'little private' and freaked out. He got out of bed, smashed his arms against the radiator in his room until the casts broke to pieces. He tore off the bandages on his 'little private' and off went the skin with it.

It was then that the Private shrieked in pain. The staff on the floor ran to his room to find him straddled across the sink trying to run water over his 'little private' as it was burning something awful. It took three attendants to hold him down as a nurse administered a shot.

When the sedation took hold, they wheeled the Private back to the operating room. The bones in his arms were reset, the casts were replaced and Dr. Wilcox grafted skin off the Private's bottom for his 'little private'.

When the Private woke up a second time, he did the same exact thing.

While Dr. Basil Wilcox was operating for the third time on the 'little private' he told the nurses he was putting the Private under an induced coma as he was due to play in a golf tournament and wasn't about to miss it to repair the 'little private' a fourth time.

There was a further reason Dr. Sorenson wanted to err on the safe side with Bobby Wallington. His 'little Bobby' was not so little. Placing Bobby in an induced coma for a few days would prevent the shock of his seeing his not so 'little Bobby' in a mummified situation.

Dr. Sorenson was hands on with giving Nurse Shipley a solution to her missing patient problem. He took the comatose soldier's file, enlisted two attendants to put him on a gurney and lied to the nurses on the second floor that he was transferring Private Wallington to the third floor. Bobby was rolled into the elevator and the good doctor pressed the fourth floor button.

***

About the time Dr. Sorenson was taking Bobby Wallington to the fourth floor, the Sergeant was driving his car off Exit 9 of Rte. 28.

The workers transferred the logs that were going to be telephone poles onto another flat bed. Milton's rig was lifted from its side position and out of the ditch it made as it came to a halt.

41

The deer was buried by one of the motorists waiting along with the other travelers. Being a vegetarian, he thought it was the right thing to do.

The salesman came back from the meeting with his potential customers. After returning the borrowed car, he proceeded down to the RV and told everyone he had made the sale.

The roadway was cleared and everyone was able to go. Those who were indulging in the donations put on the table at Fred and Pansy Framer's RV moved their vehicles to the side of the road and continued on with the festivities.

It wasn't long before the food ran out. The stranded motorists were enjoying themselves so much it was planned that all who cared to would meet once more at Grandmother Wimpole's Restaurant off Exit 9.

The Sergeant not wanting to be a killjoy, and in no particular rush to get where he was going, joined them. He even offered to drive Milton as his rig was now being towed to the nearest truck shop.

About sixty people met at Grandmother Wimpole's Restaurant. It became one of those random events that happen in life, and as Wimpole's served food family style, this hungry party of travelers was not going to be a problem.

Fred and Pansy Framer, as they were on vacation, with a generosity of spirit, secretly told the Waitress to give them the bill.

***

At the Rustic Lodge, Russ was serving Sally a third round of drinks when the attendant got the nerve to ask about the PR's car and soldier patient Bed No. 42's need for it.

"Tuscaloosa, family, back on the nineteenth, give or take a day or two."

"Geez," retorted Sally. "That could be a problem."

Instead of drinking a fourth round they walked over to the table where Nathanial Seltingbaum was sleeping.

"Wake up, Nathanial!" shouted Sally.

The PR lifted his head off the table and looked at the two concerned faces.

"What is it?"

"You're wanted. PR," the attendant answered.

"Really?"

"Mr. Flack himself wants to see you," added Russ.

"Mr. Flack? Really?"

The two men nodded. Nathanial pulled himself together. He stood up.

"I'll be going to the gent's first."

The two men watched as he swayed, fell over tables, and kicked chairs out of the way as he crossed the room.

"Got coffee?" asked Sally.

Russ nodded in the affirmative.

***

While the PR was being filled with coffee, Mr. Flack was pacing in his office. He'd stop only when he thought he heard his phone ringing or someone knocking on his door.

He'd hear a sound and pause. Not hearing anything he'd go back to pacing. Finally there was a knock on the door, not knowing if it was real or his imagination he kept on pacing. It was when she knocked for the third time that Betty Lu Donohue, patient coordinator, opened the door and walked in.

"Mr. Flack, I need to speak with you."

He grabbed his chest.

"Are you okay?"

"Indigestion."

"Espresso," murmured Betty Lu.

"What?"

"Nothing."

"Why are you here?"

"I need to speak to you about something."

Mr. Flack thought it best to take the reign of power. He offered her a seat and went around his desk. By the time he sat down, she was holding an intense gaze on the picture of a woman with three children that was before her.

"How's Mrs. Flack?"

"My mother's fine."

"I meant her. Your wife."

"Oh."

"Those are your children?" Betty Lu made sure to put an emphasis on the word your.

"Yes. That's little Benjamin, Hermoine and T.J."

They sat there in quiet, she contemplating the peccadilloes of the administrator, he contemplating the possible loss of his job and benefits.

"The reason I'm here," Betty Lu began.

Expecting her to speak about the missing patient soldier Bed No. 42, Michael A. Delaquot, he was taken off course when she continued.

"Someone has been using my computer."

He looked at her, she looked at him - really looked at him. His brow furrowed a definite sign of guilt in the eyes of the patient coordinator.

"It wasn't me."

"I didn't say it was you," retorted Betty Lu.

"Oh."

"What are you going to do about it?"

"I'll have Mac Treeter look into it."

"The computer technician? Is that all you're going to do? Aren't you going to call the FBI?"

"The FBI?" choked Mr. Flack. "What in heaven's name for?"

"My computer can only be used by someone who has security clearance and that's me. My computer has been tampered with. It could have been terrorists. That's why."

"You have patient medical records on your computer. It's not like you're linked to any -- "

Mr. Flack had no clue what he was about to spit out as his mind was racing with the thought of soldier patient Bed. No. 42 being a terrorist and what it would mean if the press got a hold of news like that.

"Where is Nathanial Seltingbaum?" he shouted.

Just then there was a knock at the door. And the hung-over PR was pushed into the room by Sally.

***

On the fourth floor, attendants were transferring Bobby Wallington from the gurney to Bed No. 42. Standing by were Nurse Shipley and Dr. Sorenson. After the attendants rolled the gurney out, Bryan took Holly's hand and gave it a squeeze.

"I appreciate your help," she cooed.

"Anything for you, doll."

"See you at the lodge?"

"Surgery at four, soldier patient Bed No. 16, woman with a bulging hernia."

"Poor thing."

"I should be there around ten," noted the doctor.

They looked intently at each other and kissed. Bobby Wallington's right eye gave a flutter. The doctor's pager went off and he left the room. Nurse Shipley was taking something out of her uniform pocket when he came back.

"Nearly forgot. Be sure to keep an eye on the wounds. If you see any swelling that looks out of the ordinary, give me a call."

"Yes, Doctor."

He left again. The nurse took a patient identification bracelet out of one uniform pocket and a pocketknife out of the other. She spoke softly to Bobby.

"There now soldier boy after what you've been through this shouldn't hurt a bit."

She sliced the id bracelet with the name of Robert Wallington off the comatose soldier and slipped a freshly made id bracelet with the name of Michael A. Delaquot on his wrist.

"You sleep tight now. I'll be in to check on you and change your dressings."

***

Back at Grandmother Wimpole's Restaurant, everyone was having a grand old time. Drew Wimpole, who inherited the eatery from his grandma, churned out many a pancake for the party of sixty and the waitresses were kept busy on refills of coffee.

With so much caffeine in their systems, the salesman and Milton were like old buddies. Fred and Pansy were regaling folks with their numerous RV adventures.

The Sergeant after his third plate of grits sat back and looked at the party of motorists that surrounded him. After years in the service protecting those at home, it made him feel good to see the results of his work.

Eventually, he remembered his many years deceased momma. She always said it was good manners to know when to leave. With her words in mind and a tear in his eye, he bid his new friends a fond farewell and promised to keep in touch.

With two hours to go till sunset, knowing he'd be able to make some good time if there were no more accidents along the way, the Sergeant hopped back in the convertible and headed toward Route 28.

It was also two hours before the male nurse had to be on duty. The alarm clock went off, he set his feet on the floor, turned off the alarm, made his way to the bathroom, came out of the bathroom, went into the kitchen and made himself some breakfast.

A bit later while eating eggs, a side of grits, hash browns and bacon, he contemplated the sanity of going to work that evening.

The wound was fresh. He had left his co-workers on the evening shift in a lurch by not warning them about the missing soldier. He had left the morning shift in a similar lurch by not warning them.

As he saw things, it was very unlikely he'd be greeted with enthusiasm when reporting for duty, even though he was a standout employee who had perfect attendance.

Take the occasion when his daddy died as an example. The poor man had developed a fatal case of blood poisoning when a hook caught him in the leg as he was casting during a fishing tournament.

The male nurse didn't miss a single day of work. Those same co-workers he shafted only hours before got together and traded hours from their shifts so he could work around his daddy's wake and funeral.

His head hung in shame at the thought he had let his colleagues down.

"I have to own up to my shortcomings!"

Finishing his breakfast, he did the dishes, made the bed, dressed, plugged the phone cord back into the wall, retrieved the cell phone from the freezer, took up his keys, got into his car and went to work.

***

After he was pushed into the room by Sally, Nathanial stumbled to the floor. Mr. Flack and Betty Lu helped him to his feet. Knowing Mr. Flack wanted to see him, Nathanial Seltingbaum was a little taken aback to find Ms. Donohue in the office. His thoughts went right away to the notion that this was not about why he wasn't at his desk, but had to do with a patient. He smiled with the anticipation he'd finally have some PR work.

"You wanted to see me, Mr. Flack?"

"Yes, yes I did. Betty Lu would you excuse us, there's a matter I need to speak with Nathanial about."

"What about my...."

"Like I said I'll get Mac Treeter on it right away. And for the time being I would treat it as hush hush. Can you manage that, Betty Lu?"

"Yes, I think I can," she said with a huff.

"Good."

The administrator saw the patient coordinator to the door. Betty Lu knew when she was getting hustled. She looked from Nathanial to Mr. Flack to the picture on the desk.

"Betty Lu --"

"I'm going."

Standing in the hallway, Betty Lu paused. Was that the door locking? Looking around to be sure no one was watching she tried the doorknob. It was locked all right.

The patient coordinator's mind went completely off the breach of security her computer recently underwent and onto the fact that she had been so blind not to see what was under her nose. In lieu of going back to her office, she sought out her best friend Julie Binder, who worked the switchboard.

1600 hrs
MAY 15th

Sitting at the nurse's station desk, Nurse Shipley looked up from soldier patient Bed No. 42's file.

"I need to speak to you."

The male nurse stopped tiptoeing. He had parked his car in the parking lot, walked into the medical facility and took the elevator to the fourth floor, all without being accosted by a single angry co-worker.

"Come with me," said Nurse Shipley.

Like a puppy dog, he followed her into soldier patient Bed No. 42's room. No one could have been more surprised to find the bed occupied.

"He's back!"

"Who's back?"

"No one."

"This is not Michael A. Delaquot."

"It's not?"

Nurse Shipley shook her head.

"This is Robert Wallington. He had surgery and is now in an induced coma. Do you happen to know where Michael A. Delaquot is?"

The male nurse replied with a hangdog shake of his head.

"You were the one who discovered he was missing. And you didn't tell anyone did you?"

He didn't answer.

"You left knowing all was not well on your shift."

"I can explain."

She got in his face.

"I don't want to hear it. Listen to me. We have a situation. Michael A. Delaquot's not here. He's not anywhere in this building. Now the members of the staff who know this are keeping it to themselves. The only person who doesn't know about it is Betty Lu. She's been led to think Mr. Flack has a special interest in Sergeant Delaquot."

"Why would she --?"

"Don't ask questions," retorted the nurse. "Before I leave I will have Betty Lu come up here and make sure that she sees Michael A. Delaquot is in bed and that it was impossible for him to be having an affair with Mr. Flack due to the fact that we have to keep the sergeant drugged up so he won't hurt himself."

"That sounds good," said the male nurse.

"It is not good. It is so far from being good."

Bobby Wallington's left eyelid fluttered.

One would think the male nurse took a step back in order not to be belted by the nurse's fist, but he was only allowing her room to pace.

"Making a few calls on the QT, I obtained information from Sergeant Delaquot's superiors that he's never been crazy a day in his life. As he walked out of here on his own two feet, there was apparently nothing wrong whatsoever, and the reason he was here at all was to use his time in our ward for his own purposes. I can only surmise he had some very important business that took him outside of our facility, and more than likely when that business is taken care of he'll be returning. Rather than reporting him AWOL, I'm willing to give him the benefit of the doubt."

"That's very nice."

"Did I ask your opinion?"

"No, Ma'am."

"So this is what we're going to do," Nurse Shipley continued. "We are going to give the sergeant a bit of time to do what it is he went to do and get his butt back here. For the moment, Private Bobby Wallington is going to be his replacement. You will keep an especially good eye on Private Wallington. Do I make myself clear?"

The male nurse nodded.

"We'll check his bandages together and then I will get Betty Lu up here so she can see for herself soldier patient Bed No. 42 is okay. As the workday is over, I will personally walk her out of the building. After we leave, you will take the identification bracelet off Private Wallington and put this one on. Using a gurney you'll take him back to the second floor where he belongs. Do you understand?"

"Yes, Ma'am."

Nurse Shipley handed over her pocketknife.

"If there is any trouble, I want you to call me. I'll be next door."

"I'll call you right away."

She left the room to get Betty Lu. The male nurse exhaled.

***

After he locked Betty Lu out, Mr. Flack gave Nathanial details of the looming PR scandal the facility was ensconced in.

"The reason I called – we seem to have misplaced a patient."

"A patient is missing?"

"Keep your voice down. This is a matter of the utmost secrecy. Do you understand?"

"What do you want me to do?" questioned Nathanial.

"I want you to do what a good PR does. Keep it out of the newspapers."

"But -- "

"No buts. This is why we pay you. We – are counting on - you."

The PR nodded. He got up from his seat. Mr. Flack put his hand out. Nathanial shook it.

"I'm going home now. It's been a long day."

The administrator took his hat off its hook and left. Nathanial stood there. He didn't know what to do next. No details were given about the missing soldier. He didn't have a clue what floor the patient was missing from. He didn't even get a name.

"Guess that's it," said the PR to the walls.

He let himself out. For a moment he was undecided which way to go. He looked at his watch. His work at the facility was over for the day.

Walking to the front entrance, the PR came to a rational decision. Before going home, he'd go over to the Rustic Lodge and check with Russ who always had the inside scoop on all happenings at the facility. If anyone knew about the missing soldier it would be him.

On his way out, the PR passed the switchboard where the patient coordinator was speaking to her friend, Julie Binder, switchboard operator.

The two ladies stopped their gossiping as Nathanial walked by. When he was safely through the sliding doors, they resumed their exchange.

"That was quick," said Betty Lu. "It must have been a PR issue after all."

"I met Nathanial's girlfriend at the picnic last July. Sweet girl," noted the operator.

Betty Lu could say nothing to this point as she was still shaken by the news of Mr. Flack and that her own judgment was so impaired where men with wives and girlfriends were concerned.

I'm so glad you told me about Mr. Flack," stated Julie. "I've suspected him for quite some time."

Just then the topic of discussion, who had stopped in the men's room after leaving his office, walked by. The two ladies stopped talking and really, really looked at him.

"You did?" questioned Betty Lu when the coast was clear.

"Certainly, look how he dresses. Like a dandy."

Just then the switchboard buzzed and Julie being the good operator she was dropped the issue of Mr. Flack's sexuality to answer it.

"Can I help you? Yes, she's still in the building. I'll tell her." Julie hung up. "Nurse Shipley wants to see you."

"Michael Delaquot. I forgot all about him."

"What about him?"

"Mr. Flack asked to see his file."

"You don't think?"

"That's what I'm going to find out."

Betty Lu left her friend and took the elevator up to the fourth floor. Julie's shift ended and her replacement came on.

"Donna, it's just what we suspected," stated Julie.

"The hotdogs they serve in the cafeteria aren't kosher," retorted Donna.

"I haven't had a chance to check on that yet. I'm talking about Mr. Flack."

"Oh," said Donna. "You mean…?"

Julie nodded her head.

"Will wonders never cease."

The two women stood there in thought. The switchboard buzzed and Donna set aside the meanderings of Mr. Flack's sexuality to answer it.

***

It wasn't long after leaving his new friends that the Sergeant realized the several helpings of grits he had eaten at Grandmother Wimpole's Restaurant were causing havoc.

While debating the need for an emergency pit stop, the Sergeant tried to remember how many feet comprised the human intestinal system. It wasn't long before he had to put these scientific ponderings to the side. Counting backwards from ten, he came to a screeching halt, jumped out of the car and ran into the woods.

Squatting among the pines, he reminisced about younger days and how he could eat anything he wanted without concern, including multiple servings of grits. Youth had its virtues in the Sergeant's mind and his approaching middle age was starting to take them all away.

It was like the bi-weekly shaving of his head. Most days he only took a fleeting glance at himself and then only if there was a mirror handy. If he was lucky enough to have a barber doing the honors, he'd be handed a mirror, and looking closely he couldn't fail to notice that his hairline was receding and there were snippets of gray hair poking through his skull.

It was dark among the pines when the grits made their last hurrah through the Sergeant's intestinal tract. In need of materials to wipe with he hunted for leaves that weren't poisonous. During the search he ruminated on the idea of having to give up grits for the rest of his life.

With the darkness came another aspect of approaching middle age that the Sergeant found himself dealing with - the loss of his eyesight. Not wanting to take a chance that he'd pick a hunk of poisonous leaves to wipe with, the Sergeant took off his boots, then his pants. Finally he took off his drawers and used them to wipe with.

These roughshod attempts of toiletry have to be seen through the Sergeant's point of view. He had nothing but the most altruistic reasons for using his drawers as toilet paper. Those reasons being, he had borrowed the car belonging to Nathanial Seltingbaum and would not desecrate it.

After he was done, he buried his draws using the bed of pines the forest provided. With his shirt covering his privates, the Sergeant went back to the car to get a clean pair of drawers out of his duffle.

"Maybe it's not the grits, but the lard they mix them with," he thought as he dressed. "That could be the cause of my digestive problems."

Happy with the thought he may not have to give up grits after all, the Sergeant gained his equilibrium back.

It was dark, his guts were sore, and so he decided to call it a night. Getting in the back seat he found a blanket Nathanial kept under the front seat, and wanting no surprises, he locked the doors. Wrapped tight in the blanket, he promptly fell asleep.

***

At the same time the Sergeant was laying his head down for the night, the patient coordinator and fourth floor nurse were standing over the occupant of Bed No. 42.

"He's sleeping like an angel," said Betty Lu.

"Yes he is," said Nurse Shipley.

"There's no way…"

"None," said Nurse Shipley. "Maybe Mr. Flack got a call from his family and because of their concerns he chose to check on Sergeant Delaquot personally to be sure we were doing our best."

"That's probably it," said Betty Lu. "Even though he is of a certain nature, Mr. Flack has always been conscientious of the patient's well-being."

"I'm off duty. We'll go down together."

Nurse Shipley went to get her bag and tell the night nurse she was leaving. Her real intent was to give Betty Lu time to check the identification bracelet on Bobby Wallington's wrist.

When the nurse left the room, Betty Lu didn't hesitate. She went to the side of the bed and picked up Bobby's arm. Reading the name Michael A. Delaquot on the bracelet filled Betty Lu with satisfaction that all was well in the patient coordinator world she lived in.

"I'm ready," Nurse Shipley called from the doorway.

Betty Lu dropped Bobby's arm. The nurse smiled to herself.

The two ladies rode the elevator together. Holly waited as Betty Lu closed up her office. They passed Donna at the switchboard, walked out the sliding doors and into the parking lot.

"Want to stop for a drink?" asked Holly.

Betty Lu's mind worked quickly. She already had the scoop about Mr. Flack and Holly had made no suggestion there would be further news forthcoming.

Taken by surprise the way she was, Betty Lu knew she had a need for education. With so much to learn, she felt her evening would be better spent watching TV. There was that show where men of a certain nature help save the relationships of men who weren't of a certain nature by insisting they get a good haircut and shave, dressing them in more stylish clothes and teaching them how to cook. The show ran in repeats Monday through Thursday at eight on a local channel.

"I'm tired. Think I'll go home," Betty Lu yawned.

"Good night then."

"See you tomorrow."

***

The moment the male nurse saw Nurse Shipley and Betty Lu get on the elevator; he took a nearby gurney and rolled it into Room 423 where Bobby Wallington was impersonating Michael A. Delaquot.

His adrenaline flowing, the male nurse was able to pick Bobby up singlehandedly from Bed No. 42 to the gurney. He rolled the private out of the room, looking both ways to make sure no one was watching.

It wasn't till they arrived at the second floor the nervous gurney pusher asked himself, "Where does this guy belong?"

The dread of being found out was draining the blood from his brain cells. He had only to go in his pocket and look at the id bracelet to find out the needed information; instead he left Bobby near the elevator and walked down the hallway to the nurse's station.

Cheryl Chelswick, the nurse who had mistakenly given Sally an enema as he was sleeping in Bed No. 42, came off the elevator. Not looking where she was going she bumped into Bobby Wallington. As it was evening and all patients were in their rooms, Cheryl, being the sweetheart that she was, checked the patient's identification bracelet.

"Why Sergeant Delaquot, what in heaven's name are you doing here?" she asked the sleeping private.

At that moment a night attendant came walking by.

"Would you help me get the sergeant back to the fourth floor?"

Enraptured by the nurse's batting eyelashes, the attendant did as he was asked. To ensure there were no problems, and as the attendant was particularly handsome, Nurse Chelswick accompanied them on the trip up to the fourth floor.

***

Things were hopping at the Rustic Lodge. More than three-quarters of the day shift were partaking of house specials before heading home.

Nathanial Seltingbaum had tried to question the bartending former soldier to see if he knew anything about the missing soldier, but to no avail as Russ was extremely busy. He decided to hang around until things died down a bit.

Russ, remembering the promise he made to the Sergeant, lined up a row of house specials in front of Nathanial with the promise to speak to him as soon as there was a lull in the crowd.

Nurse Shipley took her house special and as she was expecting Doctor Sorenson, she planted herself in the booth, in the back, in the corner, in the dark, to wait for him. Receiving no calls, she was especially pleased that everything was going according to plan.

On the second floor of the medical facility, the male nurse was about to ask where the private belonged when he remembered the identification bracelet that was in his pocket.

Nurse Happenstance was waiting impatiently at the desk. She wasn't working overtime; she was waiting for Cheryl Chelswick. The two nurses were going over to the Rustic Lodge where two attendants were waiting to dance the night away. She looked up at the male nurse.

"Never mind," he said.

"Never mind what?" she questioned.

"Nothing."

"Okay."

Going back to the elevator, he discovered the gurney was no longer where he left it. The male nurse panicked.

"How could this happen to me a second time?"

"What?" questioned Nurse Happenstance who was on her way to the fourth floor to see what happened to Nurse Chelswick.

"Nothing."

"Don't you belong on four?"

"Yes. Yes, I do," replied the male nurse as he jammed his finger against the elevator button.

"I'll ride up with you."

He cursed his luck.

"What?" questioned Nurse Happenstance.

"Nothing."

Before they could talk further, the elevator doors opened and out popped Nurse Chelswick.

"Sorry I'm late, Dee,"

"That's okay. Let's take the stairs."

The two nurses took the stairway. The male nurse took a fit. Eventually he had to stop as he was attracting the attention of the staff on the second floor.

Unsure of what to do next, he figured it would be better to be back on the fourth floor in order not to raise suspicion.

The elevator doors had closed without him getting on so he pressed the up button again.

The doors opened, he got on, rode up and was about to let himself in the locked doors when his bravado failed him. Actually, he threw up from the stress.

His co-workers began to gather on the other side of the door when they heard the gut wrenching sounds coming from that direction. Through the door's window, they watched in awe as the male nurse's projectile vomiting, containing his mother's favorite stew recipe and his recent addition of eggs, bacon, grits and hash browns, went in all directions.

When he finally stopped and wiped his mouth, the male nurse looked up to see he had an audience. He was about to put his key into the door lock when his co-workers screamed, "NO!"

Thinking it was some sort of viral and/or bacterial virus he was suffering from, they encouraged him through the pane of glass to go home.

The male nurse looked at his co-worker's panicked faces, and not wanting to distress them even more so with the news of another missing patient, he turned away from the door, went down the elevator, through the lobby, out to his car in the parking lot and drove home.

The psyche ward staff when they saw the male nurse get on the elevator breathed a sigh of relief. They called the custodians to do the honors of cleaning the mess up and went back to their duties.

***

Surgery on the female soldier with a hernia was successful and while Dr. Sorenson was stripping out of his surgical scrubs, he had a concerned thought for Bobby Wallington's welfare. The doctor stopped by Bobby's room on the second floor and found he was not back yet.

"It's not like Holly to forget," commented the doctor.

Sure that Nurse Shipley no longer had a need for Bobby, he decided to go up to the fourth floor with a couple of attendants, put the private on a gurney and return him to the second floor where he belonged.

In Room 423 that held Bed No. 42, the doctor and the two attendants found Bobby Wallington sound asleep. Dr. Sorenson first checked his wounds.

"Nurse Shipley is one damn fine nurse," commented the doctor on the re-bandaging technique used on his patient. "Go ahead, fellows."

He was already late for his date. Riding down in the elevator, Dr. Sorenson gave the attendants instructions on what to do with the sleeping patient. They got off on the second floor, Dr. Sorenson got off on the first. Saying goodnight to Donna, he stepped through the sliding doors and slipped a cigar in his mouth. He chose not to put a match to it as he was only a minute away from the lodge.

Russ saw Dr. Sorenson walk in the door, "Got your drink right here, Doc."

"Thank you."

"How'd your day go?"

"Brilliantly, if I say so myself."

"Good. Have another."

"Don't mind if I do," stated the doctor.

He took his second drink with him as he sauntered over to the booth where Holly was waiting.

"Hey, doll."

"Hi, Bryan."

He slid into the booth and gave her a kiss.

"How'd your day go?" he asked.

"Fine. How's the hernia patient?"

"On top of the world good. How'd Bobby do?"

"He accomplished his mission."

"That's the key to a number one performance, the right actor."

The doctor raised his hand and one of Russ' men came over to the booth with two more house specials.

As Dr. Sorenson and Nurse Shipley were enjoying their drinks, on the second floor of the medical facility, night nurse, Honoria Cantone, was making her rounds. She was in charge of giving meds to the patients.

During her days as a student, Honoria had mistakenly given a mega dose of aspirin to a patient who was on blood thinning drugs. It was a bloody mess for all and almost cost her a place on the honor roll.

The investigation that ensued tracked a typo in the computer records and Honoria's standing as one of the leading students in her class was saved. Never wanting to relive that nightmare, she made sure to be especially astute in following protocol when it came to handing out meds to her patients.

She would check a patient's identification bracelet to confirm the name of the patient. Then she checked the meds book to see if that patient's name and bed number were on her list. If the two did not match, the patient did not get medication.

She was working on the second floor when she discovered the name on the wrist of soldier patient Bed. No. 65 did not correspond with the name in her book.

Nurse Cantone went to the nurse's station and onto the computer to be sure there was not a typo of some sort. Her book and the computer matched, the patient who should be in Bed No. 65 was one soldier patient Robert Wallington, private.

Taking matters into her own hands and the stairs to the fourth floor, Nurse Cantone conferred with the ward's staff and was told about their missing soldier patient Bed. No. 42, Michael A. Delaquot. Nurse Cantone told them she knew the whereabouts of soldier patient Bed. No. 42. That he was in the bed of soldier patient Bed. No. 65.

The crew on the fourth floor were ecstatic that their missing soldier had at last been found. Two attendants accompanied Nurse Cantone down to the second floor. They placed Bobby Wallington, on a gurney and rolled him up to Room 423 on the fourth floor.

***

The male nurse, now back at home, had taken a bromide for his hurting stomach. Head in his hands, he spent some time looking at the identification bracelet sitting on his kitchen table and beating himself up over his recent shortcomings.

He had failed Nurse Shipley miserably he thought to himself. How could he go back to the medical facility after such a failure?

Unable to think straight about where Bobby Wallington could have vanished to, he got down on his knees and prayed for a miracle. As all prayers are eventually answered in some way or form, his brain cleared, a bright light shone through and the thought came to him that maybe when he left the gurney in the hallway someone had recognized the face of the private and without looking at his wristband returned him to his room on the second floor.

Vowing to go back to church if this was the answer he needed, he came up with a plan of action.

After a couple of hours sleep to let the pain in his gut subside, he would go back to the medical facility and up to the second floor, cut Michael A. Delaquot's name off of Bobby Wallington and put the right identification bracelet on his wrist before anyone found out.

It was going to be a long night. He set his alarm clock.

Sally was in the medical facility elevator going up to the fourth floor. With him was Private Blue Morgan, a resident of the medical facility morgue.

Private Morgan had not seen battle. He had not been overseas fighting for his country. Blue had died from the results of self-inflicted chemical poisoning, or so it stated on his autopsy report.

This was not entirely true.

Private Morgan had made it through basic training and during his first leave the private and his buddies went to a bar and got wasted. Blue bet his fellow soldiers he could drink them all under the table.

He could.

His buddies, who were passed out on the floor, abandoned the private to his own devices. After drinking the equivalent of a barrel of beer, the private went in search of a bathroom.

Mistaking the exit door for the bar's bathroom door, Blue left the bar, made his way to the middle of the road, unzipped his pants and proceeded to urinate. By the time the approaching student driver saw him it was too late.

The said student driver, who we will leave unnamed, was told by the local police and his driving instructor that it was not his fault; the demon rum had done the private in. The student driver wanting to work as a pizza delivery person got back in the car and eventually got his license.

The events that brought about Blue's death happened exactly six months ago. When his mother, Mrs. Morgan, heard that her son got himself killed by the act of taking a piss in the street, she contacted a lawyer and began a wrongful death lawsuit on behalf of her son against the United States Army.

The documents submitted to the court accused the army of self-serving motives in undoing the toilet training methods used by Mrs. Morgan, thereby jeopardizing her son's welfare and causing his eventual death. She was looking for recompense and an apology.

She also felt strongly that it would be a waste of time to bury her son before the lawsuit was settled. Having a talent for reading people's faces, she told her lawyer if even one juror didn't look sympathetic to her case they were to drag Blue into court so they may see him for themselves. Her attorney pointed out to her that this extreme action would not be necessary.

Blue's family didn't care one way or another about his burial, but they did insist that the Morgan family tradition of holding a memorial service at the dead relative's favorite bar be upheld. On this point only the grieving mother conceded.

During the memorial service, Mrs. Morgan told one and all that if Blue hadn't been broken of the potty training she so carefully instilled in him as a child, her son would be alive today.

One and all who attended testified that during his evenings spent drinking he never once went outside to pee in the road and always made use of the bar's facilities. Blue's mourners were entirely sympathetic with Mrs. Morgan and the legal situation she now found herself embroiled in.

Seeing how the grieving mother refused to claim her son's body, the board for the medical facility held an emergency meeting. They voted on the issue and it passed 7-0. The medical facility would be responsible for Blue Morgan until a decision was made in the wrongful death lawsuit.

For the record, the board's vote to keep Private Morgan took place before Mr. Flack was hired as an administrator and after he was fired from his job at the lobster and shrimp shipping company,

After voting was finished, the board members went over to the Rustic Lodge, where each confessed to why they voted the way they had. It turned out half felt badly that nothing could be done to bring Private Morgan back to life when he was delivered DOA to their doorstep. The other half agreed it was the least they could for a serviceman in need.

Unlike the board members who kept Blue on ice in the morgue, Sally had no altruistic reasons for bringing Private Morgan up to the fourth floor to take the place of Sergeant Delaquot while he was away. It was purely selfish motives combined with drinking too many of Russ' house specials.

Sally didn't want anything to happen to Nathanial Seltingbaum. If he lost his job, a PR that felt it was his duty to come to work each day may replace him. That would leave the attendant with nowhere to romance the nurses and kitchen workers like Mildred Harrington.

The thought of losing the office now that Mr. Flack was putting in a heater, leather couch, microwave and refrigerator upset Sally so much, even in his intoxicated state, he knew he had no choice but to take a stand.

After getting the low-down from Russ about the missing soldier, he had a few more house specials, weaved back to the medical facility and snuck into Betty Lu's office. Using her computer, he printed out an id bracelet in the name of Michael A. Delaquot.

He then went down to the PR's office to meet Mildred as he had told her they would hook-up again to make up for Mr. Flack interrupting them that same morning.

After Mildred left the PR office and the very drunk attendant, she went to meet her husband, Stan, as he was going off duty. Sally stayed to sleep it off. Several hours later, he woke up still intoxicated and fully devoted to following through with his plan.

Knowing no one would be looking for Private Morgan, and as he was in no condition to complain, Sally cut off his id bracelet, put the new one on and placed Blue on a gurney.

He gained access to the locked ward when he told the night attendant that Private Morgan was on his deathbed and wanted one last time to visit with his best friend, soldier patient Bed No 38. The attendant asked no questions and went back to his business.

With no one suspecting anything, Sally went into the room that held Bed. No. 42. He rolled Private Morgan up to the bed and was about to place him in it when he discovered there was already someone there. Unable to see in the dark, he turned on the lights. Bobby Wallington blinked ever so slightly.

"Who are you?" questioned the irate attendant. "There's something fishy going on here."

Remembering how that very morning Nurse Chelswick had accosted him in the same bed, he assumed the comatose private was a fellow medical facility employee catching a few zzz's.

"Wake up," shouted Sally.

Bobby Wallington blinked. As he was not given his night meds by Nurse Cantone, he was coming around a bit.

"What's your name? Who are you?"

"Wallington, Robert, Private First Class," whispered Bobby.

Sally thought. And he thought. And he thought some more. Nothing. Finally, he took out his cell phone. It took him three calls before he got the right number.

"Medical facility, Donna speaking," the recipient of the call said.

"What room is Bobby Wallington in?"

"Room 222, I'll --"

Sally hung up.

"You my friend are in the wrong place. Let's get you back where you belong."

The attendant put the gurney next to Bed No. 42. He turned Bobby and Blue this way and that. It was a slow process and one of heavy lifting, but with the incentive of the

66

leather couch egging him on, Sally transitioned the two fellows.

With Private Morgan now in Bed No. 42, Sally wished him a good night and turned out the light. He then pushed Bobby Wallington to the elevator and took him down to the second floor. He shouted to the nurse sitting at the desk that Bobby was back and without stopping pushed the gurney into Room 222. A wave of good feeling came over Sally. Maybe he had done a good turn after all in saving Nathanial's job.

Tired from a night of romancing kitchen aides and turning soldiers this way and that, also remembering how Blue Morgan left his world, Sally went back down to the PR office to sleep it off.

***

After a couple of hours sleep, the male nurse woke to the buzz of his alarm clock. He made himself some tea and toast, changed his clothes, took the id bracelet and Nurse Shipley's knife off the kitchen table, put them in his pocket, got in his car and went back to the medical facility.

Donna was dozing when he walked past the switchboard office. Visiting hours were long over, so there was no one manning the reception desk. Thinking he might run into someone on the elevator, he took the stairway.

All was quiet on the second floor. Taking advantage of the time afforded by the sleeping soldiers, the staff members were enjoying a little camaraderie in the break room. As he passed, the male nurse could hear them laughing and talking about the upcoming company picnic and of picnics past.

He quickly made his way to Room 222, sliced the bracelet off the private's wrist and replaced it with the one given to him by Nurse Shipley.

Private Wallington, with only a few flutters of the eye, had served his country well.

Dr. Sorenson had taken Bobby from the second floor to the fourth floor.

The male nurse had taken him from the fourth floor back to the second floor.

Nurse Cheryl Chelswick had taken him from the second floor back to the fourth floor.

Dr. Sorenson had returned Bobby back to the second floor.

Nurse Cantone took Bobby from the second floor to the fourth floor.

Sally took Bobby from the fourth floor back to the second floor.

Lastly, the male nurse put Bobby's correct identification bracelet back on his wrist. Satisfied that the job was done to Nurse Shipley's specifications, he went into the stairway just as Nurse Cantone was exiting the elevator. She had medicated all the patients trusted to her, and in her journey was told by the staff on the third floor that Bobby Wallington was not in their care.

Nurse Cantone, being a stickler for details, decided to go back to the second floor and see if the staff had located their missing soldier patient. When she saw all was quiet and the staff members were on break, she decided not to bother them and went directly to Room 222.

She found a soldier sleeping in Bed No. 65. Checking the wristband and her book, she found a perfect match and was then able to administer Bobby's meds.

The private's time impersonating Michael A. Delaquot was over. He fell into a deeper sleep, and in a week or so to come, Dr. Sorenson gave the word that his not so 'little Bobby' was mostly healed and he could be brought out from the induced coma.

Upon awakening, those around him would question how it felt to be in a coma and if he had any dreams. The private answered honestly, he didn't remember how it felt, but in his dreams he sure did a lot of riding in elevators.

Leaving Room 222, the male nurse had walked past the break room to the stairway, past the receptionist desk where Donna was still snoozing, out the sliding doors, back to his car and when finally at home he laid his head down on his pillow and slept the sleep of one who had been redeemed.

***

While all this was going on, Dr. Sorenson and Nurse Shipley had been dancing and drinking the night away. When the jukebox took a break, the doctor looked at his watch.

"It's getting late."

Holly knew what that meant, their time together was over. Bryan would go back to the medical facility, check on his hernia patient and call it a night, more than likely falling asleep on the couch in his office. Feeling particularly frisky after averting what could have been a catastrophe, she cuddled closer.

"I know of an empty bed," Holly whispered seductively.

The good doctor, feeling particularly frisky from a day of operations gone well, agreed.

"Let's go."

Behind the bar things had slowed down. Nathanial, after downing several house specials, felt it was a good time to question Russ about the missing soldier.

"Russsssss!" shouted the PR.

"Keep your voice down, boy."

"Sorry!" he shouted.

"That's okay."

Nathanial motioned for Russ to come closer. He grabbed the lodge owner by the shirt. Two of the former soldiers seeing their commander being set upon came right over. Their leader held up his hand and the men stopped in their tracks.

"All hell is breaking out and they want me to cover it up," spluttered the PR before passing out.

Nathanial's head landed in the bowl of pigs in a blanket that were kept on the bar for the customers. Russ motioned to the former soldiers.

"Be gentle with him," he said as concern for the welfare of his clientele always came first.

They carried Nathanial over to the booth in the back, in the corner, in the dark, that was recently occupied by Nurse Shipley and Dr. Sorenson.

Feeling mischievous, when Bryan and Holly came through the sliding doors, they went over to the switchboard office and the doctor slammed his hand against the desk, causing Donna to wake up with a jolt.

"Oh, it's you Dr. Sorenson," said the night operator as she wiped the drool from the side of her mouth.

"How are you tonight, Donna?"

"I'm fine. Thank you for asking."

"Any emergencies?"

"Oh, you're teasing me. I would have called you."

"I know. I'm going to check on a patient and get some shuteye. If you need me just buzz."

"Sleep tight," said the operator as her head fell upon the desk.

The two took the elevator up to the second floor. Dr. Sorenson looked in on his hernia patient; Nurse Shipley went in to see how Bobby Wallington was doing.

"Sleeping like an angel."

Holly took that moment to see if the male nurse had followed her instructions to the letter. Taking up his wrist, she read the name of Robert Wallington on the identification bracelet.

"Thank you, soldier," she whispered.

Leaving Bobby to his dreams, she left the room and met her date at the elevator. Together they went up to the fourth

70

floor. Nurse Shipley opened the locked door with her key and not seeing anyone they were able to go to Room 423 without interference.

Bryan closed the door and Holly threw herself at the good doctor. They kissed as if it was the first time, which it most decidedly was not. Wrapped in an embrace, lips locked, he led her across the room and they both fell onto Bed No. 42.

If Holly had not been in a lip lock with Bryan as they fell upon the bed she would have screamed when they dropped onto the body of Blue Morgan.

"Who the hell is that?" questioned the doctor after switching on the light.

"I have no idea."

He looked at the identification bracelet.

"Michael A. Delaquot."

The two looked closer at the face of Blue Morgan.

"Can't be," said Dr. Sorenson. "How long did you say Delaquot was missing?"

"Only this morning."

"This man's been dead for some time. This is not who the wristband says it is."

"Bryan, I have a little matter to take care of."

"Sure, doll. You don't need my help?"

"You've helped me enough today."

"You know where to find me."

Nurse Shipley was angry that the missing soldier patient was now becoming a nuisance. She unlocked the door for her date and went to the nurse's station.

"What are you doing here?" questioned Constance Blake, the fourth floor night nurse.

"Did you happen to notice there's a dead body in Bed No. 42?"

"Really, anyone we know?"

"No idea, but I think I know how he got there. Have two attendants meet me in Room 423."

"Right away," said Nurse Blake.

The two attendants shifted Blue Morgan onto a gurney and along with Nurse Shipley they took him back to the morgue. There was no one on duty. Needing a clue as to who the dead soldier on the gurney was, they did a quick search.

Nurse Shipley found an employee name tag.

"Salvatore Krishnecki," she read.

One of the attendants, being a sharpshooter in his earlier days, spied an id bracelet on the floor. He handed it over.

"Blue Morgan," read the nurse.

Telling the attendants to keep an eye on him, she went to the main floor. Using a hairpin, she unlocked the office door of patient coordination, and helped herself to Betty Lu's computer. Within minutes she was back in the morgue replacing Blue's identification bracelet.

With Private Morgan back where he belonged, the two attendants took the elevator up to the fourth floor and Nurse Shipley took the stairs down to the lower level.

Without knocking on the door, she let herself into the PR office. Finding Sally asleep on the desk, she took a magazine that dealt with the subject matter of business relations that lay on a table next to a lamp. Rolling it up, she then smacked the attendant on the head with it.

The hit didn't wake him up. He only turned in his sleep. Exasperated and in no mood for an argument anyway, she gave Sally another smack for good measure and threw the magazine to the floor. She then went up to the second floor, stopped to get clean bedding from a cart and knocked on Bryan's office door to let him know that Bed No. 42 was no longer occupied.

0100 hrs
MAY 16th

The hour was growing late and the only customer left in the lodge was Nathanial who was sleeping in the back booth. With no one to wait on, Russ called for a meeting of the minds with the former soldiers who worked for him.

"I need someone to impersonate a soldier gone AWOL. The soldier is attending to family business in Tuscaloosa and will be returning by the nineteenth give or take a day or two. Do I have any volunteers?"

Each man raised his hand.

The lodge owner was a proud employer of former soldiers. Instead of picking someone who closely resembled Michael A. Delaquot, he chose to give one and all a fair shot at doing a good deed for a soldier in uniform.

"You'll draw straws," said Russ.

He prepared the straws. The former soldiers chose. It was Blinky Billington who drew the long straw.

Russ took the identification bracelet out of the cash register. As he had sliced the bracelet to get it off the Sergeant's wrist, he turned to Tom Chase, a former supply officer for the army. Tom never failed to be prepared for any situation. He took out of his pocket two bonding agents, one for porous and one for non-porous materials.

Matt Cohn, a former detonator expert who hadn't lost his steady hand, took the porous bottle and without a drop going on the long straw holder's wrist, he glued the identification bracelet back together.

Blinky blinked at the information on the bracelet, "Fourth floor."

"Psyche ward," confirmed Russ.

"Covert operation," said Matt.

"Without a doubt," added Tom.

"It needs a name," stated Matt.

"Can't have a mission without a name," agreed Tom.

"This will take some assessment," stated Russ.

So he went to the bar and mixed up a large batch of the house special. Never having the opportunity to name any of the missions the army sent them on, the former soldiers had a good time throwing names to the wind and shooting them out of the air. After an hour, it was decided the only fair way to settle the matter was to pick a name out of a hat.

"Who's going to do the picking?" asked Tom

Russ looked at the men around him. They looked back at him. He got up and made another pitcher of house specials.

Another hour later, and after much discussion on each other's trustworthiness, it was decided they'd have no choice but to find an honest man by putting each of their names on a slip of paper and one of them picking from a hat.

The next hour was spent having several elimination rounds of rock, paper, scissors to see who would win the chance to pick the name of an honest man out of the hat. Russ was the rock, paper, scissors champ. He picked the winning honest man out of the hat, which was Louie Dombrowski.

To be sure things were kept on the up and up, and even though they told Louie to his face that they trusted him as much as they would trust their own mothers, they made the former soldier strip to his shorts before they would allow him to pick the mission's name out of the hat.

While Louie stripped down to his skivvies, the former soldiers wrote all their name choices on small pieces of paper, folded them up and tossed them in.

"Operation Skunk."

"That stinks," said Matt.

Louie pulled another paper, "Operation Bedside Manner."

"Who here has ever had a woman tell them they have a good bedside manner?" questioned Russ.

The men looked at each other and shrugged.

"Next!"

"Operation Its Your Lover Boy."

"Which one of you sexist pigs put that in?" bellowed Blinky.

"Next!"

"Operation Wolf in Sheep's Clothing."

"Okay, which one of you guys has an animal complex?" questioned Russ.

***

While the former soldiers were picking names out of a hat, most of the parties to the previous day's events were sleeping – some peacefully some not.

By the side of the road, Michael A. Delaquot found it was tough going to try and sleep as it took some time for his intestines to quiet down from their overload of grits made with lard.

Down in the PR office, Sally had woken up. He looked at his watch. In the process of saving the PR's job by bringing Blue Morgan to the fourth floor, he had missed his date with Rhonda Blisnick, a day nurse from the third floor, who had gone off duty and was supposed to meet him next door.

Rhonda known for being trouble if stood up, would not be happy with Sally and as he would have to lie about why he wasn't there to meet her and his brain was all used up on thinking of a plan to save the PR's job, he decided to stay where he was and fell back to sleep on his - Nathanial's desk.

Back at the lodge, Nathanial woke up. Determined to sleep at home in his own bed, he veered across the lodge dance floor. He waved a goodnight to the former soldiers. With their minds concentrating on the naming of the mission, they sent him on his way with a message to get home safe. Just as he reached the door, Russ remembered the AWOL soldier was making use of Nathanial's car.

Russ called out to Louie Dombrowski who was just coming in from taking a cigarette break. On the ruse, that he was their hundredth customer and had won a pitcher of house specials, Louie escorted the PR back to the booth.

Having never won anything in his life, Nathanial was not about to give up his winnings for his soft bed at home. Russ made the pitcher of house specials extra strong and Nathanial slept peacefully.

Blue Morgan continued to sleep with the angels.

A newly medicated Bobby Wallington was sleeping heavily.

With no callers to speak of, Donna was sleeping peacefully at the reception desk.

As for Betty Lu, she had gained the needed knowledge about men of a certain nature and had stayed glued to her set to watch two reruns of ER, which was her favorite show. She was now in bed sleeping peacefully with her cat beside her.

The male nurse who had the night off thanks to his bout of projectile vomiting was sleeping peacefully at home.

After making mad passionate love, which they did quietly in order not to disturb the patients and staff members, Holly and Bryan were sleeping peacefully in Bed. No. 42.

And what about Mr. Flack?

His sleep was not so peaceful. Tossing and turning, his conscious mind was trying to wake up while his sub-conscious mind was dreaming about man-sized lobsters taking over the medical facility.

The lobstermen had invaded his office. They dragged him down to the PR office where the three wives of his former boss were waiting for him. They tied him to a chair and the wives bombarded him with the question - "How could we not know?"

When he couldn't answer them, the lobstermen tortured him by making him eat plate after plate of fried shrimp. Telling them he had to use the bathroom, they untied him and he made a break for it.

Running up the stairs to the fourth floor he ran into Room 423 and jumped into Bed No. 42, which was occupied by the lobster and shrimp shipping president who was hiding under the covers.

His former boss pushed him out of the bed at the same moment the shareholders from the lobster and shrimp shipping company slammed into the room with two lobstermen. The hard-shelled creatures carried him out of the room and down to the boiler room.

The three wives were waiting. Someone opened the door to the boiler and as they threw him into the fire he heard someone shouting,

"Let him burn!"

That's when Mr. Flack woke up in a cold sweat, which was okay because by this time it was morning.

***

It took several pitchers of house specials and many slips of paper added to the hat before Louie picked a name they could work under. Operation AWOL Soldier, they all agreed, was very professional and had nothing to do with animals.

With that taken care of, they were on to the next bit of business, Blinky's face. It was generally agreed upon that those who worked in the medical facility not only knew Blinky by name but by face, therefore, he would have to go in with his head wrapped in bandages.

The next question arose – Why would the AWOL Sergeant have his head wrapped in bandages?

Being romantics at heart the men came up with this tall tale.

Michael A. Delaquot had left the medical facility to see his girlfriend who was going to marry someone else. When he got to his girlfriend's apartment, he yelled out that he forbid her to marry another man. The other man, asleep in the bedroom, woke up when he heard the soldier yelling. He came out and gave the Sergeant a beating about the head to shut him up.

When the other man was done beating Delaquot, the girlfriend called 911. An ambulance came and took him to a civilian hospital for fixing up. After taking care of his wounds, the hospital staff put the Sergeant in an ambulance and shipped him back to the medical facility.

There was a glitch to the plan.

If the Sergeant came back into the medical facility with bandages wrapped around his skull, the staff would have no choice but to call his wife and give her the sad news that her beloved husband had met with an accident.

After the former soldiers shed a few drunken tears over how they would feel if their women cheated on them, Russ poured more house specials and they came up with a solution to the glitch.

Blinky, while posing as the Sergeant, would beg them not to call his wife, as he didn't want her to find out about his prowling escapades to see his girlfriend. As most wives have an instinct about their husband's philandering, the staff would be reluctant to deal with a woman who lived in denial and that would keep them from calling Mrs. Sergeant Delaquot.

With the Sergeant's reason for leaving the facility and explanation of bandages decided, the former soldiers dried their tears. Actually, this story was based on a true-life incident that happened to a friend of Matt Cohn, the detonator expert. It was reassuring to the men of Operation AWOL Soldier to know that.

Looking into the small details that come along with missions of this type, the men questioned the next part of the plan. Should they steal an ambulance from another medical facility, have two of their crew dress as ambulance drivers and drop Blinky off at the facility or just walk next door, steal a wheelchair and have him roll up to the door on his own?

The better part of the night was spent weighing the pros and cons of stealing an ambulance or using a wheelchair. In the end, it was the former soldiers' enjoyment of getting back into a covert operation that made them decide to steal an ambulance and dress like drivers.

As a former supply officer for the army, Tom Chase was unanimously voted the honor of heading a group in pursuit of obtaining the aforesaid ambulance. He chose Matt Cohn, detonator expert, and Louie Dombrowski to accompany him.

The sun rose and Operation AWOL Soldier was put in motion. Tom, Matt and Louie were hyped about the mission they were undertaking. It was to be the first since giving up their various positions with the military. And as much as they liked working for Russ, they all agreed it felt good to be back in the saddle again.

Russ made a pot of coffee. Matt went to the men's room to splash water on his face. Tom went to the medical facility kitchen to obtain some hydrating drinks for the road. And Louie programmed the GPS in his car.

Giving and receiving claps on the back and pats on the butt like professional ball players do when they win or just feel the urge, the three chosen men left their buddies and set out for Township Forkship, which was twenty-five miles off the Witchitauki Highway.

***

As the former soldiers approached the Witchitauki Highway entrance ramp, those who had spent the night in various degrees and places of sleep were starting their day.

The Sergeant was waking up on Rte. 28. His back was stiff, but the sun was shining and that was always a good thing where he was concerned. After relieving himself in the woods, he got back in the driver's seat and took off with the hope of finding a diner as he was especially hungry.

On the fourth floor of the medical facility the occupants of Bed No. 42 awoke to find they were entangled in an embrace. Holly, not wanting Bryan to smell her morning breath, forgot she was in a single bed and turning over fell on the floor.

Her shift over, the night nurse was passing Room 423 on her way to the elevator. She heard a whelp and walked into the room.

"Morning, Constance," said Dr. Sorenson who lay there naked as Holly, in the process of falling off the bed, had taken the covers with her.

"Morning, Bryan."

She peeped over the bed to see who was on the floor. Holly looked up and smiled. Constance smiled back.

"Are you okay?"

"Fine."

"Good. I'm going off duty. All is as I found it when I came on duty. You know what I'm speaking of?"

Having just rolled out of bed, literally, Holly knew Constance was speaking about the person who should have rolled out of this same bed. Looking up at the night nurse, the day nurse nodded her head in understanding.

"Have a good day you two."

With that the night nurse left the room.

"Well, our day has gotten off to a running start," said the smiling doctor as he helped his bed companion off the floor.

On the main floor, Betty Lu was coming through the sliding doors. She headed right for the switchboard office where she found Donna who was just waking up. She stopped to chat on the comings and goings of the night. The night operator reported that it was slow with no new patients arriving. As they were speaking, Mr. Flack came through the sliding doors. The two women stopped speaking as they watched him cross the lobby.

The administrator's nightmare had unsettled him, so he wasn't his usual dandy self. With the only clear memory of his dream being the three wives putting him in the medical facility boiler, upon waking he was so distraught he put on the same clothes he wore the day before.

When he walked around the corner, Betty Lu and Donna analyzed the sad state of dishevel that was their fearless leader. And the two women didn't miss a trick that the clothes Mr. Flack wore to work today were the same clothes he wore yesterday.

Down in the PR office, Sally was waking up. He found his head hurt like he had been hit with something. Not one for long suffering, he got up from the desk and went up to the main floor. He avoided the kitchen altogether and took another exit on his way to the Rustic Lodge.

Russ was behind the bar. He greeted the attendant with a bright good morning and a house special. Sally sat down at the bar and downed it. Russ poured him another.

"We came up with a plan."

"A plan for what?" questioned Sally.

"To take care of the missing soldier problem."

"That's already taken care of."

He held out his glass and Russ poured him another.

"Right now there's a stiff in Bed No. 42," stated Sally as he gulped his drink.

Actually, the attendant was partially right; there was a stiff in Bed No. 42. When Nurse Shipley came out of the bathroom, she saw 'little Bryan' standing at attention.

Tossing a blanket over the randy doctor, she saluted and said, "At ease!"

***

81

Russ was confounded by Sally's admission that he had taken care of the problem of the AWOL Sergeant. Checking his watch, he was willing to bet the Rustic Lodge to any takers that the men who went on a mission to obtain an ambulance were at this moment on schedule and driving said ambulance in the lodge's direction.

He poured a house special and was about to drink it down when Nurse Shipley came slamming through the door.

"Sally!"

Seeing she was a spitfire of rage, the attendant ran behind the bar in order to obtain the added protection of the former soldier.

After leaving Room 423 and the two Bryans, Holly had gone to the nurse's station. While making sure that the changing of shifts had taken place with no problems, she noticed her patients were not partaking of breakfast. Knowing Sally was more than likely nursing a hangover and in need of the hair of the dog that bit him, she told the staff she was going to find out what was delaying the morning meal.

"My soldiers are waiting for their breakfast, Sally," said the nurse, as she stood on the customer side of the bar.

"Gee, I forgot all about them."

The concern for the soldier patients momentarily overtook Sally's concern for his own safety. He came out from behind the bar. In his eagerness to get to them, he passed Nurse Shipley just close enough for her to swing her fist into his jaw.

Down he went.

Caught between breaths while swallowing a house special, Russ began to splutter.

"Are you okay?" the nurse asked.

Russ nodded. And since he wasn't turning blue, she turned her attention to the floor where the attendant lay.

"Don't you ever again think about putting a dead soldier in a bed on my floor. Blue Morgan is back where he belongs.

I will deal with the problem of Michael A. Delaquot. Do you understand me?"

With the back of his head and his chin wracked with pain, Sally could barely nod. Having made her point, Blinky, who had taken over Louie's post, opened the door and she stormed out.

Taking a moment to be sure the coast was clear, Russ helped his customer off the floor, made him another house special, and an ice pack for his chin.

***

Following several billboards promising good eats that were strategically placed along the roadway, Sergeant Delaquot took the required exit and promptly missed the turn-off. After driving several miles along a dirt road he circled around and found the advertised eatery. When asked if he wanted grits with his eggs, bacon, sausage, biscuit, wheat toast and hash browns, he declined the offer.

The waitress poured him several cups of coffee with his meal. Being the place was well known for their jailhouse strength beverage, it wasn't long before he was feeling his mettle again.

Being sure to leave a hefty tip for the waitress, who at that time of the morning was as pleasant as the sun shining amid the blue sky, the Sergeant left the diner and took a look at his surroundings.

"Think I'll stretch the legs a bit."

So he made a left and walked down the street to explore the small town of Ridleyville.

As the Sergeant was making his tour, Betty Lu was knocking on the administrator's door.

"Come on in."

"Good morning," declared the patient coordinator.

83

Fuzzy headed, Mr. Flack just looked at her.

"I wanted to remind you about Mac Treeter."

His look became a blank stare as his mind was occupied with the thoughts of the three wives and how in the past they cost him his job and most recently a good night's sleep.

"My computer... It was broken into," reminded Betty Lu.

"I'll get right on it."

When she didn't turn around and leave the way she had come, Mr. Flack took it upon himself to escort her.

"Anything else?"

"No," said Betty Lu. "How are your children?"

"Wilfred received a 90 on his algebra test. Celeste has a role in the school play and Luke is going to graduate to the second grade after all," Mr. Flack answered as he led the meddlesome woman to the door.

As she stood on the threshold, Betty Lu attempted to squeeze in the last word. "Your wife must be very..." The door shut in her face. "...proud."

Mortified by his treatment, she could swear she heard the door lock from the inside. Making sure first that no one was looking, she tried the doorknob. It was locked. Walking back to her office, she could only ponder the added insult for a moment as she began to remember something.

"I thought he said his children's names were Benjamin, Hermoine and T.J."

Excited that she found him in a lie, she by-passed her office and went to the personnel office to check his file. On the inside of the locked door, Mr. Flack sat down at his desk and put his head in his hands.

The phone began to ring.

He stared at it. Worried that it was reporters calling to find out about the missing soldier, he didn't answer. When the phone stopped ringing, he picked up the receiver and dialed the public relations office. No answer.

"Where is our PR man?" He left his office to look for Nathanial.

Over at the Rustic Lodge, Nathanial was being served a cup of coffee.

"Thanks, Russ."

"Don't want you to be late for work."

"I appreciate that. Especially as we have a matter of PR going on right now that needs seeing to."

"It's about the missing soldier, isn't it?"

"How'd you know?" asked Nathanial.

"Word gets around."

"Well if this word better gets around it could mean my job."

Just then Tom, Matt, and Louie came through the back door. The three, just returned from their mission to secure an ambulance, gave Russ the thumbs up.

"I don't think you'll have to worry much longer about the missing soldier," said Russ.

"Really, why do you think that?" questioned Nathanial.

"Something tells me he'll be back and right soon at that."

***

Nurse Cheryl Chelswick, tired from a night of dancing with the attendant of her dreams, was making her morning enema rounds.

In no mood for this part of her job, she wanted to make the duty of sticking an apparatus up the anal cavity of soldiers in need a quick one. She barged into Room 423 without the ritual good morning. Seeing a body in Bed No. 42 she got right down to business. Cheryl lifted the sheet and jabbed an enema into the rear of the occupant.

The occupant yelled, "What the hell you doing there, girl?"

"Dr. Sorenson, I didn't realize it was you."

"Indeed you didn't," said the doctor as he sat up.

With the enema in her hand and her job on the line, she froze.

"Nurse...?"

"Chelswick."

"Nurse Chelswick, in the future I suggest you look at the patient's identification bracelet before jabbing them with your excrement inducing cocktail."

"Yes, Dr. Sorenson."

"Now if you'll excuse me, I have to use the little boy's room."

"Yes, Dr. Sorenson."

She stood there still frozen. The doctor looked at her and smiled.

"You're dismissed," he said kindly.

The nurse smiled back and took the excrement inducing equipment with her when she left.

"Can this day get any more unusual?" asked the doctor as he rushed into the bathroom.

***

In his search to find the PR, Mr. Flack went down to the lower level office. As was typical on a workday, Nathanial wasn't there. Not wanting the trip to be a waste, the administrator took this opportunity to check out the ancient k-rations that sat on the shelves.

He jumped when the phone began to ring.

Not wanting to answer it, the phone kept ringing and Mr. Flack's brain went into post-traumatic stress syndrome. He flashbacked to the part of his dream where the three wives had him tied up in this very room and lobstermen were force-feeding him fried shrimp.

Panicked, he dropped the k-ration, ran out of the room all the way back to his office and locked himself in.

Minutes later, Mr. Flack, sitting at his desk terrified and sweating, jumped out of his seat when he heard a knock on the door. He looked at the door hoping to see through it, but not having super powers was unable to.

There was another knock.

"Come in already," screamed the administrator in a shrill voice.

The person on the other side tried the door but it didn't open. Mr. Flack stood there.

"Mr. Flack?"

"Nathanial? Is that you?" he rushed over to open the door. "Thank God, you're here."

He pulled the wayward PR into the office by way of his collar just as Betty Lu was passing by holding his personnel file. She couldn't believe her eyes.

"It's daytime and so early in the morning."

She quickly turned direction and headed to the reception desk to speak to Julie Binder.

Needing answers, Mr. Flack grilled Nathanial. "What's going on with our missing soldier? Do the newspapers know about it already?"

"No. Nothing's been leaked out."

The administrator sat down at his desk, and looking heavenward, loudly thanked his higher power.

"You're welcome," said Nathanial.

"I didn't mean…well actually…good job. Was there anything else you needed to see me about?"

"No," answered the PR.

"Keep up the good work then."

Nathanial left closing the door behind him. He picked up the newspaper that he had left on a table before going into his boss's office.

It was this local newspaper that didn't carry a headline or article on a missing soldier at the medical facility that caused him to answer his boss honestly that nothing had been leaked.

The only matter of PR being well in hand, Nathanial stood in the hallway pondering his next move. As he was hungry, he decided to go to the coffee shop and get some breakfast.

Walking in, he was unaware of the stares he was receiving from Betty Lu and Julie. The operator had been late for work and only on duty forty-five minutes before taking an emergency coffee break.

"That was quick," said Betty Lu about Nathanial's appearance in the coffee shop.

"I told you he has a girlfriend," said Julie.

"That in my book in neither here nor there."

She looked around. Being the coffee shop was empty except for her, Julie and the lone member of the public relations department, Betty Lu felt free to open Mr. Flack's personnel file.

The two women read it over quickly. They looked at each other.

"It's just as I suspected."

"Files don't lie, that's for sure."

The two ladies kept their eye on Nathanial as he poured an espresso.

***

Blinky Billington sat still as Matt, the former detonator expert, wrapped his face and head in bandages.

"Any problems requisitioning the ambulance?" asked Russ.

"Piece of cake," answered Tom, the former supply officer for the army.

Blinky changed into a pair of hospital scrubs that were stored behind the bar for an attendant who always managed to spill house specials on his attire.

The former soldiers took inventory of their replacement for the AWOL soldier.

"Bracelet on?"

"Check."

"Bandages?"

"Check."

"Scrubs?"

"Check."

"Slippers?"

No answer.

The former soldiers looked at Blinky's bare feet.

"Think anyone will notice?" questioned Russ.

The men looked to each other. They shook their heads.

"We're ready then."

The former soldiers synchronized their watches. They led Blinky out the back door. They put him into the ambulance. Then they stopped in their tracks.

Who was going to drive?

This was an angle that wasn't covered during the planning stage of Operation AWOL Soldier. It wasn't just Blinky who could be recognized, they were all known by the medical facility staff.

The former soldiers opened the doors of the ambulance. They escorted Blinky back into the lodge. Russ mixed up another pitcher of house specials and the men contemplated their dilemma.

Several pitchers later, they came to the conclusion it was highly unlikely that Michael A. Delaquot would show up at the emergency room door in the presence of two ambulance drivers who had their own heads wrapped in bandages.

"Sympathy bandaging," argued a drunk Blinky.

The other former soldiers, though drunk, had the presence of mind to know that sympathy bandaging was not a good idea. They would have slapped Blinky across the head the fourth time he yelled, "I'm for sympathy bandaging," but they knew it was pointless as his head was bandaged.

The more they drank the more the members of the team saw a vague hint of validity in Blinky's idea.

"There may be some neurotic ambulance workers who take on the complaints of their journeyers," added Tom as he fell off his chair.

They picked him up from the floor and told him to be quiet.

"I did hear a story about an ambulance driver who believed in reincarnation and that in another life he was the king of England. After putting on forty pounds and growing a beard, he had a costume specially made and went to work every day dressed as Henry the Eighth," said the former detonator expert.

The men looked at Matt with interest.

"Another driver, when he got wind of it, requested a transfer as he was a fan of Robin Hood," added Matt. "King Henry would drive while Robin Hood would regale the sick with stories of how he robbed from the rich and gave to the poor. Depending on the speed he was driving and the seriousness of the health issues faced by the patients, Henry would oft times bellow he wanted his money back. It was very uplifting for the patients."

Over more house specials, Russ and the former soldiers gave some serious thought to where they could rent costumes on such short notice.

***

Satisfied that the news of the missing soldier had not been leaked out of the facility, Mr. Flack was once again able to answer his phone when it rang.

"Administration, how can I help you?" he answered with some ease.

"This is Alicia Morgan, Blue Morgan's mother," answered the woman on the line. "You still got my boy on ice over there?"

90

"Yes Mrs. Morgan, Blue is being well taken care of," answered Mr. Flack.

The administrator knew all about Private Morgan's lethal combination of self-inflicted chemical poisoning and mistaking the middle of the road for a bathroom which caused his untimely demise.

"Good. The lawsuit on my son's behalf has been settled for an amount I will leave unnamed."

"I'm glad to --"

"That'll teach the army not to be so quick about undoing a mother's toilet training," cut in Mrs. Morgan.

"You're absolutely --"

"I'm sending my boy's Uncle Wally and Cousin Randle to pick him up. Have him ready," and with that Mrs. Morgan hung up the phone.

"Right-o," said Mr. Flack to the empty line.

He put in a call to the morgue to have Blue ready for when his Uncle Wally and Cousin Randle arrived. Back in a work groove and wanting to keep up on things, he also made a call to Mac Treeter, the facility's expert computer person regarding the patient coordinator's computer.

***

On the fourth floor, Nurse Shipley was having a sixth sense feeling of impending danger. The standing hairs on the back of her neck were right; Betty Lu was getting off the elevator. She rang the buzzer to be let in.

"Don't touch that?" cried the nurse to social worker, Penny Carlough, who was sitting next to the door button and was about to press it.

Thinking they hadn't heard her buzzing, the patient coordinator banged on the door.

"Let me in. I need to speak with Sergeant Delaquot."

"Damn that woman, she's going to be the death of me," stated Nurse Shipley while walking down to the locked door.

"What did you say?"

"I need to speak with Sergeant Delaquot."

"He's taking a shower. Can you come back later?"

"I don't want to be a bother."

It was tough for the nurse not to respond to that comment. The two women stood on either side of the locked door for a very long minute.

"I'll come back later," Betty Lu finally said.

"Can't wait," mumbled the nurse under her breath.

Betty Lu walked back to the elevator and pressed the down button. Nurse Shipley kept an eye on her through the locked door's pane of glass. The nosey woman waved. The putout nurse waved back and didn't move until the elevator doors closed with her inside.

The elevator reached the main floor and the doors opened. Sally was waiting to get on with his rack of breakfast trays. Betty Lu stood to the side to make room.

"What floor you going to?"

"Fourth," he answered.

She smiled at him and pushed the fourth floor button.

"So am I. I was just up there. Forgot my book."

Sally's chin and head were hurting, so he didn't respond to her admittance of forgetfulness. When the elevator stopped at four, he pushed the rack of trays over to the locked ward door. Ringing the bell, he was quickly buzzed in.

Betty Lu tried to make herself as small as possible as she followed behind Sally as he went through the door. He stopped at the first door on the left, took a tray off the rack and went into the patient's room. She peaked out from behind the rack. No one was looking. She scooted quickly across the hall and ducked into Room 423.

The bed was empty, but it also looked like it had been slept in. With nothing pending at the moment, she decided that she would wait for the Sergeant to come back from his shower so she could find out the details about his relationship with Mr. Flack.

The patient coordinator was about to get comfortable in a chair when she heard the toilet flush. She was nearing the bathroom door when she heard the sound of someone whistling as they washed their hands. She had her ear to the door when it suddenly burst open. Leaning a bit too forward, Betty Lu fell into the arms of Dr. Sorenson.

"Good morning," said the doctor.

She looked up into his twinkling eyes. Being that Dr. Sorenson looked so much like one of the doctor/actors on a hospital drama, we will leave unnamed, she always had a bit of a crush on him.

"Morning," she giggled.

"Steady on your feet old girl."

Betty Lu giggled some more and tried her best not to look as the naked doctor walked across the room to retrieve his clothes from the floor. She had the biggest grin on her face when he turned her way carrying his clothes.

"You have a good day now you hear," said the doctor as he took his clothes into the bathroom and closed the door.

"You…"

Betty Lu couldn't get the rest of the words out. She left the room in a hypnotic state.

Nurse Shipley came out of the common room into the hallway and saw the patient coordinator standing on her side of the door. She went up to Betty Lu who grinned at her. The nurse smiled back. The dreamy-eyed woman pointed to the door and the nurse let her out. She watched with some amusement as Betty Lu pressed the down button and got on the elevator.

"What's got into her?"

Her question was quickly answered. Dr. Sorenson came out of Room 423 and walked out the door she was still holding open.

"Betty Lu just saw me naked as a jay bird," said the doctor in a matter-of-fact way.

"Oh, that explains it. You know she has a crush on you."

"I believe today I fulfilled one of her secret fantasies."

"Bryan, you are so full of yourself."

"Don't I know it," laughed the doctor as he pressed the down button. "But don't you worry none, I only have eyes for you, doll."

Nurse Shipley blushed. Dr. Sorenson got on the elevator and back to work.

***

Mac Treeter was sitting at Betty Lu's computer when she got back to her office. Upon arrival at the medical facility he had met with Mr. Flack in his office.

"You are to look at the computer and report back to me," said the administrator. "Do not, and I repeat, do not tell Betty Lu of your findings. Do you swear?"

Mac looked at him. Seeing how earnest he was the computer expert swore to secrecy and promised to report any findings to Mr. Flack and Mr. Flack only.

"Oh, hello," said the woman who was still glowing from her recent run-in with a certain doctor.

Mac looked at her. He couldn't understand why the administrator was being so secretive, she seemed innocent enough.

The computer expert's words, "Looks like someone's been messing with your computer." snapped Betty Lu from her fantasies about Dr. Sorenson and back into the patient coordinator world she daily worked in.

"Really?" she asked in a non-committal type of way.

"From what I see," answered Mac, "it looks like your machine allows access to several people."

"What does that mean exactly?"

"There's more than one user name and password allowed into your computer."

"Oh. What does that mean exactly?"

94

It was the second "what does that mean exactly" that brought back his remembrance of the oath of secrecy he had made not more than twenty minutes ago. Mac looked up at Betty Lu. What seemed like a sweet woman in a flower print dress a minute ago now looked like a wolf in sheep's clothing.

"He swore me to secrecy. I'd better not say anything else."

"Mr. Flack you say?" questioned Betty Lu with a flap of her eyelashes.

Suddenly, Mac felt the hairs on the back of his neck rise. He didn't know what was going on here and he wanted no part of it. Lucky for him at that moment his cell phone rang.

"Hello," he answered.

"It's me. Did you find anything?" questioned Mr. Flack on the other end.

"Why honey, I told you not to call me during business hours," answered Mac. "No, I'm not with another woman. I'm at work. No, you can't smell another woman's perfume over the phone lines. I told you that a hundred times. Well yes, I am working on a woman's computer. No, you don't have ESP. What? Is the woman whose computer I'm working on in the room? Yes, yes she is."

During this ongoing monologue, Mr. Flack questioned the sanity of Mac Treeter, computer expert. That is, until he mentioned that the woman whose computer he's working on was in the room. When the administrator heard that bit of news his nerves and arteries constricted at the same time causing a block to the blood flow to his heart.

"Sharp pain in chest!" were the last words Mac heard over the phone line. Without another word Mr. Flack dropped the receiver.

"Hello. Hello, honey." Mac closed his cell phone. "She hung up. I don't know what I'm going to do with that woman, she's as jealous as a fox in a hen house."

"Have you given her cause to be jealous?" questioned Betty Lu who couldn't let go of a good story until she knew all the details.

"To be truthful… Between you and me…"

The patient coordinator leaned in.

"A couple of times," Mac lied.

"Do you want to talk about it over a cup of coffee?" questioned Betty Lu.

Seeing he now had a way out of his dilemma of answering her questions about who had been on her computer, and this supplied by Betty Lu herself, Mac answered he would indeed enjoy a snack and the opportunity to lift himself out of the misery and guilt he had been enduring. Betty Lu was in her glory.

"It'll be my treat."

She latched onto his arm.

"You're hurting me," said Mac in anguish.

"Sorry."

She let up on her grip.

The two went down to the coffee shop. Mac, being a fiction writer in his spare time, over coffee and chocolate croissants, regaled Betty Lu with the first three chapters of a book he was writing about a jealous lover and her wayward computer expert boyfriend.

He was calling the book - If You Love My Computer So Much, How Come You Can't Love Me.

***

The Sergeant, while working off his breakfast, was enjoying his tour of Ridleyville. It was a friendly place. Folks said hello everywhere he went. He practically glowed as he enjoyed his walk through the heartland of the country that he swore to protect with his life.

"It gives a man something worth dying for," he said to an old codger he stopped to talk with.

The old codger, a veteran of many wars and a few skirmishes, agreed with the soldier wholeheartedly. After he was through giving an update on life in today's army, the Sergeant walked to the far end of town and to his continued delight saw all the trappings of the Ridleyville Annual Fair. On a billboard it stated the coming events of the day. The words 'Pie Eating Contest' caught his eye.

"God, can this trip get any better?" he asked of his higher power.

If there was one pleasure the Sergeant missed while being a cog in the military machine it was food-eating contests.

As a boy he had a voracious appetite caused by the growing up of his limbs as they made their way into manhood. He had sat down at many a dinner table and did his best to do his mother's cooking a good service. But he felt substantially subpar in the eating department when he witnessed the prowess of those folks who took part in eating contests held at state and county fairs.

Much of his adulthood being spent in the service, the Sergeant had sat at many a table where his fellow servicemen could down rations of food that would easily make most people puke. Yet he still had the capacity to be amazed at the human physique when it came to those civilians who entered eating contests and the amount of hot dogs, corn on the cobs, hard-boiled eggs, beer and pies they could down at one sitting.

"Wonder if they have funnel cake?"

The Sergeant went up to the ticket booth and inquired about the possibility of the fair containing a stand where funnel cake was made and sold. The ticket seller assured him there was such a stand owned by Conrad Haney, the local taxidermist.

As it was morning, kids were in school and folks were at work. Sales being rather slow, the ticket seller took the time to tell the soldier how Conrad became the town's expert in funnel cake preparation.

Like most businesses, the taxidermy season came each year in the winter months. It was then that numerous hunters riding in from the surrounding counties would come to Ridleyville seeking the expertise of Conrad Haney. Their vehicles would be decorated with various species of dead animal, which was especially off putting to the local ladies sensibilities.

Hunting season coincided with three major holidays, Thanksgiving, Hanukkah, and Christmas. The town ladies hated the idea that the trucks laden with various species clashed with their street decorations, so they took their complaints to the town council.

Not wanting to upset the local economy as these hunters partook of other businesses in the community, with all good intentions toward the ladies and Conrad's choice of career, the town council decided to donate to the taxidermist a piece of property just outside of town that was adjacent to the local dump.

Conrad was very much appreciative of the thoughtfulness of the townsfolk and he enjoyed many happy years in his field of endeavor. Eventually though he found himself to be lonely, and with time passing, getting older. Remembering the promise he made to his mother to one day marry and have children, he set out to find himself a mate.

When Conrad went into the town in search of a woman to woo, he found they were either taken or pretended to be as no woman wanted to live next to the dump. The only thing for him to do was send for a mail order bride. He got a catalog and decided upon a woman named Dorcus.

When she stepped off the train, Conrad and the entire town of Ridleyville was there to meet her, including Judge Chambers, who in his fifty years on the bench never took a day off. Having never seen a mail order bride before, the judge thought it was high-time to take a break.

It seemed to the happy couple that fate had brought everyone together, so they chose to tie the old knot without delay. Before her bags were taken off the train, the two were married.

The groom then drove his bride to her new home. The first thing she did was to unload the kitchen appliances that she brought with her. After she was done, he took her on a tour of his work establishment. They entered the barn that was only steps from the house. Dorcus took one look at the dead animals that were waiting for taxidermy and went back to the house, packed up her stuff and demanded Conrad take her back to the train station.

The train was still at Ridleyville Station as it was the last stop on the line and they weren't scheduled to make the return trip for another quarter hour.

Many of the townsfolk were still gathered there, including the man who married them. Before her husband could empty his truck of her possessions, the just married-bride got an annulment from Judge Chambers and had taken her seat on the train.

The townsfolk waved goodbye to Dorcus as the train pulled away. Conrad had only been married under an hour but it might have been ten years the way people, especially the ladies, carried on.

A good many of those ladies not wanting the taxidermist to make the same mistake twice gave him advice for the future. It would be best when contacting brides listed in catalogs to let them know at the get go what his line of business was.

Those words of wisdom weren't to be needed. After the train carrying his ex-wife pulled away from the station, Conrad went home. He was going to fix himself a grilled cheese sandwich when he realized Dorcus had left behind her funnel cake apparatus - a top of the line specially made pitcher with an integral funnel-like spout.

He forgot all about his grilled cheese sandwich and took his mother's old cookbook off the shelf, where he knew he'd find a recipe for funnel cake.

"To make a long story short," continued the ticket seller, "Conrad became the best funnel cake maker for miles around. He works every county and state fair from here to Topeka. As he makes a good living off fried dough the taxidermy business became just a hobby. He even met a nice lady and today they have five children all under the age of five."

"That was a damn good story and one with a happy ending to boot," declared the Sergeant.

With an affectionate heart for a country where a taxidermist can rise to become a leading state and county fair funnel cake maker, the Sergeant, excited about the thought of eating fried dough covered in powdered sugar and the chance to root the contestants of the pie-eating contest onto glory, bought his ticket and walked into the fair.

***

Back at the medical facility, Mr. Flack was walking into the coffee shop. The agonizing pain he had felt in his chest when he heard the news from Mac that Betty Lu was standing next to him as he checked her computer had passed so he attributed it to gas. As he wiped the sweat off his brow, he remembered he had forgotten to eat breakfast that morning due to the agitated state caused by his dream about lobsters taking over the facility.

Looking over Mac Treeter's shoulder as he continued his story about love gone wrong, Betty Lu eyed Mr. Flack walking toward the espresso machine.

"Mr. Flack," she called.

He stopped in his tracks. He knew that voice. It was the same voice from his dream that shouted, "Let him burn!"

"Mr. Flack. Over here!"

The administrator turned slowly. His body began to quake. Across the room, the patient coordinator was waving for him to come over. He took a languid step toward the table. When he saw Mac Treeter looking like a deer in the headlights down he went.

Dr. Sorenson was crossing the threshold of the coffee shop and saw the administrator hit the floor. He rushed over and began CPR. Betty Lu forgot all about her computer, Mac Treeter and Mr. Flack.

"Hello Dr. Sorenson," she said with a giggle.

He switched from breathing into the mouth of Mr. Flack to pounding on his chest.

"One…two…we meet again…three…."

"Want me to order breakfast for you?" inquired Betty Lu.

"Two egg whites scrambled, one slice of ham and rye toast skip the butter," replied the doctor who went back to breathing down the administrator's mouth. "Oh, and if you would, send for a cart and a couple of attendants."

"It would be my pleasure," she giggled.

Betty Lu put in the doctor's breakfast order and then called for help. Hearing it was Mr. Flack, a stampede of qualified staff and bystanders crowded into the coffee shop.

A resident physician who was on duty in the ICU, and hadn't slept for forty-two hours, ran in with the cart. Holding up the paddles, he was ready to shock the living daylights out of the patient, but Dr. Sorenson blocked him.

Wanting to give Betty Lu a good show, the doctor paused. Everyone in the coffee shop held his or her breath.

"He's going to be okay."

The room exhaled.

Two attendants lifted Mr. Flack off the coffee shop floor and Betty Lu was serving Dr. Sorenson his breakfast when Blue Morgan's Uncle Wally and Cousin Randle walked through the sliding doors of the medical facility. They stepped up to the reception desk where Bridget, an elderly volunteer, was waiting to assist them.

"We've come to take Blue home," stated Uncle Wally, who was always one to get down to brass tacks.

"Well, that's just about the nicest thing to hear. A soldier's going home. What's Blue's first or last name?" asked Bridget.

"Morgan, last name," chimed in Randle.

"Morgan, Blue," repeated the elderly volunteer as she perused index cards.

After several minute of this, Wally began to get impatient. He wanted to ask why in blue blazes the woman was not using the computer, but having been raised to respect his elders, he held back.

"You got my nephew here or not?" he finally blurted out.

"I don't see the name. Take a seat won't you and I'll double check."

The two men took a seat. They watched as the elderly volunteer slowly made her way over to the switchboard window.

"Julie, I've got a problem here."

"I'll be glad to help if I can."

"Do you know of a patient named Morgan, Blue?"

"Why yes you silly thing, everybody knows about poor old Blue," answered Julie. "Why do you ask?"

"His family's here to pick him up."

"Seriously?"

Bridget pointed and when the operator eyed the pair, it was love at first sight. Wally Morgan was one of those big homegrown men and just the way Julie Binder liked a fellow to look.

"Why don't you take the switchboard for me and I'll help the gentlemen."

The elderly volunteer had never worked the switchboard. Always willing to learn a new thing or two, she sat down at the desk. Julie checked her lipstick, adjusted her dress and walked over to the waiting relatives of Blue Morgan.

"Can I be of service to you?" she asked.

"We've come to get Blue," retorted Uncle Wally.

He looked at Julie – really looked. She smiled a big smile. He was smitten.

"I'm Wally Morgan. This is Randle."

"Julie. Julie Binder, switchboard operator."

She offered her hand. Wally took it and held onto it. Randle rolled his eyes. He had seen this happen a hundred times with women when they first saw his uncle.

"That's a mighty important job you have, Julie," said Blue's Uncle Wally.

"Yes, it's the heart of the entire operation that you see here before you. Are you thirsty?"

Wally nodded and Julie took his arm.

"You're hurting me," said the big man.

"Oh, I'm sorry."

She let up on her grip and aimed him toward the sliding doors.

"What about Blue?" Randle questioned.

"He's waited this long," replied Uncle Wally, "he can wait a little longer."

And the sliding doors closed behind them.

***

After serving Dr. Sorenson his breakfast, Betty Lu sat down to keep him company. Downing a second helping of coffee he knew the time limit was running out and if he sat with her much longer the gossiping would start. It would be blown out of proportion as such things always were. The story would be spread like wildfire to the fourth floor, and Nurse Shipley in particular, that he was having a tête-à-tête with Betty Lu in the coffee shop. Not one to intentionally hurt a woman's feelings, he reminded the patient coordinator that it was time for her to get back to business.

"You have a new patient needs caring for," said Dr. Sorenson.

"I do?"

"Mr. Flack," he reminded.

103

"I'm such a silly thing. I'd better go. I hate to leave you sitting here alone."

"Why you sweet thing, you emit caring powers you know that?"

She giggled in response.

"Get going now, the man in charge needs you."

She got up and didn't take her eyes off him as she walked backwards to the door. Standing on the opposite side of the coffee shop window, she gave him a wave.

"She's a good egg," stated the doctor as he helped himself to another cup of coffee.

Betty Lu went to her office to make up an id bracelet for Mr. Flack. She found Mac Treeter sitting at her computer and her mind snapped back into patient coordinator mode once more.

"Are you still messing with that old thing?"

"Almost done."

"Hurry now, Mr. Flack's waiting for his bracelet."

The computer expert wasn't finished, but at the mention of the administrator he remembered Betty Lu's unanswered questions waiting to be asked. He gathered his stuff and ran out of the room.

"Queer little man," she thought.

She made a bracelet for Mr. Flack and went to the ICU to put it on him. As she was passing the elevator, Sally, who had finished serving breakfast to the soldier patients, was getting off.

"Did you hear about Mr. Flack?"

"No," answered the attendant.

She held up the bracelet.

"Where is he?"

"ICU. Possible heart attack."

She went on her way and he double-timed it to the kitchen, shouted to the kitchen staff that Mr. Flack had a heart attack, slammed out the back door, and ran over to the Rustic Lodge.

"Nathanial, your boss is in ICU," yelled the attendant.

"What? What'd you say?" slurred the PR.

"Your boss may be kicking the bucket at this very moment."

"My horse has spilled his feed bucket, you say?"

"Something like that."

"I'd better get back to my office."

"Go with all speed," said Sally

Nathanial stood up, took two steps, and as he fell to the floor he hit the back of his head on the table.

"Whoops," said Sally. "Russ, we have a problem here."

Those who drank too much were always falling down, so the drunken former soldiers went right into rescue mode. They went over to the booth and picked their customer up.

Blood spurting profusely on the lodge floor aided the men to make a quick decision. Tom and Matt would help Sally carry Nathanial to the medical facility.

As they were carrying the wounded man across the dance floor, Russ saw the front door starting to open.

"Louie!" he yelled.

"Present and accounted for, Sir!" shouted the former soldier as he lifted his head off the table and dropped it back down again.

The premises being unsecure, Russ order Blinky and his bandaged head to hide as he quickly blocked Nathanial's upper torso with his body. The door opened fully and Julie Binder walked in holding tightly to the arm of a stranger.

"One minute men," whispered Russ.

He nonchalantly walked towards the bar. On the way, he picked up Louie's head from the table and let it drop with a bang.

"How may I help you Switchboard Sue and who's your friend?" asked Russ as he started making a new batch of house specials.

"I thought you said your name was Julie?" Wally questioned.

"It is my big strong man," Julie replied as she pinched his cheek. "Morning, Russ. This is Wally Morgan, Blue's uncle."

"Well, well, well. You here to visit with your relative?"

"I'm here to take the boy home."

"Then you need some fortification." He waved to his men. "House specials all around."

"Who's that they're carrying out?" inquired Julie.

"Nathanial. He tripped over the cat and hit his head."

"I didn't know you had a cat."

"Neither did I," he mumbled. "You two hungry? I could rustle up some pigs in blankets."

"That would be delightful," squealed Julie.

"Most appreciated," chimed in Wally and he downed his drink.

"You need another," said Russ.

"Don't mind if I do."

There was nothing Julie Binder loved more than a big strong handsome man enjoying his drink. She downed her house special and held especially tight to Wally's arm.

"You're cutting off my circulation again," he declared.

"I can't help it. You're ringing my phone. Do you think it would matter much to you if I kissed you?"

"Are you thinking to make it a habit?" inquired the big man.

"Yes," declared Julie with certainty.

"Then go to it." He puckered up and she laid a kiss on the big lug.

Blue's cousin walked in the door. He held it open for the guys as they made their way out with Nathanial. When Randle saw Julie kissing his uncle's lips like she was a deep suction vacuum, he shook his head at the wonderment of women who were always throwing themselves at him.

"Wish some of what he's got would rub off on me," thought Randle.

"Drink, son?" Russ asked.

"Don't mind if I do," stated Randle.

106

Blinky was feeling a little left out what with Tom and Matt helping Sally with Nathanial and Louie passed out at a table. He toddled up to the bar and sat down next to Randle.

"Looks like you've seen trouble."

Blinky didn't know how to answer. Soon he'd be in the medical facility covering for the AWOL soldier. In need of some practice he decided now would be as good a time as any to get in character.

"My girlfriend told me she was marrying another man. I went to stop her and he beat me about the head."

"I had that happen to me once. See this scar on my head," pointed Randle. "After her fiancé was done beating me, my girlfriend called the ambulance to come and get me. The folks at the hospital had no choice but to call it into the police. I told the officers what happened; they swore to me they wouldn't tell my wife. That's why I'm still married today. Them guys were okay."

"What happened to your girlfriend?" questioned Blinky.

"She married him. I still see her on Tuesdays and Thursdays," Randle replied.

1200 hrs
MAY 16th

The concerns for the missing soldier who belonged in Bed No. 42 were taking a momentary back seat to the medical emergencies afflicting various members of the hospital staff. As Sally, Matt and Tom carried Nathanial through the sliding doors, Dr. Sorenson was coming out of the coffee shop.

"What happened to him?"

"He tripped," said Sally.

"On his way down..." added Tom.

"...he did a head slam," finished Matt.

"A solid case of cause and effect," stated the doctor. He took the penlight from his pocket and looked into the PR's eyes. "Can you hear me, Nathanial?"

Being a little too close when the PR cried out, "Where's my horse?" the doctor got a good whiff of alcohol.

"He's pickled. Saved him from doing considerable damage I don't wonder. As he's one of ours, take him to ICU. They'll keep a good eye on him there."

An attendant came by with an empty gurney. The three men passed as they wanted to follow through on their personal care of the PR.

In the ICU, Betty Lu was fastening the identification bracelet on Mr. Flack as he slept. Shortly before when he was rolled into the ICU, the resident physician had to sedate the administrator as he was in such an agitated state he couldn't be examined properly. Whenever the resident physician came near, Mr. Flack kicked him away, accusing him of being a lobster in disguise.

The ICU nurse was used to Russ sending back the walking wounded and drunken staff members. She barely looked up when Matt, Tom and Sally came in carrying Nathanial.

"Where should we put the PR?" inquired Sally.

"Bed No. 3 next to his boss."

When they placed Nathanial in the bed next to Mr. Flack, Betty Lu's mouth dropped.

"What happened to him?"

"He heard the news about Mr. Flack," answered Sally.

Tom was about to add his recollection, but she stopped him.

"Don't say another word," said Betty Lu. "I have to see Julie Binder about something."

"He's gonna need a bracelet," yelled Sally as she ran out the exit.

Coming out of the bathroom and seeing he had a new patient, the resident physician rushed over with the cart and paddles. Before he could shock the crap out of Nathanial, Sally told him why it wasn't necessary.

Seeing his job was done, the attendant bid his goodbyes to Tom and Matt and went to the kitchen to get the lunch trays and to update the staff on the latest developments.

***

At the Ridleyville annual fair, the Sergeant was enjoying his fourth helping of funnel cake. He had appreciated the adventures of Conrad Haney so much, he listened a second time as the taxidermist told the story about how he became a world famous funnel cake maker and found true love in the process.

"I never get tired of hearing about the success of others," said the Sergeant as the littlest Haney slept peacefully in his arms.

Seeing the fair worker surrounded by the love of his family caused the AWOL soldier to pine for his own brood. Conrad wrapped up a dozen funnel cakes to go and on his way out of the fairgrounds the Sergeant decided to make use of the portable toilets that dotted the fair's landscape.

In the next portable toilet over from his, the Sergeant saw one of the contestants for the pie-eating contest preparing for the upcoming challenge. He thought for sure it was a contestant as the young man had a number around his neck and his fingers down his throat as he threw up.

"So there's a trick to it," acknowledged the Sergeant. "What's your name, boy?"

"Alfred A. Cummings," the boy choked out.

"I'll be rooting for you, Al."

"I…appre…that," answered Alfred.

The Sergeant took care of his business. When he came out of the portable toilet he had a momentary dilemma between the recent pining in his heart for his family and finding a bookie that was laying odds on the winner of the pie-eating contest.

It was Alfred A. Cummings who was working hard to clean out the contents of his stomach that made up his mind.

"That's a boy worth betting on," exclaimed the Sergeant.

Knowing his family would be home no matter when he got there, and it would be extra pleasing to them if he came back with his pockets loaded with winnings, he went in search of a bookie.

At the medical facility, Betty Lu was caught in her own dilemma. Nathanial needed a bracelet and she was anxious to tell Julie Binder the news about him and Mr. Flack before anyone else could.

Her concerns for her job won out. She rushed back to her office, got on the computer, it spit out the bracelet and she ran back to the ICU to slap it on the PR's wrist.

When she got there, Mr. Flack was fighting his sedation. He saw Betty Lu messing with his bedmate and shouted, "The lobsters are attacking!"

The resident physician and ICU nurse came over to the bed and while he held Mr. Flack down, she gave him another round of sedation.

Betty Lu took no mind to Mr. Flack's outburst. She raced to the lobby. Catching her breath, she was surprised to see Bridget, the reception desk volunteer, sitting at the switchboard.

"Where's Julie?" Betty Lu panted.

"She's seeing to Blue Morgan's family. I think she took them to the lodge," answered Bridget. "I have to use the little girl's room."

Betty Lu looked at her. She looked at the sliding doors. Seeing the poor old woman was jiggling, she took her place at the switchboard.

"Hurry back," the patient coordinator yelled.

The volunteer gave her a wave as she crossed the lobby to the ladies room.

In Ridleyville, the Sergeant crossed the fairgrounds to the area where the pie-eating contest was to be held. Seeing a crowd gathered in a circle waving dollar bills, he knew he'd found his bookie. He ate one of the funnel cakes he was holding for his family as he waited to place his bet.

***

At the Rustic Lodge bar, Wally Morgan was enjoying the clutching attentions of Julie Binder as was Randle Morgan enjoying the company of Blinky Billington.

Filled with a pot-load of coffee, Louie Dombrowski was back at his post. He opened the door for Tom and Matt who reported to their boss that the mission to get Nathanial into capable hands was accomplished. Russ hustled up some more house specials as the lunch crowd from the medical facility was starting to come in.

111

Matt was enjoying a well-deserved drink when he heard the sound of familiar laughter.

"There's a mule in the room," he shouted at the top of his lungs. "Could it be Randle Morgan, First Class?"

Blue's cousin stopped in mid-drink when he heard his name and past rank. He turned to see who had called. A familiar face leaned out from the line-up at the bar.

"Matt Cohn, Chief Petty Officer, detonator expert and all around chump," shouted Randle.

"Seems this world ain't big enough for the two of us," shouted Matt.

"Then you better make for the moon, son," shouted Randle.

The two men hugged and clapped each other on the back. Russ poured them house specials. They clinked glasses and got around to updating one and all.

"This is the guy I was telling you about," said Matt.

Those within hearing distance gave Matt a vacant look as he was always telling stories about some guy he once knew and their various escapades.

"The guy who had a wife and a girlfriend. The one that got beat about the head by the fiancé," added Matt.

The former soldiers nodded their understanding. Randle, being the show off that he was, gave them all a look at the scar on his head.

Being around all this male testosterone was upsetting Julie Binder as it was taking Wally's attention away from her kissing. She took her drink and his and Wally followed her to the booth in the back, in the corner, in the dark.

At the medical facility, Bridget had taken twenty minutes to get to the bathroom and back to the switchboard. By the time she made it to the chair, Betty Lu was out the sliding doors and on her way over to the lodge. Louie saw her charging headlong across the parking lot, which reminded him of the local moose. He quickly opened the door for her.

Betty Lu continued her charge to the bar and ordered a house special. While catching her breath she eyed Blinky's bandaged head. The former soldier had her full attention.

"Damn," Russ mumbled under his breath and he turned in the other direction, drinking down the house special he meant to serve.

"I see that you've been hurt. May I hold your hand to solace you?" Betty Lu said in her sweetest patient coordinator breath.

As Blinky always had a thing for Betty Lu, and she had never given him the time of day, he was astonished that she wanted to hold his hand. Forgetting that he had bandages on his head and the identification bracelet on his wrist, he gave his hand over.

"Michael A. Delaquot," read the patient coordinator aloud.

Blinky pulled back his hand. He had been betrayed by the sweet lamb's voice that was hiding a wolf in sheep's clothing.

"Michael, why are you not in your bed?"

Those around the bar stopped speaking when Blinky began to splutter. Russ poured him a drink. Betty Lu took it away, wagged her finger at the lodge owner and drank it herself.

"He's with me," spoke up Randle.

Russ drank down another house special.

"Who are you?" questioned Betty Lu.

"Randle Morgan, Blue's cousin. I came here to take Blue home and when I found out my old soldier buddy was a guest in your facility, I offered to take him for a drink."

"Really," responded Betty Lu.

"Really," Randle cut back. "A man with problems needs to have a little repast."

"See this." Betty Lu held up Blinky's arm. "This bracelet makes this man a ward of the medical facility. He's officially in our care, that's where he should be," retorted the patient coordinator.

Randle saw he was in for a fight. He thought of his uncle and what he would do. With that in mind he took a step up to Betty Lu, grabbed her and kissed her.

Betty Lu, with eyes crossed, looked at the man who was kissing her and when he let go she almost fell down, but he caught her.

"My name's Randle Morgan."

"Betty...Betty...," she responded.

"Well Betty Betty, how about I order us some drinks and we get better acquainted?"

Holding both their drinks in one hand, Randle escorted the fainting woman away from the bar. When they were out of hearing distance, Russ hurried over to Blinky.

"Hide yourself and don't come out until she's gone."

***

After a thorough examination, the resident physician came to the conclusion that Mr. Flack did not have a heart attack. He made notes about the extreme anxiety exhibited regarding lobsters and their taking over the medical facility. Diagnosis - the administrator for all appearances was in the midst of a nervous breakdown.

With no surgeries scheduled, Dr. Sorenson took the time to check on Mr. Flack. When told his heart was fine, but he'd been shouting to his fellow patients to beware the lobstermen who had infiltrated the medical facility, the doctor told the resident physician it was in the best interest of all concerned to transfer the patient to the fourth floor.

The resident physician thought this was an extreme measure until Dr. Sorenson assured him Mr. Flack would be in the gifted hands of Nurse Shipley and her crew of crackerjack staff members. To be sure, before making the transition, the doctor would go to the fourth floor to confer with the nurse about his decision.

114

On the psyche ward, Nurse Shipley was having a time of it, but not with her patients. She had warned the staff that she was to be called before anyone could be buzzed in, so she had spent most of the day inspecting visitors to be sure Betty Lu was not attached to them.

The inability to get her work done ticked the nurse off considerably. Sally was aware of this when he left the floor after picking up the used breakfast trays and now he had to go back on the ward to deliver the lunch trays. Lucky for the attendant, Dr. Sorenson was taking the same elevator.

"What's for lunch today?"

"Split pea soup, grilled cheese, fruit cup and jellyroll for dessert."

"I know someone who loves jellyroll. Got any extras?"

The attendant lifted a piece of cake from one of the trays and gave it to the doctor. The elevator doors opened. Knowing what lay ahead of him, he was insistent Dr. Sorenson get off first.

"No, my good man, you first," said the doctor.

"I insist," stated Sally.

"What's the matter?"

"Nurse Shipley has it in for me."

The doctor got off the elevator first. He went over and rang the bell. Peeking through the window, the doctor watched as Nurse Shipley stormed to the door. On her side all she could see was Sally and his tray cart.

"You again," she blurted upon opening the door.

"Look what I brought." The doctor held out the piece of cake.

"My favorite, c'mon in."

"Can my friend do his job?"

Nurse Shipley smiled, "I'm sorry. It's been one of those days."

"Tension that's all it is," said the doctor. "I have a cure for that."

He put his arm around the nurse and walked her to Room 423. Impressed, Sally made a mental note regarding the benefits of jellyroll cake while serving the soldier patients their lunch.

***

Out of the dozen funnel cakes the Sergeant had Conrad pack for him only five were left, which was enough for one and all of his participating family members. He enjoyed eating seven funnel cakes as he watched Alfred A. Cummings scoff down sixteen blueberry pies. The winning contestant had broken the longtime Ridleyville fair's record of fifteen pies held by Mortimer Vicksburg.

Alfred's entire family was present to cheer their favorite son onto victory. Receiving a check for $1,000 and a silver cup, he then made the mistake of bowing before the crowd. Alfred was so well practiced from bending over and puking before the contest, when he bent from the waist he promptly threw up.

The Sergeant was delighted with the added public exhibition and the fact he was getting his money's worth of entertainment. That is until the judges ripped the check and cup from Alfred's hands.

"We have to look over the rules of the contest," Judge No. 1 announced.

"There may be a rule regarding the time blueberry pies are spent in the digestive system of the winner," concurred Judge No. 2.

The judges were booed off the stage. Alfred's family was especially demonstrative with this turn of events. So much so, they were throwing the contents of their lunches at the judges.

The police were called when the situation became a riot. The next day's headline would refer to the afternoon's event as the Ridleyville Fair's Blueberry Pie Debacle.

The Sergeant was sure the judges would rule in favor of Alfred, so he stood on line to collect his winnings.

Alfred's family became more frenzied as they too had placed bets on the family favorite. They made their way through the crowd that was waiting for their winnings. When they got near enough they picked the bookie up and turned him upside down in an attempt to dislodge the winnings from his deep pockets.

As the bookie protected his head from being slammed to the ground, the police surrounded the melee and the Sergeant was quickly swept up and tossed into the back of the wagon. It had been years since he had been carted off to jail. He went along for the ride with no complaints.

Ridleyville was used to this sort of thing from Alfred's kinfolk, as they were a boisterous lot. Carting the members of the Cummings clan off to jail would mean keeping them overnight and serving them a couple of hot meals. This was an added treat whenever the family members were incarcerated as they were big eaters and there wasn't a decent cook among the Cummings wives. In order to save the taxpayers' money, the police made it a habit to drive them directly to the courthouse.

Judge Chambers banged his gavel in order to quiet down the crowd. He wasn't at all surprised to see who was at the center of things. He allowed the bookie to speak first.

"Willie."

"Your Honor, I have to get back and find out who won…else my reputation --"

"Yes, yes, I know all about your reputation," interrupted Judge Chambers. "Who started the commotion?"

Several members of Alfred's family bowed their heads in pretend shame. Like eating popcorn during a movie, the Sergeant was munching on funnel cake.

"No eating in court, soldier," said Judge Chambers. "That is unless you have enough for everyone."

"I'm sorry Judge, I only have about three left."

"Give one over then. Court was busy today and I haven't had lunch yet."

The Sergeant stepped up and handed the bag to the judge. He helped himself to a funnel cake.

"We're a lucky group to have Conrad living in our neck of the woods," stated Judge Chambers as he took a bite. "Did anyone tell you the story about his first wife? She was a mail order bride. First one I ever --"

"Your Honor," pleaded Willie.

Judge Chambers gave a little cough and wiped spilled sugar off his robe. He got on with the proceeding.

"What's your part in all of this?"

"Innocent bystander waiting to collect his winnings," answered the Sergeant.

"Give Willie back his money," declared Judge Chambers, who was now in a lenient mood thanks to the fried dough covered with powdered sugar.

The Cummings, one and all, handed back the money they took from Willie.

"Now apologize," declared Judge Chambers.

"We're sorry," said the oldest Cummings.

"That's okay. Honest, your Honor, I have to get back or my name will be mud and no one will ever bet with me again."

"That would indeed be a disservice to the community," replied Judge Chambers. "Case dismissed."

"That is what I love about this country, swift justice," commented the Sergeant. He cheerfully handed over what was left of his funnel cakes to the judge.

The members of the melee were loaded back into the police wagon. It was the arrestor's pleasure to give all the arrestees a ride back to the Ridleyville fair as they also had bets on the various pie-eating contestants and wanted to see what the final outcome was.

As the Sergeant was being returned to the Ridleyville fair, the Rustic Lodge was doing a good afternoon's business. Randle introduced Betty Lu to his Uncle Wally. They took a seat with him and Julie and the foursome spent the afternoon enjoying each other's company.

The medical facility ICU was hopping and the resident physician and nurses were kept busy with patients. Mr. Flack was sleeping deeply thanks to mega doses of sedation.

One bed over Nathanial was awakening. Head swimming from drink and the wallop he took on the back of his head, he thought he was in Mr. Flack's office when he saw his boss. Wanting to converse with the administrator on matters of PR, he got up.

"The missing soldier took my horse. All is well," reported the barely conscious PR.

With all matters of business now up-to-date, Nathanial was feeling so woozy he didn't think he could make it to his office on the lower level. He climbed into bed with Mr. Flack and fell back to sleep.

At the switchboard the phones were ringing off the hook. The calls were not being answered as Bridget, who should have been off duty hours ago, was partaking of her afternoon nap, which was usually reserved for afternoons at home after a full morning of volunteering.

At his home, the male nurse, who was feeling the results of too much sleep, was taking a shower in preparation for going to work.

On the fourth floor, Sally was picking up used lunch trays and uplifting the spirits of the soldiers in the psyche ward as he told one and all that he was making plans for their escape.

In room 423, Dr. Sorenson was feeding jellyroll cake to Nurse Sorenson.

"You are a courteous fellow," said Holly as she sat on his lap.

"It's my aim to please."

"I heard you had a tête-à-tête in the coffee shop with the patient coordinator."

"News spreads like fire in this place."

"Don't worry I didn't take it to heart."

"Good. You know I only have eyes for you, doll."

"I know. How's your little Bryan?"

"Thought you'd never ask."

***

The minutes were flying by and Blinky was still hiding in the storage room. He didn't know if it was the cobwebs or the bandages that was causing his scalp to itch. He peaked out the door.

"Are we doing this or not," he shouted to his fellow former soldiers.

Russ got on with Operation AWOL Soldier. He delivered a drink to his itchy employee on his way over to the booth where the foursome sat.

"Betty Lu, Julie, you've been here long enough, time to get back to work."

The two ladies looked up from the shoulders they were leaning on.

"What time is it?" Betty Lu questioned.

"1600 hrs," answered Russ.

"Almost quitting time," said Julie. "Will you wait for me?"

"Forever," replied Wally.

The two women said their goodbyes to Blue's uncle and cousin. On their walk back to the medical facility they made plans to get their things and walk back to the lodge together.

"Wake up, time to go home," said Julie when she entered the switchboard office.

She nudged the elderly volunteer and got no response.

"Betty Lu," called Julie hoarsely.

The patient coordinator backtracked. She saw the operator's anxious face.

"She's dead," Julie said of Bridget.

"Oh my."

"She can't be found sitting at my desk. There'll be an investigation. They'll find out where we spent the afternoon. We could lose our jobs."

Betty Lu was determined to hold only one job until she retired many years from now and that was as patient coordinator.

"What should we do?" Julie asked as the switchboard rang.

"Answer the phone. Use your name."

"Good afternoon medical facility, Julie Binder speaking. Room 19, one moment I'll connect you."

"Alibi is set. We just need to get rid of the body," said Betty Lu.

The two ladies looked out at the reception area. It was empty of visitors. The only occupant was Melanie, a college student whose work schedule was dependent upon her class schedule. She could be found behind the gift shop register or behind the reception desk depending on which day of the week it was. Betty Lu went over to her.

"Hello," she said in her sweetest voice.

Melanie looked up from her magazine.

"Have you seen Bridget? I have something to talk to her about."

"She was working switchboard when I got here."

"Oh. Well. She's not there now."

As if they had coordinated their actions, at that exact moment, Julie appeared at the switchboard window.

"She must have gone home," said Melanie.

"I'll catch up with her tomorrow then."

"Hmm," said Melanie as she turned a page in her magazine.

With the establishment of Bridget's whereabouts taken care of, Betty Lu walked back to the switchboard office.

"I have a plan," she said to Julie. "We'll take Bridget home and put her to bed. They'll think she died in her sleep."

Julie was amazed at what a fast thinker Betty Lu was. She stayed at her post as the patient coordinator left to get a wheelchair.

Back at the lodge, the former soldiers were rehashing the problem of who was going to drive the ambulance and escort Blinky into the medical facility. It would take someone who was not only unknown to the emergency room personnel, but could be trusted to keep secret the fact they were sending Blinky in for the AWOL soldier.

Wally and Randle stepped up to the bar. They downed two house specials as quick as jack rabbits. Russ knew he had found his men. Blue's relatives were sworn to secrecy and given the sordid details of Operation AWOL Soldier.

"So you see our dilemma," said Russ.

"We'll be glad to help a soldier in need," said Randle.

"That's mighty fine of you. Have you ever driven an ambulance before?"

"There's always a first time for everything," said Wally.

Russ was in agreement. They had their drivers, the plan could go forward. Once again the former soldiers took inventory of their replacement for the missing soldier patient Bed. No. 42.

"Bracelet on?"

"Check."

"Bandages?"

"Check."

"Scrubs?"

"Check."

"He's ready."

The former soldiers and Blue's relatives synchronized their watches. As they loaded Blinky into the back of the ambulance, Betty Lu and Julie were loading Bridget into a wheelchair.

"We have to wait for Donna to come and replace me," said Julie. "She should be here any minute."

As if the night operator knew her role, she stepped through the sliding doors. With the switchboard covered and Bridget's head hidden by a shawl, the two ladies rolled the wheelchair out into the parking lot. They were so busy with their own doings, they didn't notice Wally driving by in the ambulance.

Randle sat in back with Blinky. He gave the former soldier who was about to go undercover a pep talk and his personal recollections of being beat about the head and how he had convinced the hospital staff not to call his wife, who to this day doesn't know about his extracurricular activities.

***

The afternoon was waning towards evening and the Ridleyville fair was in full swing with students and working folks enjoying the rides and attractions. The matter of who had won the pie-eating contest had been determined to the satisfaction of everyone.

The judges searched high and low throughout Ridleyville for a rulebook on pie-eating contests. The library didn't have one neither did Judge Chambers when they sought him out. With no rulebook to go by the judges relinquished the $1,000 and cup back to Alfred A. Cummings.

Willie was able to make good to the bettors. The Sergeant pocketed his winnings and was once again on his way out of the fair when he remembered his family and their love of funnel cake. He stopped at Conrad's stand where there was a long line.

In no rush, the soldier decided to wait till the line thinned out a bit. The Cummings family saw him wandering alone and invited him to join them at the corndog stand for some dinner. Alfred's stomach was pretty much empty. He outdid his pie-eating feat and downed thirty-three corndogs as everyone watched in amazement.

As the Sergeant enjoyed the companionship of the Cummings clan and his dinner of corndogs, Wally and Randle were rolling Blinky through the medical facility emergency doors. At the same time, the male nurse was walking through the front doors on his way to work. Melanie looked up from her magazine as he was one of her favorites.

"Are you on duty tonight?"

"Looks that way," replied the male nurse.

"I'm off at nine-thirty. Want to meet for a drink on your lunch hour?"

He thought it over for about a second. "The lodge at eleven-thirty?"

"It's a date," said Melanie.

The male nurse dawdled at the reception desk a while longer. Seeing he was going to be late for work, he said his see you laters and went to the elevator. Waiting for the doors to open were Wally, Randle and Blinky.

The scrutiny they expected in the ER didn't come to pass as there were several real emergencies to deal with. After a few questions to the fake ambulance attendants and a quick once over, it was determined a gurney was not necessary for the return of the soldier to the fourth floor and he was transferred to a wheelchair. No one minded when Wally and Randle offered to take the soldier to the fourth floor.

When the elevator doors opened the male nurse went in first and made sure the door didn't close on the attendants and their wheelchair occupant. They rode up in silence. The male nurse opened the locked door and was immediately engaged with his co-workers as they bid him hellos and glad to see you're feeling betters. No one paid attention as Wally and Randle rolled Blinky into Room 423.

Suddenly, there was a scream.

The male nurse remembered the loss of soldier patient Bed No. 42. He grabbed his stomach when it turned. His co-workers thinking he was still with virus rushed him out the locked door. He stuck his hand between the elevator doors as they were closing, held his breath as he rode down, walked across the lobby, never breaking his stride as he broke his date with Melanie before going out the sliding doors.

When he made it back to his abode, the male nurse took off his scrubs, put on his pajamas, jumped into bed, and pulled the covers over his head.

Upon entering Room 423, Blinky had hopped out of the wheelchair and onto the bed where he slam-dunked into the sleeping bodies of Nurse Shipley and Dr. Sorenson.

The startled couple handled the matter according to their sex. The frightened nurse screamed. Dr. Sorenson pushed the errant body off the bed.

"What in blazes! Can't a fellow sleep! What kind of facility are we running here?" the doctor questioned as he stepped over Blinky on his way to the bathroom.

"Who are you?" Nurse Shipley questioned as she covered herself with the bedding.

Having seen this woman naked, combined with the many house specials they had drunk, temporarily disabled the thought processes of the two make-believe ambulance attendants. Wally and Randle stood there like stone.

According to the instructions given them by Russ, there was to be no occupant in Room 423, whereby there would be no problems. There being two bodies in Bed. No. 42 was not an anticipated detail.

It was Randle who finally spoke up. "We brought Michael A. Delaquot back."

The bathroom door opened, Dr. Sorenson stepped out. Nurse Shipley looked down at the bandaged head on the floor.

"Let me see his bracelet," she demanded.

Wally picked Blinky up off the floor. Randle picked up his arm and held it out so the nurse could see the id bracelet.

"If your head wasn't bandaged, I'd punch you!"

"There, there, Nurse Shipley, remember my Hippocratic Oath," stated Dr. Sorenson. "I'd have to step in and take the punch for him…I think. I'll have to look that up."

"Bryan, what are you babbling about?"

"All's well that ends well. Don't you think so, Nurse Shipley?"

It never ceased to amaze Holly how quickly Bryan bounced back from adversity and that he actually could be jovial about the recent turn of events.

"What happened to him?" questioned the doctor as he pulled on his pants.

"His girlfriend's fiancé beat him about the head," lied Randle.

"That's too bad. Who are you?"

"Ambulance drivers," lied Wally.

"What hospital?"

The doctor sat in the chair and pulled out a cigar from his jacket pocket. Wally and Randle were not prepared for questioning. They stood there.

"He's getting heavy. Why don't you put him in the bed," said the doctor.

Nurse Shipley wrapped the sheet tighter and slid out of bed. She gathered her clothes and went into the bathroom. The two men placed Blinky in the bed. The doctor opened the window and lit his cigar.

"Who sent you?"

"Russ."

"That former soldier is top shelf in my book. Who's that in the bed?"

"It's me, Blinky."

"Russ put you up to this?"

"I got the long straw."

"Good man. Are you staying till the soldier gets back?"

"That's the plan," answered Blinky.

"Splendid. Let's keep this to ourselves, men."

Nurse Shipley came out of the bathroom. The men became quiet as she walked over to the bed. Afraid that she was going to follow through on her threat to punch him, Blinky closed his eyes and leaned away. He would have fallen on the floor if it weren't for Wally having the foresight to catch him. While Blinky was cradled in the arms of the big man, Nurse Shipley came as close as she could to the errant patient.

"Do you need anything, Michael?" inquired the nurse in a tone that made the neck hairs of every man in the room stand on end. Frightened, Blinky kept his eyes shut and shook his head.

"I'll let everyone know you're back and check on you again before I leave. Gentlemen."

Randle was in the nurse's path. He went left as she went right. He went right when she went left.

"Stand still!" she ordered.

Randle obeyed. She walked past him and left the room.

"What a woman," said the doctor as he took a drag on the cigar. "I wouldn't be here when she gets back."

"See you, Blinky," said Randle.

"All the best," said Wally,

With their well wishes done, Wally and Randle quickly left the room and hightailed it back to the lodge. The former soldiers gathered around as Blue's relatives gave details of the mission, including seeing a naked nurse. Russ' men were devastated that they had to miss out on all the action.

In Room 423, the doctor continued to smoke his cigar. Blinky made himself comfortable. They enjoyed a good laugh or two as they discussed the comings and goings at the facility and the lodge.

It wasn't long before Nurse Shipley came back to check on the soldier patient. What she really came back to do was take Michael A. Delaquot to task for leaving the facility which caused so much drama to her and the staff members of the ward. But seeing the love of her life smoking so peacefully, she gave up the notion of revenge.

"Will I be seeing you over at the lodge, Bryan?"

"Being I was so busy this afternoon, I'll check on my patients first. Have a house special ready for me will you, doll."

"It'll be my pleasure." With a – "sweet dreams soldier" - she left the room.

"Think she really meant that?" said the former soldier who drew the long straw.

The doctor took a drag on his cigar. "Let me put it this way. When Michael Delaquot stepped out of the door of this facility, he stepped on the ego of Nurse Shipley. I don't think that was a good thing."

Blinky sunk into the bed. Dr. Sorenson blew smoke out the window.

***

It was getting late. Wally and Randle decided not to wait for Betty Lu and Julie to come back before finding a place to stay for the night. They left the lodge leaving word for the ladies that as soon as they got settled at a motel they'd return.

Betty Lu and Julie had gotten the dead volunteer home and settled in a chair, which they took to be Bridget's favorite as it was right across from the TV set.

"No cats," said Betty Lu when she came back from checking the rooms.

"Good. I guess we can be going," said Julie.

"We just can't leave her here," said Betty Lu as the patient coordinator in her came back on duty.

"What do you propose we do?"

"Call the authorities," and she picked up the phone receiver.

Julie understood her motives. The thing a single woman fears most is being alone when they die and no one discovering their body for days, weeks, or at the worst months. As Betty Lu spoke to the operator, Julie pulled up a chair next to Bridget and turned on the TV.

When Betty Lu hung up the receiver she opened the front door and turned on the porch lights to make it easier for when the police arrived. Then she pulled up a chair on the other side of Bridget.

"Are they coming?"

"The police department has one car and it's currently being used to transfer drug smugglers to the county line. According to the operator, Bridget is third on their list. I told her there was no hurry. What's on?" inquired Betty Lu.

"Unmarried Women of Duran County."

"I love that show. I wonder if Bridget has anything to munch on?" said Betty Lu and she went into the kitchen to see.

Sally was weary and really wanted to get a good night's sleep in his own bed, but instead he was at the lodge sitting at a table with Rhonda Blisnick, the day nurse he had stood up the night before.

He was doing his best to get back on the good side of Rhonda. She was a nurse whose uniforms didn't quite fit her body. They were always very short in length, too tight and had buttons popping open in all the right places. For most of the fellows who worked in the facility, she was candy for the eyes. Those she deemed with a first date for some reason never had a second. Sally wanted to know why. He had asked her out several times and she had always said no.

The attendant had the feeling she was not going to take being stood up lightly, so he stopped at the gift shop when he got off duty and bought her a little something.

"What is it?" Rhonda asked as she undid the wrapping paper.

"I want you to be surprised," said Sally.

She got down to the box and turned it over.

"Condoms! You stood me up last night and now you buy me condoms."

"Not a good thing?" he questioned.

In answer, she took her drink and poured it over his head. Holly was standing at the bar waiting for a house special. She watched as the day nurse walked out the door, then walked over and sat across from the attendant.

"Whatever you did, don't worry about it. Rhonda's a frustrated actress."

Sally nodded as he wiped his brow.

"Guess who came back?"

"The Sergeant? You're kidding?"

"Saw him with my own two eyes."

"Glad to hear it. Look I'm really sorry about Blue."

"Water under the bridge," said Holly.

"Sally!"

"I've got to go. Thanks for the news. Coming Rhonda," said the attendant in his rush to get to his date.

"Heard the Sergeant came back this afternoon," said Russ as he put Holly's drink on the table.

"What Sergeant?" she asked.

The lodge owner realized he had let the cat out of the bag and now it was hanging on the cord by its tail.

"I'll be right there," said Russ pretending he heard his name being called. "We'll talk later."

He practically ran behind the bar. Holly sipped her drink and waited for her date.

Unmarried Women of Duran County was over and just in time as a man of the law was knocking at Bridget's door.

An officer, who was tall, dark, and handsome, was standing on the porch. Betty Lu made sure her hair was in place and her slip wasn't showing before letting him in.

"I have a report of a dead person."

"What's your name?" inquired Julie.

"Lieutenant Skip Turner."

"You make my heart skip a beat."

"Like he never heard that one before," said Betty Lu.

"What's wrong?" asked Julie.

"What about Wally?"

"What about him?"

"Ladies."

They turned their attention back to the officer.

"How tall are you?"

"Julie Binder, can you not focus on the situation at hand," said Betty Lu.

"What situation?"

Lieutenant Turner stood there as the two ladies bickered back and forth. The sound of a loud burp brought the fighting to an end. Betty Lu and Julie looked at each other. They looked to the officer. All three looked to the only other person that was in the room.

"Time for dinner," said Bridget as she got up from her chair.

The previously dead woman walked into the kitchen. Betty Lu fainted into the arms of Lieutenant Turner. Julie looked into his eyes.

"Hazel with specks of gold," she noted.

***

At the Rustic Lodge, Holly sipped her drink and waited for her date. At the medical facility, Dr. Sorenson was busy leading two attendants to the fourth floor as they pushed a gurney with Mr. Flack on it.

The doctor had forgotten why he had gone up to the fourth floor earlier that day. In the midst of helping Sally make his lunch deliveries, enjoying jellyroll cake in the company of the nurse he loved, and then dealing with Blinky and the two fake ambulance drivers, Mr. Flack had gone completely out of his thoughts.

Figuring he'd tell Holly about her new patient when they met up later at the lodge, he took it upon himself to requisition a second bed for Room 423. He then went to the ICU and personally saw to the administrator's transfer.

The resident physician had earlier stopped by Mr. Flack's bed in order to check on him and saw the administrator cuddled up with the PR.

"This is definitely a tight knit group," he said to himself.

He didn't have the heart to separate the two and gave orders to the staff to let the fellows be.

When Dr. Sorenson came to get the administrator he met with the resident physician who had not a drop of sleep for well over fifty hours. The two men walked over to Mr. Flack's bed.

Having been a party to some recent bizarre happenings on the fourth floor, Dr. Sorenson was not surprised to see peculiar happenings in the ICU when he gazed upon the two cuddling men.

"What's that saying about strange bedfellows?"

"Misery acquaints a man with strange bedfellows," the resident physician answered.

"What's that from?"

"The Tempest."

"Bill Shakespeare. He was a talent."

The resident physician agreed. He also agreed to the transfer of Mr. Flack to the fourth floor. The two attendants parted the sleeping couple, putting Nathanial back in his bed and Mr. Flack on the gurney. With Dr. Sorenson leading the way, the administrator left the ICU for higher ground.

***

At the Ridleyville fair grounds, the Sergeant was saying his goodbyes to Alfred and his family.

After the corndogs, he was challenged by the eldest Cummings to a shooting match at one of the booths. The Cummings patriarch lost sixteen times before the two called it quits.

Being a good sport, the Sergeant passed all but two of his winnings to the various Cummings children. Armed with stuffed animals for his wife and daughter, plus a dozen funnel cakes, he got back into Nathanial's red convertible and continued the ride to his home in Tuscaloosa, which was only two hours away.

***

Around this time, Betty Lu and Julie were driving back to the lodge.

Being there was no dead body to contend with, Lieutenant Skip Turner had vacated Bridget's premises shortly after Julie presented the officer with her phone number.

"You had us worried," declared Julie to Bridget who was sitting before the TV enjoying her evening repast.

"My late husband always said I sleep like the dead," chuckled the elderly volunteer.

Explaining how she got home and their endeavor to save their jobs, Bridget enjoyed a good laugh at the foolishness of the patient coordinator and switchboard operator.

Waiting a decent interval to make sure Bridget was really okay, Betty Lu and Julie said their goodnights and they pulled up to the lodge just as Wally and Randle were also pulling up.

The foursome went in together, ordered four house specials at the bar and took a seat in the back booth. The ladies took turns telling the story about the dead volunteer. Wally and Randle especially enjoyed the part where Bridget burped and came back to life.

Tom, the former supply officer for the army, delivered more house specials to their table. As he placed the drinks down, Wally was speaking.

"We can beat that. Why just a few hours ago we were…"

Tom dumped a drink on Wally's lap. "Geez, I'm sorry. Why don't you and Randle come with me and I'll help you get cleaned up."

"You didn't spill any drink on me," said Randle.

Tom gave him a look that Randle, being a one-time army lackey, recognized.

"Let's go Uncle Wally."

The two got up and Tom led the way over to the bar.

"We have a problem here, Russ."

Tom explained the latter situation to his boss and Russ explained the former situation to Blue Morgan's relatives. The former soldiers spoke about Betty Lu being the patient coordinator and how she could get them all in trouble for sending someone into the medical facility impersonating a soldier patient.

"I'm powerfully sorry," stated Wally. "I didn't realize."

"We'll be on our guard," added Randle.

"I'm sure the Sergeant will appreciate what you've done for him."

As the ladies were watching, Russ made the pretense of helping Wally to dry his shirt. He made them another round of house specials and sent them on their way.

"Good catch, Tom. Think we can count on them?"

"They're okay in my book," and he went back to work.

"You were going to tell us about tonight," reminded Julie.

Wally looked at her, smiled, got closer and kissed her. That was enough needed to change the subject and the women took the stage again with their exploits.

Louie Dombrowski held the door open for Dr. Sorenson when he arrived. Seeing Holly waiting for him, he went right over to the table, downed his drink and gave a wave to Russ for another round.

"How you doing, doll?"

"Better now that you're here."

"I forgot to tell you something."

"What's that?"

"Mr. Flack is now a resident of your ward."

"I thought…"

"It wasn't a heart attack. More like a nervous breakdown. The man keeps shouting about lobsters taking over and being forced to eat shrimp."

"I always saw him as hyper-wired."

"We all have our breaking points. You'll see to his care?"

"Only the best for one of ours," replied Holly.

***

Shortly after Mr. Flack was transferred out of the ICU, Nathanial woke up in the ICU. The last he remembered he was having drinks at the lodge.

"What happened?" asked the PR.

"You bumped your head. You'll be okay," answered the resident physician.

"Can I go home?"

"Sure enough."

With that good news, Nathanial got up from the bed. He stretched.

"I feel…good."

He walked out of the ICU and immediately bumped into Sally who was coming up from the PR office with Rhonda Blisnick.

"Hey there Nathanial, how you doing?" asked Sally.

"Right as rain."

"How about joining us, we're going over to the lodge."

"Don't mind if I do."

On their way out they passed the reception desk where Melanie was doing her nails. Nathanial was unaware of his past cuddling with the administrator. He was feeling particularly frisky that he chalked up to having had a good sleep. On a whim he invited Melanie to go with them.

"What's your name?" he inquired as they stepped through the sliding doors.

This foursome walked over to the lodge. Nathanial by force of habit led the party to the booth in the back that was occupied by the other foursome.

"Hey, Betty Lu. Hey, Julie," said Sally. "Good news the missing soldier's back."

"That is good news," said Julie who didn't have a clue what he was talking about.

Betty Lu's antenna went up. She looked at Sally with such a look her eyes reminded him of a wolf.

"We'd better find another table," he said.

The foursome went on their way. Betty Lu got up from the table.

"If you'll excuse me, I have to check on something."

Wally and Randle, having been given the details of the covert operation from Russ and Tom, recognized trouble when it was afoot. Randle whistled a sharp note. Even with the fifties music playing on the jukebox it was heard throughout the lodge. The shrill noise stopped everyone, including Betty Lu, in their tracks.

"Will you marry me?" Randle called out.

Everyone, including Betty Lu, turned this way and that to see who he was yelling at. Finally Betty Lu pointed to herself. Randle nodded yes. She jumped into his arms and kissed him.

"More house specials," cried Wally.

After a round of clapping for the newly engaged couple, the occupants of the lodge went back to their own business. Wally went up to the bar to get a tray of house specials.

"Well, this is a turn of events. You guys come here to bring Blue home and now one of you is bringing home a bride," said Russ as he poured the drinks.

"I wonder what Randle's wife is going to say about it," Wally mumbled as he took the tray to the booth in the back, in the corner, in the dark.

Nathanial was enjoying a house special in the company of Melanie as the escaped soldier was turning into his driveway.

The house was dark except for the flashing lights of the TV in the living room window. Looking in, he saw his wife curled up in a blanket as she sat on the couch.

Not wanting to disturb her he used his key. All was quiet. Placing the stuffed animals on the bench seat, he took off his boots, went into the kitchen, got a plate, placed one of the funnel cakes on it and helped himself to a beer.

He walked into the living room and sat down on the couch. Rosie put her feet in his lap.

"I see you got my letter."

"Yes, I did. Funnel cake?"

"Thank you."

"What's that you're watching, Rosie?"

"Married Women of Duran County."

The Sergeant took a drink of his beer.

"You're prettier than them."

"You think so?"

"I know so."

"Good to have you home."

She pecked his cheek and took a bite of cake.

137

***

It was an early night.

Bryan walked Holly to her car. She went home and he went back into the facility to check on his patients. Passing the switchboard he couldn't help himself. Seeing Donna was fast asleep, his hand slammed down on the desk.

"Oh, it's you," she said sleepily.

"What's new?" questioned Dr. Sorenson.

"Patient came into the ER."

"Resume position."

Donna put her head back down.

Lucky for Sally, Rhonda Blisnick quickly got over being stood up and the stupidity of his gift. He walked his date to her car and followed in his car to her home in Lawton.

Melanie and Nathanial were leaving the Rustic Lodge. Russ was taking a catnap in the backroom, leaving Louie to keep an eye on the PR. The member of the covert operation watched as he walked Melanie to her car and when he saw Nathanial looking for his own car, Louie called him back on the pretext that he needed to speak with him on a matter of PR. Seeing the two come through the door, Tom mixed up a new batch of house specials.

"Don't mind if I do," said Nathanial when offered a drink.

Betty Lu was glowing from her recent engagement and the house specials she celebrated with. Wally and Randle had to remind her and Julie that they had work in the morning. The two men dropped the ladies at their respective homes before going to their motel. Betty Lu wanted her fiancé to spend the night, but Wally told her it was against Randle's religion. Not wanting to jinx her upcoming marriage, she kissed her future husband goodnight and went inside. Randle closed the screen door and got back into his uncle's truck.

"If I wasn't married already, I'd marry that girl. She's a sweetheart."

Before putting the car in gear, his uncle slapped him upside the head.

Blinky was fast asleep in Room 423. He had enjoyed the dinner of turnip greens, fried chicken and chocolate pudding. In the bed next to him lay Mr. Flack. As he didn't appear to be waking up anytime soon, Blinky ate his dinner too.

Mac Treeter, computer expert, walked through the sliding doors of the medical facility. He looked in on Donna who was fast asleep. Using a credit card he opened the patient coordinator's office door and helped himself to the computer.

In the small town of Tuscaloosa, the Sergeant was kissing his wife's neck as she watched TV.

"Am I prettier than that one?"

"Uh huh."

"How about her?"

"Uh huh."

"What do you think about the one with the short hair?"

"Is this show gonna end soon?"

"It was over an hour ago."

The Sergeant looked at the TV. A documentary was on about snakes in the wild. He looked at his wife.

"I live to tease you," she smiled.

"Oh, you do."

He took the remote, turned off the TV and picked her up.

"Do you want to see your children first?"

He put her down in the hallway and opened a bedroom door. The oldest, Caroline, was sleeping peacefully amid a room packed with stuffed animals. The Sergeant went back to the bench. He placed the panda he won at the Ridleyville fair next to his daughter and gave her a kiss.

"She's grown."

"Nineteen this September."

Rosie closed the door and the Sergeant opened the next door where his two sons were sleeping.

"Look how Michael Jr.'s feet are hanging over the bed."

"He's six-three by last count."

The Sergeant wiped a proud tear from his eye. He placed the covers back over Jeremy who had kicked them off.

"Where's the little one?"

"He's still a night owl. So I moved him to his own room."

"That's cause he was born at night during a lightning storm. The lights went out as he was coming. Remember that?"

"Yes. That was a fun night."

"You're a trooper."

He kissed his wife. She opened the door to their youngest child's room.

"Your daddy's home," said Rosie.

Their five-year old popped out from under the bed.

"Hey, daddy."

"Hey, yourself."

Rory ran over and jumped in his father's arms.

"Whatcha got for me?"

"Funnel cake. Want some?"

"Sure."

The three went into the kitchen. Rosie gave her youngest a glass of milk and poured two cups of coffee. They spent the next two hours eating funnel cake and listening to their son, who had been born in the dark during a lightning storm, as he told all about the goings on since his dad was last home.

0700 hrs
MAY 17th

It was an early morning.

Nurse Chelswick was making her rounds. She stopped in Room 423. The two previous days she had given enemas to Sally and Dr. Sorenson. Not wanting to make the same mistake a third time, she was carefully checking id bracelets.

She went up to the first bed and checked the band with her list. The occupant was not on it. She went over to the second bed. The bracelet's name matched the name on her list.

With confirmation made that this was the soldier patient she was to fill with life affirming liquid, she lifted the sheet pulled down the scrubs, and injected the sleeping soldier patient.

"Well hello there," exclaimed the patient.

"Good morning, Sergeant."

The injection of liquids done, Blinky sat up. He blinked into the eyes of the nurse and it was love at first sight.

"I'm Blinky."

"I thought your name was Michael. Don't tell me I got it wrong again."

He looked around and remembered the mission he was entrusted with.

"Blinky's my nickname."

Nurse Chelswick gave a sigh of relief. Her smile lit up the former soldier's heart.

"I have to go."

"Will I be seeing you later?" he asked.

"I'll be around."

He didn't have to think long as the mixture was fast acting. He made a mad dash for the bathroom. The slamming door jarred the sleeping subconscious mind of Mr. Flack who screamed, "The lobsters are coming!"

When Nurse Chelswick gave Blinky the enema he wasn't surprised by the action but by the fact that he wasn't the one doing the work. The former soldier suffered from chronic constipation. This was the ill effect of his time in the service and the refusal to have his bowels move just anywhere. He had learned a few tricks to stop nature's process.

When he got out of the service, his guts were not the same. Unlike Mrs. Morgan, he saw no point in suing the army for undoing the work of his beloved mother.

The former soldier who was impersonating soldier patient Bed No. 42 was able to stop in mid-bowel-movement when he heard the voice of his roommate screaming to those within hearing distance to take up arms against the coming lobsters. With pants down about his ankles he opened the bathroom door. Mr. Flack was standing on the bed wielding the only weapon near enough which was his pillow.

"Stay away! You have no power here. Take your specially designed just for lobsters spacecraft and go back where you belong."

Hearing the screams, members of the staff rushed the room. Blinky held up his hand to stop them from pouncing on the administrator.

"I'm going to do what you said. I'm returning to my spacecraft and I'm never coming back here again."

"You promise."

"I swear. See I'm holding up my claw." Blinky held up his arm. "Goodbye. And I'm awful sorry I scared you."

"That's okay. Take your fried shrimp with you."

"They're already buckled in their seats."

"Good. Get going now."

"Goodbye."

142

Blinky backed into the bathroom and closed the door. He sat on the toilet to finish his business. Having held it in that way the contents of his guts came shooting out. The sounds that came from the bathroom placated Mr. Flack, who mistook the noise for the lobster craft taking off into outer space.

The staff members, knowing what the sounds meant, grimaced, but they were satisfied that the administrator was not going to need to be sedated again as he lay back down on the bed and proclaimed, "It's over."

Due to the smell that was coming from under the bathroom door, the staff went back to their duties. When he was done, Blinky came out, closed the door softly, opened a window and got back into bed.

***

Betty Lu had spent a good part of the night being romanced by her fiancé, and in sleep, dreaming of the wedding to come. She woke up knowing the future was finally on the course she had always hoped for.

Preparing for work, her thoughts were on where the reception would be held. By the time she got on the bus it came to her - the festivities would take place at the Rustic Lodge where she got engaged.

As his fiancé was making plans for wedded bliss, Randle was sitting in a diner booth. Over a hearty breakfast, his Uncle Wally was taking him to task on his sudden engagement to a woman he just met and how Hazel was not going to like it when she got the news of her husband's impending marriage.

"What were you thinking, boy?" mumbled Uncle Wally as he stuffed a hotcake in his mouth.

"I only wanted to protect a fellow soldier."

"You protected him alright and now you're in a pickle. Hazel isn't going to take to the idea of having to share you."

"I know. I know. I'll get out of this somehow."

"I'm thinking it's about time we hightailed it out of here with Blue."

"What about Betty Lu?"

Wally gulped down another pancake. He was about to wipe his mouth with a napkin instead he handed it to his nephew and used his sleeve as a replacement.

"Waitress!"

The waitress sauntered over.

"What can I get you?"

"Another stack of pancakes and a pen."

Bridget was at her post and Julie was at the switchboard when Betty Lu got to work.

"Can you take a break, Julie?"

"If Bridget will cover for me."

The elderly volunteer was in the midst of telling the guard the story of her recent run in with the law and her astonishment upon waking to find an officer in blue standing over her thinking she was dead.

As she had seen more excitement as a switchboard operator than she ever had at the reception desk, Bridget called on another volunteer to cover her spot. She chuckled and mumbled something about the stupidity of the two women as she sat down to answer the phones. With the upcoming wedding on their minds, the previous night was a thing of the past. Betty Lu and Julie paid her no mind and went to the coffee shop.

Over pound cake and lattes, the two friends were going over the details of the wedding.

"Alleluia, I can finally stop watching Unmarried Women of Duran County and start watching Married Women of Duran County," said Betty Lu.

"There's not a single woman on the planet that can enjoy watching a show about married woman having fun when they weren't one of them," agreed Julie. "That's something to celebrate."

They clinked coffee cups.

"We'll have the reception at the Rustic Lodge."

"Where you got engaged."

"That's exactly what I thought."

"What about the moose heads?"

"I'll talk to Russ about taking them down and putting something more --"

Betty Lu stopped in mid-sentence. The cause – Sally had just walked through the door.

The attendant could have gotten a cup of coffee from the kitchen, but didn't have the strength to walk that far. His time with Rhonda Blisnick went well until he followed her home.

This was his first date with the nurse and he swore to himself there wouldn't be another. Rhonda was the type of woman who thought if she allowed a man the pleasure to wine, dine and have his way, he should also have to listen to her. And the woman could talk.

When he got to her home, Rhonda turned on the lights so Sally could see her clearly as she updated him on her life starting from the time she was two as she didn't remember much before that.

 She kept up the talking till three in the morning when he made his excuses that he had to be at work in a few hours. Bleary-eyed, ears ringing and thoroughly exhausted, Sally came in through the sliding doors where the smell of fresh brewed coffee caught his senses. Feeling he couldn't take many more steps without a good jolt of caffeine, he followed the aroma to the coffee shop.

As he helped himself to a cup, Betty Lu's mind was trying to compartmentalize information. She put the thoughts of her wedding to the side and tried to remember what it was. Something about a soldier. Something about someone missing. Something about her computer and Mr. Flack. She gave her head a couple of hits as the wedding plans were fighting her thought process.

"Soldier, missing, computer, Mr. Flack," she said aloud.

Julie's mouth was stuffed with pound cake. "Sold, miss, comp, flack," she repeated.

"That's it!" cried the patient coordinator. "The missing soldier was Michael Delaquot, he ran away because of Mr. Flack."

"Wha bout com?" Julie questioned as she chewed.

"I don't know," replied Betty, "But I'll find out. I have to get to work."

***

At the Delaquot home, there was a mad dash for the Sergeant when Caroline, Michael Jr. and Jeremy came out from their rooms and saw their dad sitting at the kitchen table.

"So you haven't forgotten me."

Big as they were, the kids jumped all over him for that remark. Being Rosie and Rory were fast asleep, he made breakfast while his three oldest ate funnel cake and gave him an update on what had been happening since he'd last been home. Later, he took a breakfast tray into his sleeping wife.

"This is not a hotel you know."

"I figured you being home and all you could take care of things."

"Don't I always?"

"Yes, you do. I'll eat later."

She turned over. He left the tray, closed the door, took a towel from the linen closet and went into the bathroom. He came out, went back to the bedroom and woke his wife up again.

"I thought you and Caroline got rashes from scented soaps and perfume."

146

"We do."

"Then who does this belong to?"

Rosie came up on her elbows. He put a bar of purple soap to her nose.

"Do you really want me to answer that question?"

Getting no response, she dropped back and was asleep before her head hit the pillow.

As the Sergeant showered he tried to figure out which of his sons enjoyed smelling like a girl, while back at the medical facility Betty Lu was trying to figure out the shenanigans that were taking place right under her nose.

After leaving Julie at the coffee shop, she went straight to the ICU. Forgetting she saw Nathanial at the lodge the night before, she included him when asking the resident physician, who had gone without sleep for slightly over sixty hours, about Mr. Flack and his whereabouts.

"Where are the administrator and the PR?"

"Who?"

"Mr. Flack and Nathanial Seltingbaum."

"Fourth floor, back into the world," responded the weary resident and he fell back onto one of the beds and conked out.

In her panic, Betty Lu tried to shake him awake, "Did you say fourth floor?"

The resident physician was down for the count. The patient coordinator ran out of the ICU shouting, "I have to save him."

The ICU nurse thought she said, "You have to save him." She ran to the bed saw the resident physician lying there and thinking he had a heart attack she hurried to get the cart.

With no doctors in sight, the flustered ICU nurse shocked the resident's heart while on the fourth floor Betty Lu was holding her finger on the psyche ward door buzzer.

Some of the soldier patients who were in the hallway went up to the window to see who was trying to get in. Without

147

warning, she smashed her face against the window and screamed, "Let me in!" The visibly shaken soldiers thinking they were under attack ran back to their rooms.

The staff not knowing what to make of it looked to Nurse Shipley who had walked in the door only minutes before. Tired from a late night her radar had been in sleep mode.

"Damn. I haven't even had my coffee yet. What room is Mr. Flack in?"

Four twenty-three was the answer she received.

"Damn. Damn. Damn. Which one of you did that?"

"I did," said Dr. Sorenson as he walked out of the common room.

The previous night after checking in on the newest ER arrival, the good doctor had looked in on his patients. Among them were the service woman with a fixed hernia, Bobby Wallington and his 'little Bobby' and lastly Mr. Flack. As all the patients were on the mend or heavily sedated, he felt jovial and in need of a smoke. He sat down on the couch in the common room and before he could light up he had fallen asleep with the cigar dangling in his mouth.

"Did you sleep on the couch again, Bryan?"

"Guilty."

"You don't get enough rest."

"I get what I need," he grinned wickedly.

The nurse blushed. On the other side of the door, Betty Lu was having a hissy fit.

"Dr. Sorenson, they won't let me in," she shouted.

Like a western hero in an old movie, the doctor took a breath and slowly strode to the locked door. There were several members of the fourth floor staff that wished the doctor had a holster with a gun so he could put the woman out of her misery. What they didn't know about Dr. Sorenson was he had the ability to fire with the one weapon that always worked; he opened the door wide and shot her a compliment.

"Betty Lu, you sure do look pretty in the morning."

The patient coordinator giggled, "That won't work on me anymore. I'm getting married."

Nurse Shipley and the staff were silent where they stood. They barely breathed.

"Who's the lucky fellow?" questioned the doctor.

"My fiancé's name is Randle Morgan."

***

The diner waitress eventually came round with more pancakes and a spare pen.

No matter how dumb their members were, the Morgan family held to the belief that substantial food intake would boost brainpower. The only conclusion their minds could muster up was Randle's fiancé Betty Lu took in so much drink the night before there was no way she would get to work on time. This would enable them to leave a note, put Blue in the truck and get the heck out of there without any fuss.

With only the word 'goodbye' written on the diner napkin, they entered the doors of the medical facility and dropped to their knees. Randle crawled over to the switchboard office and peaked in. Bridget was still covering for Julie who seemed to be on an extended break.

Seeing their plan was working, he crawled back to his uncle and gave him the thumbs up. The two men got off their knees and made themselves known to the elderly volunteer.

"May I help you?"

"Where does Betty Lu hang her hat?" Wally questioned.

They had to wait two phone calls before Bridget pointed the way. Walking across the lobby, Blue's relatives passed the coffee shop where an interrogation was in progress.

"I told you, I don't know anything," cried Sally.

"You expect me to believe that?" retorted Julie

149

After a night of listening to Rhonda Blisnick and now having to submit to the torture laid out by the switchboard operator in her effort to find out the latest happenings, the attendant had had his fill - literally.

Julie went to the coffee pot to pour Sally a sixth cup. The truth warranted he be of a sober disposition with none of the alcohol he lived on giving support. On her way back to the table she saw Wally and Randle walking by.

"Wally honey," Julie called out.

The two men stopped in their tracks. The last person they wanted to see besides Betty Lu was her best friend. Wally slapped Randle in the head and they took off running.

The coffee in this shop was not only known for being jailhouse strong, but exceedingly hot to the point of scalding. When Julie saw the big guy run, she dropped the cup spilling the contents on Sally.

He screamed as the hot liquid splashed his pants. Luckily he was wearing a pair of scrubs with elastic in the waist, with one motion he was able to drop them. The operator had dated the attendant a few times, so she took no mind to his baring all and ran out the door in search of her new love.

Although the area around his private parts were feeling pain, seeing his chance to escape, Sally tried to run. Trapped by pants that were wrapped around his legs, he fell to the floor. Taking off his shoes, he kicked the pants off and ran out of the coffee shop, through the sliding doors and with all the haste his bare feet could muster hurried over to the lodge.

Seeing the half-naked attendant coming his way, Louie flung open the door and Russ seeing Sally's distress handed over the entire pitcher of house specials. The attendant downed the concoction anesthetizing the pain of Rhonda's talking marathon, Julie's interrogation, and the burnt skin surrounding his you know where.

With the switchboard operator hollering their names, Wally and Randle went through the first exit door they came upon which was the stairway to the below ground level. They took the stairs two and three at a time and without stopping to see if they were being followed, they ran down one of Major Tripington's long-abandoned tunnels.

***

As the two relatives of Private Blue Morgan were running in the dark, the sun was shining brightly over the Sergeant as he waited in his driveway. There were many things he missed while serving his country and driving the kids to school was one of them. His oldest Caroline was the first to come out.

"I have my own transportation, Daddy. Did mom tell you I'm quitting college and leaving on an extended fact finding trip?"

Her dad, who didn't have a clue, shook his head.

"I didn't think so. These are the brochures for all the countries we're going to."

"We?"

"My social sciences professor. He's wonderful. I have to go."

She kissed her dad and got in a car that was parked in the street.

"We'll discuss it later," she shouted and drove away.

"I'll be here," he barely managed to squeak out.

A cloud was beginning to form in the Sergeant's sunny day. He looked down and saw he was holding in his hands travel brochures for every war torn country of the last twenty years.

His brain needed to quickly escape 'family world' and get back into 'army world' so he could handle the forthcoming father/daughter battle with a sound plan. Before his soldier's way of thinking could kick in Michael Jr. came out. He stuffed the brochures in his back pocket and opened the passenger side door.

"Your chauffeur's waiting."

"I already have a ride."

A car pulled up with a young girl at the wheel. Michael gave his dad a 'good to have you home' hug before jumping into the waiting car's passenger seat.

Watching his son ride away, the Sergeant found he was enveloped in a cloud of toxicity. He sniffed the air. A combination of scented soap, body spray, and quadruple X, or was it O, for odepu, deodorant hit his nose. Unable to breath, he began coughing. Mystery solved – it was Michael Jr. who owned the perfumery in the bathroom.

When the air cleared, he wiped his sweaty brow touching the bristly rim of his receding hairline. This loss of hair combined with two of his children running amok, and no longer needing a driving service, brought back the reality of his passing youth.

The cloud in his previously sunny day darkened considerably when his third child came out the door and shocked the Sergeant back into the present.

Jeremy, a student in middle school, was obviously in the midst of an identity crisis that showed up in his wardrobe.

With many social groups to choose from, the student was hard pressed to decide which one he wanted to belong to, so he chose them all. He was wearing a plaid shirt and pocket protector for the geeks, a baseball cap for the sports crowd and blackened eyes for the gothic crew. It was the pants hanging off his butt that caused the Sergeant the greatest concern.

He stood there speechless.

"I'm gonna be late, Dad."

"Son, you forgot your belt."

"It's the style," said the youngster.

With that report on the latest fashion trend Jeremy got into the car.

"Dad!"

The emphasized word snapped the Sergeant out of his reverie. He closed the passenger side door and slid into the driver's seat.

"Where to?"

"School."

"You're going to school dressed like --?!"

"I'm gonna be late!"

"We wouldn't want that," said the stunned father of four. He turned on the motor and got going.

***

"My heart is broken."

Betty Lu forgot all about trying to save Michael Delaquot, patient, from Mr. Flack, administrator. She was enraptured with Dr. Sorenson who seemed to be taking the news of her engagement so personally.

"I want you to tell me all about it," he put his arm around Betty Lu's shoulder and steered her toward the elevator.

Pressing the button to go down to his office on the second floor, the doctor took note of the gaping looks of the psyche ward staff as they crowded around the door. He winked at Nurse Shipley, which brought her back to her senses. She shooed her fellow workers back into the ward and closed the door gently.

The elevator doors opened and the two stepped on. It was then the nurse breathed a sigh of relief and went to the break room to get the cup of coffee she so desperately needed.

After two cups, she felt steady enough to tackle the day. Walking into Room 423, she found Mr. Flack and a head full of bandages body in the next bed over.

"Who the hell is that?" Nurse Shipley asked herself before charging to the nurse's station.

"Who the hell is that?" she repeated.

"Who, where?" questioned Penny Carlough, social worker.

"The person in Bed No. 42?"

"Michael A. Delaquot, sergeant," was the reply.

"I need a drink."

Nurse Shipley left the ward and while waiting for the elevator tried to focus. As she rode down the memory of being slammed by the wayward sergeant while she and Bryan were sleeping in Bed No. 42 came to her.

Louie could see Nurse Shipley was dazed; he opened the lodge door without a word. Russ poured a house special. Holly drank it down. That's when she saw Sally at a table with his head resting upon it. Russ poured another; she took it with her, sitting across from the attendant. The two looked at each other and downed their respective drinks.

"The men are in need of their breakfast."

Sally nodded. They held up their empty glasses. Russ came over and filled them. In unison, they drank them down. Sally rose. The nurse saw he was naked from the waist down.

"Are you okay?"

He nodded, walked out of the lodge and back to work. Nurse Shipley put her head down on the table. She pondered the losing of her mind. Michael A. Delaquot was back, she had seen him last night. No, he had jumped on her last night. How could she have forgotten?

It was Betty Lu. The strain of dealing with the woman was driving her crazy.

***

While the Sergeant was re-acclimating to his family, Dr. Sorenson was pasting together his broken heart, Nurse Shipley was tying one on in order to hang on, and the fugitives, Wally and Randle, had finally reached the end of the tunnel. Unable to go forward, they caught their breath and listened. The only sound they heard was the dripping of water through a crack in the cement.

"What are we going to do now?" questioned Randle.

"We'll just wait down here until the coast is clear," answered Wally as he wiped his sweating brow.

With a plan in hand, they walked back the way they came. Several minutes later they were standing near the stairway wondering whether it was safe to go up. The dread of running into the switchboard operator was too much and the decision was made to wait it out a while longer.

They began opening doors to see if there was a comfortable place for them to stay. When they came upon the public relations office, Wally flicked on the light. They were amazed to find a desk, chairs, and most of all a Morgan family favorite - k-rations.

Looking in the desk, Wally found bottles of liquor that Sally kept on hand for his dates with facility nurses and kitchen aides.

"We can live down here forever," noted Randle.

They were opening packages of k-rations when the phone rang. With his mind distracted by the smell of beef jerky Wally, out of habit, picked up the receiver. Was he dreaming or did the voice on the other end of the line belong to his sister.

Upstairs, Julie had given up the search and went back to her switchboard. She had tried her best to connect Mrs. Morgan to Mr. Flack, but wasn't aware the administrator was currently incommunicado on the fourth floor. As the phone rang in the administrator's office, the operator took the time to regale Mrs. Morgan on the merits of her brother and nephew.

The ranting went on for several minutes. Mrs. Morgan thinking the operator was insane screamed to be connected with someone in authority and to do it quick. Julie switched the phone call down to public relations as Nathanial was next in line when it came to disgruntled callers and visitors.

Mrs. Morgan immediately recognized her brother's twang.

"Wally is that you?"

"Yes, it's me."

"Why haven't you brought my son home?"

"There's been some red tape."

Blue's mother went into a rampage about the army, doctors, toilet training, ranting operators and other burdens she had been exposed to. Seeing this was going to take a while, Wally took the receiver from his ear, placed it on the desk and opened a bottle of scotch. After two swigs he had the strength to interrupt his sister, who if she ever found herself in a ranting contest with Julie would surely win. He promised they'd be home with her son as soon as they could and dropped the receiver down.

After hanging up on his sister, Wally breathed a sigh of relief and got back to the delights the k-rations offered, while Julie was at the switchboard trying to catch her breath.

Out of shape from sitting at a desk all day, the operator ran out of steam before she got too far in chasing after the love of her life and his nephew. She had gone back to work, which allowed Bridget to go back to her job and then she had gotten the call from Mrs. Morgan and was further winded while going on and on about Betty Lu's future relatives.

Before switching the call down to the PR office, Julie was telling Mrs. Morgan that she looked forward to meeting her kin during the upcoming wedding. Blue's mother thinking the operator was talking about her son launched into a tirade about incompetence, the operator's stupidity and that it wasn't a wedding but a funeral that was to be the reason for the next Morgan family gathering.

Realizing Randle didn't have a chance to let his newfound happiness be known to his family, Julie thought it best not to upset the woman further and connected her to the PR office.

When she saw the switchboard lights go out on Mrs. Morgan's call, something sparked in Julie's mind. She had forgotten why Wally showed up at the medical facility only twenty-four short hours ago - Blue.

"Of course that's why Wally was in such a rush, he wanted to check on his nephew."

Putting her job on the back burner once again, Julie hurried past the reception desk, calling out to Bridget to man the phones. She ran to the morgue and slammed through the doors shouting the big man's name.

Arnold Manheim was the facilitator of this department. Being it was an unusually quiet place to work he wasn't used to dealing with the living and their emergencies. He looked up calmly from his paperwork.

"Where's Wally?" she questioned.

"Who?"

"Blue Morgan's uncle."

"Never heard of him."

Julie found it hard to breath. Thinking it was only a matter of seconds and he'd have a dead body to take care of, Arnold slid a seat her way. She plopped down and between gasps of air she made the morgue facilitator swear that if Blue's relatives did show up he would call her right away.

With nothing to lose, Arnold swore an oath. Seeing she was in no shape to walk, the kindly employee whose job it was too keep an eye over those who had gone onto greener pastures, requisitioned a wheelchair and took the time to push Julie back to her desk at the switchboard.

As the elderly volunteer had already crossed the lobby several times in a short period, Arnold before returning to his duties in the morgue, was also kind enough to transport Bridget, via wheelchair, back to the reception desk.

***

The ride to Jeremy's school was a quiet one. The escaped soldier contemplated how he had the ability to whip the most confident man or woman in his field of vision into shape rather quickly. One minute in his skillful hands and what was once riff-raff walking freely on the streets of the country he loved would be cowering frightened beings wanting to know why they joined up, and with tears in their eyes, planned how they could escape and go home to mother.

He couldn't understand how quickly he found himself to be a weakened authority when faced with a son who was a criss-cross dresser. Every attempt to voice his concerns was met with no words. He was actually too afraid to delve any closer into Jeremy's life for fear of what he would find out.

Standing on the edge of society that was the middle school his son attended, the Sergeant pondered the dress codes of the students who stood in front of the building waiting to start their educational day.

To the left was a group of nerds. He didn't have a problem with them. They looked exactly how the nerds looked when he was an attendee at this same school so many years ago.

Standing near the nerds was the gothic crowd. They reminded him of the many old Dracula movies he and his friends rented while on summer break from this same school.

The athletic crowd looked just about the same, including the requisite crew cuts and cute cheerleader hangers-on.

Then he looked to his right and saw a crowd that really put a damper on his sunny day. A pack of boys all with pants hanging down around their butts and drawers showing. They stood there on display for the entire world to see and worse yet, they seemed as proud as peacocks.

Growing up in his time, just a hint showing entitled you to a wedgie. The Sergeant's mind couldn't wrap around the striped, checkered, circles, and plain tidy whities that were blatantly exposed here in front of the same school he went to as a kid.

During his escape from the medical facility, he had in his travels recognized the America he knew, loved, and swore to protect. Standing here among the nations young, he questioned for the first time on just what the hell was going on.

What his eyes were telling him was America's kids were going butt wild. He questioned what he had been fighting for all these years. He wondered who was watching the children while he was watching the enemy.

That was when it struck him.

"Was this a terrorist plot to literally catch the country with our pants down?"

The half of the Sergeant's mind that was trained by the armed forces turned over and over with thoughts of a global nature. The half of his mind that was married with four kids did a back flip of anxiety.

The power struggle going on in his brain came to a sudden halt with the thought -

"What if there was a fire drill? No. What if there was a real fire?"

The Sergeant pictured some Neanderthal student setting the science lab on fire just like Henry Littleton did when he attended this school.

Henry had been short in stature and big on ego. He thought he had genius material that wasn't recognized. With grades ranging in the D minus to D plus range, his parents, thinking their son had reached his educational potential, refused to pay for a nationally known college where he would get a higher education. In his quest to get them to relent, Henry decided to create a stink bomb during lab class.

It turned out Henry wasn't the genius he thought he was. When the flames flickered from the garbage can and hit the ceiling, he was the first to jump out the science room window while the teacher was busy pulling the fire bell.

The Sergeant, then known as Mikey D., was an eighth grade student and in the process of taking a final in math class. He had actually been praying for a fire drill or the teacher dropping dead so there would be a delay of the inevitable bad grade he was going to earn.

With the fire bell clanging, he along with his classmates left the room and walked into a hallway of stampeding students rushing to get out of the building. Smelling smoke, he realized they were in the real thing. Mikey's Boy Scout training kicked in and he helped the teachers get the children out.

He even saved the life of Susie Sacks, who he loved from afar, after she fainted. Carrying his dream girl out of the burning building, he laid her down on the grass and began mouth-to-mouth resuscitation. Knowing he'd probably never get this chance again to save the girl he loved, Mikey refused to stop the breaths of life even after the emergency workers showed up and wanted to take over.

They finally had to pull the scout off Susie. A quick examination determined she had been in no danger at all and the life-sustaining actions he took were not merited. When Susie woke up and heard from her girlfriends that Mikey D. saved her life, she made sure her father, the mayor, gave him the Tuscaloosa merit of valor for his bravery and permission to date his daughter.

The school bell ringing took the smiling Sergeant out of his reverie. He watched Jeremy, who had been standing alone, be enveloped by the vast array of groups as they headed into the building to start their day.

Concerned for the safety and manhood of the droopy-drawed young boys, the Sergeant thought it was his civic duty to speak to America's leader of youth and find out what was going on in this microcosm of society. Not wanting to upset his son, he decided to wait till all the students were inside before going to the principal's office.

***

As the Sergeant awaited his chance to speak to the principal, Sally was delivering breakfast trays to soldiers on the fourth floor. His last drop off was Room 423. Not wanting to lose out on a leather couch, he thought it was his duty to spend some time with the administrator and give him a pep talk and a prayer for a full recovery.

Mr. Flack woke up on Sally's shout of good morning. The tray-bearing attendant opened the curtain and Blinky blinked at the light that flashed across his face.

"I'm sleeping here."

The attendant recognized that voice. It called for an inspection so he got closer to Bed No. 42. Mr. Flack thinking his bedmate was under attack shouted, "Beware the lobsters!" Blinky sat straight up and shouted, "Where's my gun?"

Sally dropped to the floor.

As the administrator hid under the sheets, Blinky grabbed hold of the tray that had spilled its contents across his bed and held it as a weapon.

"Who goes there?" shouted the former soldier.

"It's me, Krishnecki, Salvatore."

"Who?"

"Sally."

"How can I be sure?"

The attendant held up the identifying picture that dangled around his neck.

"Okay, get up slowly."

Sally stood up with hands over his head. Blinky blinked into his face. When he saw the look of recognition on the attendant's face, the former soldier put his hand up to silence him. Mr. Flack was fluttering beneath the sheets.

"Are you a lobsterman from space?" questioned Blinky.

"No, I swear it."

"I don't believe you. Get back in your space capsule and no funny tricks."

Sally stood there in surrender and a whole mess of confusion. Blinky pointed to the bathroom and led the

161

attendant into the room closing the door behind them. The former soldier flushed the toilet several times as he told of winning the long straw in order to stand in for the AWOL soldier. Sally, always quick on the uptake, realized this was the information only an hour before Julie was trying to coerce out of him.

On the last flush, Blinky came out of the bathroom and shouted, "And don't come back!"

Sally got down on hand and knees. Blinky opened the door and the attendant crawled out of the room.

"You're safe now. I made the lobsterman promise not to come back."

The administrator lowered his sheet. Blinky's breakfast and bed were in ruins, so he climbed in Mr. Flack's bed with the excuse it was for his protection in case the lobstermen tried to come back. The administrator, grateful to have his own member of the secret service, was only too happy to share his morning meal.

On the second floor, Dr. Sorenson was showing Betty Lu to the door. She was about to tell him for the third time how she had become engaged to Randle. The doctor was not one to stomp on the dreams of a nearing middle-aged woman who had a fish on the hook. He would have listened, but had to end their session together when he received a phone call that his doctor services were needed elsewhere.

He excused himself and gave the patient coordinator a kiss on the hand and threw in that Betty Lu's getting hitched was a loss for all mankind. Despite being engaged to another, the patient coordinator giggled at the flattery.

The door closed behind her and she didn't even mind when she heard the sound of the lock turning. The doctor had kissed her hand and that was enough.

Instead of living vicariously through the staffs on the many medical shows she was addicted to, she was now living the dream - engaged to one man, the heartbreaker of another.

Betty Lu was overwhelmed by the turn her life had recently taken.

The Sergeant was overwhelmed by the turn his life had recently taken. Sitting on the hood of the family car while he waited to talk to the principal, he took an account of his children.

His daughter was going on a trip to former war torn countries with a predator disguised as a college professor. His oldest son stunk to high heaven, his middle son was showing multiple personality problems and his youngest son was living like a bat.

"Nothing I can't handle," he finally said to himself.

He walked into the middle school and was promptly waylaid by a broom-yielding custodian. The Sergeant was karate trained and made it a rule never to be taken by surprise. He put two hands on the broom and gave it a hard enough twist to force the holder to the ground.

From the floor, the large burly fellow dressed in a green jumpsuit looked up at his opponent.

"Is that you Mikey D?"

The Sergeant looked down. The face, though older, was familiar.

"Mad Arthur?"

"The one and only."

The Sergeant took a seat on the floor next to Arthur. The two men shook hands and quickly caught up on old times.

Arthur was the school bully when Mikey D. attended middle school. He found the ability to reign terror over the population of students and teachers to be not only a gift, but very fulfilling as well. He felt his talents were especially appreciated when he was given the title Mad.

Thinking this was his life calling, and as he had no other aspirations, after graduation from high school he quickly applied for the position of custodian and had been there ever since.

"The first fifteen years, I terrorized the kids, kept them in line. There was no hanging out in the bathrooms or the hallways. I'd hold up my broom and those kids couldn't run fast enough to their classrooms. Teachers loved me. The past five years things changed though."

"In what way?"

"It's anarchy. Total lack of respect. Did you see those kids with their pants hanging around their butts?"

"My son's one of them."

"I didn't want to bring it up," said the custodian. "Things like that have to be handled delicately."

"I was going to talk to the principal about it."

"Won't do you much good, Lionel Thornapple's head muckey-muck."

"Lionel, the Lion, Thornapple?"

"These days he's more like a pussycat," answered the custodian.

The two men got up from the floor, shook hands and parted ways. As the Sergeant headed for the principal's office, he looked back to see Mad Arthur swinging his broom at a few of the gothic crowd. The custodian lowered his weapon and walked away when they laughed at him.

1100 hrs
MAY 17th

Russ stood over Nurse Shipley, "Shouldn't you get back to work?"

She looked up from the table with the saddest eyes the former soldier had seen in a long time.

"Can you keep a confidence?" questioned the nurse.

"My lips are sealed."

"I think I'm losing it. I had a missing patient, now I don't."

"That's a good thing."

"I had to throw Betty Lu off the trail...so I kind of inferred that Mr. Flack was...I don't know how to undo it."

"Hmm. Let me get you a cup of coffee."

Russ got up from the table. The offer of coffee was just a ruse to buy a little time. The quandary was, he didn't want to get on the bad side of any member of the medical staff and didn't know how she would take it if he confessed that the returned soldier was really Blinky in disguise. Being a former soldier who had seen battle he knew what it was like to lose a comrade in arms, find them, and lose them again. He had the scars on his lower extremities to prove it. He went back to the table holding a coffee - milk no sugar.

"Did I ever tell you how I happened to become a soldier patient?"

"I heard you were operated on in Germany before transferring here."

"That's right. Do you know how I got wounded?"

The nurse shook her head and took a sip of coffee.

"Can I trust you?"

She nodded the affirmative and he told the story of how his lower extremities came to be wounded.

Forty-five minutes later, the nurse was laughing out loud and wiping tears from her eyes. His job done, Russ took the empty glasses and coffee cup from the table and Holly went back to work.

Sally had delivered all the breakfast trays and was now in need of a little me time before lunch. He took the stairs down to the lower level and when he put the key into the PR door he found it was unlocked.

He opened the door slowly, saw the light was on and thinking the PR was back, called out Nathanial's name. Wally and Randle stopped in mid-drink.

"Who are you?" the surprised attendant questioned.

"We're relatives of Blue," said Wally.

"We've come to take him home," added Randle.

"Blue's in the morgue, I'll show you the way."

The two men looked at each other. They looked at Sally. Randle was the one to blurt out, "We can't go up there!"

Seeing the two men were in some sort of trouble, the attendant closed the door, went to the desk and took out a bottle.

"Tell me all about it."

***

"Mikey D."

"Lion Thornapple."

"They don't call me that much anymore," said the principal as he ran his hand over his bald head.

The two former students did the customary shaking of hands and reminiscing. The principal, who always enjoyed a good laugh, took it on the chin as he was kidded about his

166

age and the loss of his long golden locks from whence the nickname came.

Lion, who started out as a school teacher and never set foot outside of the country, sat in wonder as Mikey D. told stories of the travels he partook in that were promised by the Armed Forces in their 'See the World' recruiting campaign.

With years of their lives caught up on, the Sergeant got down to the reason he was visiting. Principal Thornapple took his seat behind the desk and listened with interest to the father of four's concerns about his third child.

"I've done just about everything I can possibly do to get those boys to pull their pants up. Their parent's even let me give them a month's detention and that didn't work," confessed the beleaguered leader of the young.

The Sergeant had first-hand knowledge of being a leader and how hard it was to get those under your command to conform to a way of life that was foreign in nature. But he also knew Jeremy had not been a droopy-drawed boy since he was a three-year old refusing to give up wearing diapers.

As he was speaking his mind, the thought of Rosie's battle to get Jeremy to surrender his diapers flashed through the Sergeant's remembrance. Not wanting to give his old friend heart failure, he held in the urge to shout eureka. The father of four had a plan and he knew it would work. All he had to do was get the principal on board.

"What's the cafeteria serving for lunch, Lion?"

"Mac and cheese, hot dogs."

"My favorite, your treat?"

"It'll be my pleasure," answered Lion.

Chowing down on his middle school lunch, the Sergeant was enjoying his trip back in time, while at the medical facility, Betty Lu was back in her office wondering why there were no messages from her fiancé Randle. She called Julie to make sure her phone was working and to rub it in about the doctor kissing her hand.

"Where have you been?" questioned the operator.

"I was with Dr. Sorenson. Alone. In his office. He kissed me."

As soon as the words came out, Betty Lu thought better about leading the switchboard operator on. The news that the doctor had kissed her could get back to Randle, and being he was the first man she had ever hooked in a marriage sort of way, she was not going to take a chance on losing him.

"Actually he kissed my hand."

"I don't care if he kissed your butt," replied Julie. "Wally and Randle were here this morning and they ran away from me."

That was all Betty Lu needed to hear, she dropped the phone and ran to the switchboard office to get the rest of the details in person.

"I was asking Sally in the nicest way for news on what's been going on with Mr. Flack when Wally and Randle walked by the coffee shop. I placed my cup of coffee down gently and called Wally's name. They took off like they were shot out of a cannon. I left the coffee shop and looked this way and that, but they were gone."

Somehow Julie made her explanation of chasing the two men through the facility less than it really was. That wasn't important to Betty Lu. The fact her fiancé didn't ask about her when he saw Julie was the problem. In her mind, and on TV, a fiancé always asked about the well-being of the woman he was engaged to.

On one of Betty Lu's favorite soap operas a nurse actually woke a patient prematurely after surgery to find out if her fiancé was fooling around on her. Of course the patient died from the shock, but the nurse had the truth and that's what really mattered.

"Is Blue still in the morgue?" asked Betty Lu.

"I checked. He's still there," answered Julie.

The patient coordinator breathed a sigh of relief. Down on the lower level Randle was having a hard time breathing at all. Blue's cousin was choking on a piece of hardtack that got caught in his throat.

"I told you small bites of that stuff and if you can't swallow, the rule is to spit it out," said his uncle as he slapped the recently engaged married man on the back.

The piece eventually flew out of Randle's mouth. Able to breathe again, he downed a swig and took another bite. Sally was enjoying the antics of Blue's relatives and at the same time trying to think of a way to help them. It wasn't until Wally told the story of getting Blinky to the fourth floor in the requisitioned ambulance that the attendant came up with a solution to their problem.

Tossing the empty bottles into the trash, Sally sat the two men down, told them to focus and explained his plan.

***

After their shared breakfast, Blinky escorted Mr. Flack to the common room. In order to assure the administrator that there were no lobstermen waiting to shanghai them in the hallway, the former soldier went first, making sure the coast was clear. Keeping his back to the wall as much as he could, Mr. Flack sidestepped and when it came time to cross the hall, he got down on his back and slid.

Blinky, having no experience with the administrator as he was not a customer of the Rustic Lodge, got a kick out of the man and vowed that when Operation AWOL Soldier was over he was going to invite Mr. Flack for a drink.

The sergeant impersonator aka secret serviceman checked the common room for clues the lobstermen had been there. When he asked what clues he was looking for exactly, the administrator replied, "Anything of a shrimp nature." Not seeing anything in the way of seafood, the former soldier gave the all clear and Mr. Flack slid in.

As the other soldier patients were sitting around doing nothing, Blinky took it upon himself to make a list of things they could do that day. He started with his favorite – a group sing along.

The former soldier was leading the soldier patients in a rendition of "Polly Wolly Doodle" when Nurse Shipley walked into the ward. Her disposition lightened by Russ' history of being wounded, she was happy to hear the men having such a good time and decided to look in on them before going to the nurse's station.

She took a seat and was quite surprised to see it was Michael A. Delaquot, leading the men. The nurse was mesmerized by the merriment of a patient who must be in pain, what with all the bandages wrapped around his face and head. During the song's "fair thee wells" the baritone went up to a nearby patient and held the hairbrush that was doubling for a microphone to the soldier's mouth. That's when she saw soldier patient Bed. No. 42 blink.

Nurse Shipley was a keen observer. She knew that blink. That blink had served her many a drink. That blink every once in a while winked at her when drunk.

"Oh my gosh," said the nurse as Blinky walked across the room to mike another patient. "Damn that Russ."

She rushed out of the room and before anyone could question her, she was out of the ward and out the sliding doors on her way back to the Rustic Lodge to have a talk with its fearless leader.

The trials and tribulations in Tuscaloosa and the medical facility were ongoing and so it was for the male nurse. Overtired from all the rest he had been getting lately; he was preparing for work and wondering how things were going on the fourth floor. Out of curiosity, and not wanting to drive all the way to work and have to drive back again, he decided he could save time and gas by calling in for an update.

The only problem – who to call?

The answer to that was Sally. But the male nurse didn't have a cell phone number or a phone extension for the attendant and if he called the medical facility Sally would be paged over the loudspeaker by the operator. While waiting for him to pick up, Julie being the snoop she was would question who was calling and why. That was too dangerous.

He could call the nurse's station on the fourth floor and take his chances with whoever picked up the phone. The thought of Nurse Shipley answering nipped that idea in the bud.

While shaving his beard, Russ, the fearless leader of former soldiers came to mind. Here was a third party with insider's knowledge with no repercussions attached. The male nurse dialed the lodge's number several times with no answer.

Like the medical facility, the lodge was a twenty-four seven operation. Thinking they must be dealing with a lingering lunch crowd, he dressed for his shift. Putting aside the time lost and gas wasted, he'd visit Russ, get the latest news and make a solid decision whether to attempt going to work that night.

As the male nurse got into his car, Sally was helping Randle and Wally change into hospital gear.

Blue's relatives came up with several arguments why they shouldn't attempt the attendant's plan. Running into Randle's fiancé and her operator friend was at the top of their list. As they couldn't think straight from all the drink they had drunk, the two men finally let worries about meeting up with Betty Lu and Julie go by the wayside. When the trio came into agreement, Sally left them while he went to the facility's laundry room and commandeered a couple of outfits used by doctors during surgery.

They say it's the man who makes the clothes, but Blue's relatives really got a kick out of the transformation the surgical scrubs made in their appearance. Both decided if there were another life after this one, they would both step out of their mundane boxes and make a big leap into the world of doctoring.

Randle was so impressed with the change in his demeanor he wanted his wife to share in the experience. Climbing the stairs to the main level, they made Sally swear they could keep the outfits.

The attendant was the first to come out of the stairway. Seeing the coast was clear, he had the two men follow him to the kitchen. It was the first time the staff had doctors visiting. As the three men made their way to the exit, they were generously handed all kinds of foods to take with them.

When they came out the kitchen door that was adjacent to the trash compactors, Blue's relatives had enough in their hands to tide them over during the trip home

***

The Sergeant took a box of toothpicks off the shelf and helped himself to one before putting the box back. With a quick swipe he was able to pick the chunk of hot dog free from the space between his front and back molars where it had lodged. He then caught up with Rosie as she pushed a cart with Rory sleeping in the bucket seat. Shopping for supplies in a store we will leave unnamed, the mother of four was trying to get the details of what the father of four planned to do to break the children of their bad habits.

Eating from a bag of chips they hadn't paid for yet, she playfully slapped her husband when he said she shouldn't worry her pea-brain about it. After years of raising her children alone, Rosie was glad to have Michael taking charge of things until he stopped to pick up a box of bullets.

"Are those really necessary?" questioned his wife.

"The only way to make real changes in the minds of children is to instill fear in them," stated her husband. "You'll thank me for this later."

He saw the look on his wife's face. Rosie was about to embarrass them both by fighting with him in the store with other shoppers and employees looking on. He beat her to it. Right there in the middle of the cereal and juice aisle, he grabbed his wife and kissed her passionately.

The women shoppers who stopped to watch thought they were a romantic couple and wondered why their husbands weren't more like that. Employees debated getting a hose from the lawn and garden department. A snide teenager shopping for his fix of sugary breakfast cereal offered a few words of advice when he quipped for them to get a room.

The Sergeant eventually let his wife go, but only when in mid-kiss Rory let out a child size snore.

"On with the plan," stated the Sergeant.

"Can't you wait till we get home?"

"No, he answered. "WAKE UP YOUNGSTER!"

The loud shout into his left ear made Rory cry. It made not a bit of difference to the Sergeant. Every day of his military career he saw men on the verge of tears when he shouted in their ears about their bad posture and jutting chins.

Rosie agreed that the time had come for her youngest to see the light of day every day. Nevertheless, she walked away and let her husband deal with the crying child.

Thick skinned from years of experience yelling terms like "sissy boy" and "mamma's boy" to grown men as they cried during training, the Sergeant cheerfully steered the cart, picked up household items and listened to the cries of his son as he yelled at the boy to stay awake.

***

On the psyche ward, Penny Carlough handed a tissue box to the crying former soldier who was impersonating the

Sergeant. The sing-along had come to a finish and now it was time to dig deep into the minds of the soldier patients.

The men were sitting in a circle with the social worker and she opened by asking for a volunteer to start them off. Blinky raised his hand and hooted for Penny's attention. As all the other soldiers had turned this way and that to avoid being called upon, she gave the enthusiastic patient the floor.

Once he started, Blinky found he enjoyed the challenge of taking on the persona of Michael A. Delaquot. Acting before a live audience gave him the incentive to make it an Oscar winning performance.

He did his best to do justice to the script that was written by the former soldiers at the lodge. Going for an added touch of realism he shed a few tears that quickly became a flood as he spoke about his girlfriend's recent engagement, taking a beating about the head by her soon-to-be husband, his inability to tell his wife about his infidelities and the awfulness of having his head encased in bandages and not being able to scratch a scalp itch.

After telling his woes, Blinky was hugged by Mr. Flack who didn't like to see his secret serviceman crying. The administrator told Penny the tears of his protector came so easily because he was tired from fighting lobstermen all night. Seeing that it was almost time for lunch, Penny told Mr. Flack they would discuss his lobster and shrimp problems at their three o-clock session.

When Blinky had dried his last tear, it was Penny's turn to give some sound non-secular professional counseling. Being a church going gal, she reminded him of his duty to God and country and what the good book stated clearly in several chapters about coveting and adultery.

She was about to warn Blinky that he was on the road to hell and damnation when a replacement for Sally entered the common room with a cart of lunch trays.

As his replacement was serving lunch to the soldiers on the fourth floor, Sally was helping out at the lodge. He had brought Wally and Randle, dressed in surgical scrubs, to the lodge in order to see if they could borrow the ambulance to take Blue out of the medical facility in style. Being Russ had a larger than usual lunch crowd show up that afternoon and he was down one man, the attendant, knowing the sacrifice Blinky was making on behalf of the AWOL soldier, donated his services.

As they waited for Sally, due to the overcrowded tables, Wally and Randle were sitting in the back booth, having drinks and sharing the food they had received from the kitchen staff with Nathanial who had woken up when they sat down.

The two relatives of Blue, who were feeling no pain, took to identifying with their surgical outfits. They regaled the PR with made up stories about cutting patients open while they were still awake. Eventually, the gory details of blood and guts spilling off the operating room table sent Nathanial to the men's room to upchuck the contents of his stomach that was filled with a bad combination of house specials and medical facility food.

Nurse Shipley was sitting at a nearby table with Dr. Sorenson. Earlier, Louie had stepped aside and allowed the angry nurse to slam through the door as she rushed to give Russ her views about his replacing the missing soldier patient with Blinky.

Dr. Sorenson had seen the alarmed look on Russ' face when Holly came through the door. He turned on his barstool. Seeing the passion in his love's eyes, he quickly jumped off the seat, grabbed the nurse in his arms and kissed her.

When he let her up for air, the nurse's temper was somewhat quelled.

"I need to speak to --"

She didn't have time to finish. Bryan was kissing her again. Seeing his chance to escape the coming wrath, Russ unfroze from the spot where he stood. Before he ran into the kitchen to hide, he ordered Matt to man the bar and Tom to key in E19 on the jukebox.

***

The afternoon hours were spent in their various forms at the lodge, medical facility and home of the Delaquot family.

At the lodge, Russ made sure Holly's dance card was kept full; he ordered Matt, Tom and Louie all in succession to dance with her. Winded and enjoying the attention of the various men, she forgot all about what led her to be there in the first place. When she finally sat down, Bryan ordered more house specials and some lunch.

On the fourth floor of the medical facility, the soldier patients were enjoying the impersonating Sergeant as he led them in charades. Mr. Flack was having a good time and no one seemed to mind that the only guesses he was throwing out were lobster and shrimp based.

Not wanting to miss Betty Lu's fiancé, she and Julie were eating lunch and discussing wedding gown necklines as they sat at a table in the morgue.

They were kind enough to bring lunch for Arnold. Over tuna sandwiches, he was able to provide designer expertise from having served as wedding coordinator for all six of his sisters when they walked down the aisle.

Arnold was a wealth of knowledge on differences between v-necks, scoop necks and strapless gowns and how they could best set off a bride's décolletage in the wedding pictures.

The two women had no idea what the word décolletage meant.

"Boobs," stated Arnold.

The Sergeant would have liked to partake of this aspect of his wife's anatomy, but he was caught up in keeping his youngest awake.

Rosie was also inclined to think her husband's little time at home would be better spent in the bedroom and not in front of the TV playing video games with a child who was trying to nod off, but the soldier was on a mission to set things right with his family in as short a time as possible, much like when training the fresh faces who stepped off the bus into his basic training capable hands. Unable to stand the call of "wake-up sissy boy" and the cries of her youngest, Rosie went to have her hair and nails done.

Having stayed up all night and seeing daylight for several hours, Rory was a mere shadow of his former day-sleeping self. His spirited crying finally stopped and he settled down as he played go fish with his dad.

The Sergeant, who had broken the spirit of many a young soldier colt, judged rightly that he was over the hill with this offspring and got on with tackling the next seed of his loins, which was Michael Jr. After the card playing ended, he enlisted his youngest and together they went into the bathroom to play a new version of basketball.

Using the garbage pail as a basket, the Sergeant and his son tossed all of Michael's smelly girly products.

"No son of mine is going to smell like he just got back from France," said the Sergeant.

Even though he didn't have a clue what France was, Rory enjoyed bonding time with his dad and was proud that he had made three baskets.

When the tossing was done and the shelves and counter top were cleaned, the Sergeant replaced the thirty-six fragrant products with one, a deodorant, which we will leave unnamed, that was used by generations of the Delaquot men and the only one that was acceptable, and rightly so, by the higher powers that be in the army.

While Rory was spending some time coloring with his crayons, the Sergeant, in order to reinforce the law of the land as he saw it, drafted a notice, which he taped to the bathroom mirror for all to see.

Only home for a short time, he wrote the message to be inspiring, strong sounding, with leadership qualities. In order not to draw attention to his oldest son by name and just in case Jeremy was also a partaker in scented materials, he went over and above the call of fatherly duty in his quest to cover all the known social behaviors, taboos and anything else he could think of. It read as follows:

TO: Men in Barracks

It has come to my attention that some of you dandies have been using materials with what could only be described as "girlie smells."
At no time should men smell like women and at all times women should smell like - like women. In other words the only people who should smell like women are women.
Got that?
Men, you have two choices.
Voluntarily give up the perfume-laden products that cause you to smell like a whorehouse in July.
Or
Continue to use the olfactory offending materials and find yourself at the mercy of the staff sergeant.

Signed,

Your Superior Officer.

P.S. As the staff sergeant has been known on occasion to be totally out of her mind – I would go with Choice One.

That done, the Sergeant moved onto fruit of his loin's number three and his pants around the butt habit. Venturing forth into the room Jeremy shared with Michael Jr., he opened all the drawers in the dresser to see which clothes belonged to whom.

Going by size, he was able to locate Jeremy's underwear drawer. Looking inside, he immediately saw the boy's problem and made it a point to remember to take his wife to task for spoiling their offspring with an excessive amount of the undergarments in question. To put some blame where it belonged, as he was not a working lad, Rosie had apparently aided and abetted their son by buying designer underwear instead of the white briefs worn by American boys for generations - a brand which we will leave unnamed.

He took out all the underwear he could find, and then scouted the hamper and under the bed for any strays and put them in a garbage bag.

Going to his own room, the Sergeant took a belt he no longer needed and placed it in his son's empty underwear drawer. Looking at his watch, he realized it was time to pick Jeremy up from school. The busy father grabbed his youngest and the bag of underwear, loaded them both in the car, and went on his way.

***

The male nurse parked his car in the medical facility parking lot and walked over to the Rustic Lodge. As it was four in the afternoon of a workday, he expected to find the place void of facility staff members.

He was wrong.

Giving a good day greeting to Louie, the former soldier opened the door and the male nurse confidently strode through the entrance. When he saw Nurse Shipley dancing with Dr. Sorenson his feet became lead.

Unable to walk backwards as other patrons were coming in, he averted his face and went to the bar. Russ had his house special ready. Taking the drink and keeping his head turned away from the dance floor, the male nurse walked the perimeter of the lodge till he got to the booth in the back where he saw Nathanial.

With agitation growing, he kept on walking. Head pointed to the ceiling while draining the glass, he bumped into Sally who was carrying a dirty tray of dishes. The tray fell to the ground, and as the song on the jukebox had stopped only a few brief moments before, the sound of the dishes crashing to the floor caught the ear of everyone in the lodge.

All eyes fell on the disturbed man. He looked at everyone looking at him, and when his circling gaze fell eye to eye with Nurse Shipley, his stomach rolled. Clamping a hand over his mouth, the male nurse ran for the door, which was open as Louie heard the crash of dishes and looked in to see what was going on. Reaching the fresh air, the male nurse bent from the waist and threw up his breakfast.

Nurse Shipley extricated herself from the doctor's embrace. Walking out the door, she was prepared to give hell that day to someone, and forgetting the last two hours, her comportment changed from one of happiness to revenge.

About to give the male nurse a piece of her mind, she stopped in her tracks when she saw him. The part of her that was all nurse kicked in. When he was done emptying the contents of his stomach, she walked him to his car, telling him not to come to work until he felt better and that she'd tell those on night duty he wasn't coming in.

Appreciative of her help, and wanting to get the hell out of there, the male nurse took off in his car as though it had a jet propulsion engine underneath the hood. He got back on the Witchitauki Highway and off the Witchitauki Highway, drove up his driveway, opened the door to his home, didn't bother to put on his pajamas and jumped back into bed.

***

With no sign of Blue's relatives, Betty Lu and Julie thought it was best to wrap up their three-hour lunch. Wanting to be of help to the patient coordinator during the wedding process, Arnold accompanied Betty Lu to the gift shop to see if they had the latest bridal magazines.

Julie called Bridget, who was in volunteer overtime, to see if she would mind taking over the watch for Blue's relatives. The elderly volunteer who had never been in a morgue before was open to the opportunity and agreed to make the switch.

The parties went their ways and Bridget enjoyed having the chance to explore the workings of the morgue without interference. After spending some time looking around and opening and closing drawers, she sat down and promptly fell asleep.

While the Sergeant was driving to the middle school to pick up Jeremy, Rory fell asleep. He had a bit of business to take care of so he didn't disturb the tyke. When he pulled up, Lion and Mad Anthony were waiting. The father of four handed over the bag and the plan was gone over again by the three men. The dismissal bell rang and in order not to raise suspicion the trio went their separate ways.

"How'd your day go, young fellow," the Sergeant asked a little too heartily.

Jeremy didn't answer. Looking his dad square in the face, his child's instinct read the paternal half was up to something. Without a word, they got in the car and his dad shouted for Rory to wake up. The overtired child started bawling and the Sergeant went into an explanation of the tactics he was using on the littlest night owl.

Jeremy, being a teenager and all, was relieved that his instincts were basically right and was only wrong about him being the something his father was up to about. He lost all concentration as teenagers do when adults are talking to them

181

and screaming at the same time. Off the parental hook, he relaxed and turned up the radio to block his dad and brother out.

The Sergeant, using his peripheral vision as he watched the road, noted the relaxed demeanor of his middle son and with a "this kid is in for a surprise" smile on his face he drove them all home.

***

With the lunch crowd for the most part gone, Russ, Tom, Matt and Louie turned their attentions back to Operation AWOL Soldier. They looked at Nurse Shipley who was still enjoying the attentions of Dr. Sorenson. After walking the male nurse to his car she had come back to her table in order to enjoy Bryan's undivided attention and another house special.

The former soldiers standing together at the bar debated the issue of telling her all about Blinky and how he got the long straw. Knowing it was better to confess their role in covering for the AWOL sergeant while the doctor was by the nurse's side, the four men held another rock, paper, scissors match to see who would be the lucky one to go over and speak to Holly.

Russ was surprised when he lost. Remembering how Holly had clocked Sally, he chickened out and waited till the nurse went to the bathroom. As a precaution, Russ gave an order to Tom - when Holly came out of the bathroom he was to distract her. Russ then rushed over to the table to talk to the doctor.

"So you men took it upon yourselves to cover for the AWOL soldier?" questioned Dr. Sorenson, who pretended not to know anything.

"Guilty as charged," stated Russ.

"Damn good of you. What would this country be without upstanding men such as yourselves. Did the soldier give you a timeline?"

"Nineteenth, give or take a day or two," replied Russ.

"I think I can be of help," said the good doctor.

The former soldier shook hands with the newest member of the team. Meanwhile, in the booth, in the back, in the corner, in the dark, another covert operation was in need of a jumpstart.

Nathanial was snoozing again. Randle and Wally were watching the PR with drunken admiration at his ability to sleep like a pretzel, all twisted like. Sally was finished covering Blinky's shift. Seeing the two men were still sitting there, he took it upon himself to remind them that they had to hit the road.

"It's time to go," declared Sally.

"Go where?" questioned Randle.

"Home...with Blue."

Wally and his nephew looked up at Sally.

"Blue's in the morgue, you're taking him home today."

Their minds couldn't get past the house specials they had drunk.

"Give me the keys to your truck."

Randle took the keys out of his pocket and handed them to the attendant. On his way out the door, Sally stopped at the bar and told Tom that the two men were to be cut off from all drinks of an alcohol based nature. Hoping they'd be sober by the time he got back, Sally left the bar, got in Wally's truck and drove it over to the trash compacter entrance that was nearest to the kitchen.

***

The Sergeant pulled up to his house. Rosie heard her youngest howling the minute the family car turned onto their block. She stood on the lawn waiting. When he saw his mother, Rory unbuckled his seat, shot out of the car and ran into her waiting arms.

"This is cruel."

"You'll thank me when he has to get up and catch the bus next fall. Are the others home yet?"

Rosie nodded. The Sergeant went into the house and as she hugged her youngest Rosie pondered over the whirlwind that was her husband. Like all army wives, whenever her husband came home on leave she had to stand by and watch as he tried to take the crooked angles of the family and make them straight.

She was the one to instigate this visit home and had no choice but to go along with things until he felt the job was done. Rosie was about to put Rory back on his own two feet when her husband came out the front door holding the rifle he won from Clyde and the box of bullets.

"I take it we're going to the rifle range?"

"You got it," answered her husband.

As he was putting the gun into the car trunk, Michael Jr. came tearing out the front door.

"Mom!"

"I'm right here."

"Do you know what your husband did?"

Rosie didn't have a clue.

"He threw away all my stuff and left me with this."

Michael Jr. held up the lone stick of deodorant that was the same brand used by generations of Delaquot men.

"Look at this."

The angry youth handed his mother a crayoned sheet of paper, she handed him Rory.

"Did you draw this?" she asked her youngest.

"That was me," answered her husband.

"Years in the service are paying off."

"Not that side!" screamed Michael, Jr.

184

Rosie's oldest son tore the page out of her hand and flipped it. She did her best to hide a grin while reading the words dandy and girlie smells. When she got to the bit about whorehouses in July she burst out laughing.

"It's not fair!" her son shouted.

"It's life. Get in the car," said the Sergeant.

"No!"

Michael Jr. stood on their front lawn in defiance. The neighbors had turned off their TV sets when they first heard Rory howling and were now sitting on their front porches. Most were betting on the man of the house to get his way.

"I said get in the car. Caroline, where are you?" her father bellowed.

Rosie had a question about the note, "Who's the staff sergeant you're referring to?"

"You."

"Me?"

"When I'm not here, you're in charge. And by the looks of things you haven't been doing such a good job."

"You say another word and tonight this staff sergeant will be taking a knife to your --"

"Caroline, get a move on!" shouted the military man. "Everyone, in the car."

"He's crazy," said Michael Jr. as he handed Rory back to his mother.

"What?" shouted his father.

The Sergeant got up close and personal to his oldest boy. They stood nose to nose. The neighbors held their breath.

This pause in the showdown between father and son might have been mistaken for wanting to make a good show of it or to look superior, but Michael Sr. was actively searching for something in the soldier part of his brain that the father part of his brain could say without looking stupid. When the two parts of his brain came together, the Sergeant felt years younger.

"What did you say?"

185

Like all kids who didn't know when to quit, Michael Jr. repeated himself.

"You're crazy!" he shouted.

"Of course I'm crazy I just got back from fighting a war!" the Sergeant shouted back.

"Atta boy!" shouted one of the neighbors.

For the first time, Michael Jr. realized he was on public display. He took a step back - stood tall - and saluted his dad.

"Good to have you back - Sir!"

The proud father saluted his oldest son. The two men hugged. Then the alpha dog put his pup in a headlock.

"Men," Rosie said to no one in particular. "I'm hungry. Will you two sentimental slobs get in the car. We're stopping for dinner first. Caroline!"

Michael Jr. felt better than he had for a long time. He missed his dad and as a watcher of the nightly news, which kept him abreast of what was going on in the world, was frankly glad to have him home in one piece. Also, he had long ago been ready to give up wearing smelly laden products, but didn't know how. Smelling like a perfumery had only started because of Jeanine Applegate, a former girlfriend who liked to sniff around a lot. He dove into the car. Hungry as all teenage boys his age usually are, he was counting on the older generation to take the younger generation to a favorite all-you-can-eat family style buffet.

Jeremy, who was told to stay in the car when his dad pulled up, climbed over the front seat just as his brother was diving in.

Rosie's dander was up, she was cursing under her breath about men, their egos, etc., etc., as she got in the front seat and buckled Rory in next to her. The overtired youngster let out a loud scream at the same time the Sergeant screamed again for his oldest.

Caroline came out of the house like she had all the time in the world. Getting in the back seat she had to push Michael

Jr. out of the way as he was hogging all the room while holding Jeremy in a headlock.

The Sergeant closed the car trunk with a satisfied slam. He turned to his neighbors, and when they started clapping, he took a bow.

1800 hrs
MAY 17th

At the medical facility, the day shift was turning their responsibilities over to the night shift.

Betty Lu and Arnold had already left for the day. After buying several bridal magazines at the gift shop they became so excited they forsook their jobs and drove to Hadleyville Bridal Boutique and Flowery. The patient coordinator wanted to show the morgue employee a wedding gown she had been making bi-monthly payments on for the last eight years.

On the fourth floor, Blinky was enjoying a dinner movie in the common room with Mr. Flack and his fellow patients. They were watching an old black and white western and every time the cowboys gave chase, the former soldier would lead the soldier patients around the room pretending to ride horses.

Dr. Sorenson was escorting Nurse Shipley to the nurse's station so she could get her things when they heard whooping and hollering.

"I'd better see what's going on."

"You are off duty and I want to get home," said the doctor.

"You're going home? You're going to sleep in your own bed tonight?"

"No. I'm going to sleep in your bed tonight," he answered. "Now you can go in that room and get all upset or you can take me home and have your way with me. Which will it be?"

The nurse hesitated. The doctor gave her a mischievous smile.

"Whoopee!" she shouted, and went and got her things.

Expecting to hear something from her wayward relatives, Mrs. Morgan called the switchboard to see if they left with her son yet. Julie was able to report in the negative. Not wanting to take part in the operator's conversation about her relatives, Blue's mother promptly hung up.

On his quest to get the private, after parking the truck, Sally had gone through the kitchen and disregarded questions concerning his whereabouts and why he had missed lunch. He passed through to the hallway, commandeered an empty gurney and rolled it into the morgue.

At first he thought no one was there, but looking closer he saw Bridget asleep at the desk. He actually could have made all the noise he wanted due to the volunteer's dead to the world sleeping habit, but he quietly pushed the gurney across the room, put Blue on it and left.

As Sally was placing the private in his uncle's truck, in a Tuscaloosa country style buffet, which we'll leave unnamed, the Sergeant was loading up on his third plate. He was enjoying his family immensely and loved seeing his wife all discombobulated by his antics.

Rory was screaming, but seeing how it was a family restaurant and at nearly every table there was a young one screaming, no one paid any attention to it. Being the type of mother that gave in to her children's whining, the continued sound of her youngest crying was driving Rosie to distraction.

"Let him sleep for a few minutes, please."

"That doesn't work with my men and it won't work with our young one. He has to make it to ten."

"Ten tonight, I'll be out of my mind by then."

"I'm looking forward to that," said the Sergeant.

His wife got up and helped herself to a third helping of chocolate cake.

"Daddy…"

"Yes, Caroline."

"About my trip."

"I read the brochures. As a matter of fact, I traveled to quite a few of those places you'll be going to. Being I was on the lookout for the enemy, I didn't have the opportunity to really enjoy the landscape. What time's your flight tomorrow?"

"Nine in the morning. I have to be there two hours before."

"0600 hours. That's a roger."

Rosie came back to the table. "What's a roger?"

"Got to head back tomorrow, dropping Caroline at the airport on my way," he said between bites.

"We haven't discussed it."

To Caroline's surprise, the Sergeant took his wife to task. What was there to discuss? He questioned. Their daughter was of age. He added. She was independent. They could no longer interfere in her life. If she wanted to quit college to travel with an ex-history teacher, an older man he had never met, and the places they would be touring were the war torn countries of the last twenty years, that was entirely her prerogative.

"Did you get your shots?"

"Yes, Daddy."

"Got your passport?"

"Yes, Daddy."

"Got money?"

"Yes, Daddy."

"You are set to go."

When he was done with his fatherly speech and the question and answer period, Rosie, who was turning scarlet, went back for another helping of cake, this time topped with three scoops of ice cream.

Caroline hugged the man who was her dad. She told him how much she loved him and was so grateful to have one parent who completely got what she was about. The father and daughter went back to the buffet together. When the

Sergeant told his daughter she should eat up as it would be a long flight, she cried out in delight and gave him another hug.

Back at the table, Jeremy was quiet. He watched as his dad and Caroline filled their plates. He looked at his mother who was loading up on sweets. He watched Michael Jr. flirt with a waitress. He listened to Rory's crying. Knowing beyond a doubt that he was not perfect, Jeremy became suspicious of the man his sister was bouncing up and down for joy with. He decided that until his dad left the house at 0600, he had better be on his guard.

***

In the medical facility parking lot, Sally was on his guard. Making sure he wasn't followed, he drove back to the lodge, and left Blue in the bed of Wally's truck while he went inside. He walked straight to the booth in the back to find Wally and Randle had joined Nathanial in a drunken slumber.

"Time to go, guys."

The two men didn't budge. He tried to shake them awake. They still wouldn't budge. This was a problem, so he went up to the bar to think.

Meanwhile, at the switchboard, Julie surrendered her post to Donna, went out the sliding doors and walked over to the lodge to see if Wally was there. She saw the truck. Giving no thought to the gurney in the truck bed, she gave Louie a cheerful smile as he opened the door for her.

Giving the place the once over, she saw Wally in the back. Not wanting to disturb the sleeping man, she stepped up to the bar to get a drink.

"Hey Sally. Russ." Julie said in greeting.

"Hey," replied Sally after lifting his head off the bar.

"Hey," Russ replied while pouring a house special.

"Mrs. Morgan's going to have a fit," offhandedly mentioned the operator.

191

"Why?" Russ offhandedly inquired.

"Wally and Randle were supposed to bring Blue home today, funeral's tomorrow afternoon."

Russ poured the operator a second drink and she went to the jukebox to play an oldie but goodie so her loved one and his nephew would have sweet dreams. This left Sally to continue with his thinking. With all the troubles he had been having lately with the female sex and still having a headache after being clocked by Nurse Shipley in the a.m. hours, the attendant had not made plans for the evening.

After a few house specials and lots of thinking, he decided his life was in dire need of good karma. The only way to up a karma quotient was by doing a good deed. As Blue was already in the truck, Sally decided he would bring the boy home to his mother as per schedule.

Seeing Julie was playing darts for the kitchen's team, he tried one more time to wake Blue's relatives. Having no luck, he left the lodge, went back to the medical facility, said hello to Donna, and let himself into the patient coordinator's office.

Sally looked up Blue on the computer, got the dead soldier's mother's address, locked the office, said goodnight to Donna, went across the parking lot, got into Wally's truck and took off for the Witchitauki Highway.

***

The tires on the Delaquot family vehicle were carrying close to the laden weight allowed for. The family did the buffet proud and was now on their way to the rifle range.

Rory was still howling. Caroline was talking about her upcoming trip and how handsome her professor was. The Sergeant insisted on reminding their daughter that he was an ex-professor. Michael was on his cell phone talking to the waitress back at the restaurant. Rosie turned up the music to shut out her family members and catching glimpses of his dad's eyes in the back mirror, Jeremy quietly contemplated what he was up to.

When they got to the range, the Delaquots unloaded and the Sergeant took the rifle and bullets out of the trunk. The range was a regular family outing when their father was home; the kids put on the hearing protectors and took a seat.

He loaded the gun as Rosie watched with Rory howling in her arms. With the ear protectors on, the child's noise was quelled, but her temper was still running hot from the idea that her husband was not going to help her stop Caroline's trip.

After loading the gun the Sergeant turned to his wife.

"Let me have him."

Not knowing what he was up to Rosie handed over her youngest. He handed her the rifle. She looked at him.

Husbands and wives who have been married long enough always have a few facial expressions that are codes. Rosie looked down at the gun and looked back at her husband's face. Then she saw it. He did this little pull of his mouth, to the right, a real quick action that would be hardly noticeable to the untrained eye.

That's when she knew. The man had a plan.

She looked at the kids watching her with their undivided attention. When their father handed their mother the rifle, Caroline stopped talking about her ex-professor turned traveling companion, Michael Jr. closed the cell phone and Jeremy took his eyes off his dad. They had never seen her hold a rifle before.

Rosie stood taller than she had in quite a while. She turned around, took the few steps to the rail, aimed and fired.

The kids stood up. They came closer. The Sergeant pushed a button and the target flew up in front of them. They looked in astonishment - right where the heart would be was a bullet hole.

They backed away from their mother. She handed the rifle to her husband and took her youngest child, who had stopped crying, out of his hands. Rosie walked proudly to the car. The Sergeant unloaded the rifle, putting it and the box of bullets back in the trunk.

"Are you kids coming?" he shouted to his three oldest.

Caroline, Michael Jr. and Jeremy unfroze. They put the ear protectors back on their hooks and got in the car.

The ride home was a quiet one.

***

It was nearing bedtime on the fourth floor and all was quiet. After the western ended, Blinky went to the nurse's station, asked for a flashlight, went back to the common room, turned off all the lights and told ghost stories to the soldier patients.

The secret serviceman and his knowledge of all things eerie more than intrigued Mr. Flack. He and his fellow soldier patients all agreed they particularly liked the story of service men and woman who never rose higher than the rank of private coming back as ghosts and haunting their former rag-assed sergeants.

Of course, not to hurt his feelings, they were quick to exempt the sergeant as they felt he was a great guy and definitely would be an exception to the ghost haunting rule.

When the administrator raised his hand, his secret serviceman was quick to acknowledge him. Having never served his country, Mr. Flack wanted to know whom he could come back and haunt.

As soon as Russ was made privy to the histories of recently hired medical facility staff members, he would give this information to the former soldiers in his employ. Blinky knew all about the administrator's grim past.

When the former soldier assured Mr. Flack that it was indeed possible to one day come back as a ghost and haunt the president of the lobster and shrimp shipping company, it thrilled him to no end.

After the ghost stories were over, Blinky made a request of the night attendant. This man, along with the soldier patients, enjoyed the Sergeant's impersonator so much he agreed.

The night attendant went down to the facility kitchen, which was closed, and hustled up two barrels of ice cream and all the fixings for sundaes. Putting all the ingredients on a cart, he rolled it up to the fourth floor. The soldier patients came together as a group and told the sergeant, because his bandaged head could be mistaken for a scoop of vanilla, he should take on the role of the ice cream man.

Touched to the core, Blinky quickly wiped the tears from his blinking eyes and got to the business of piling the ice cream bowls high with scoops of chocolate and vanilla, topping them off with bananas, chocolate syrup, whip cream, nuts and cherries.

The night attendant finished his sundae; it was getting late, he had no choice but to insist that the soldier patients turn in for the night. Blinky took charge of assigning clean up tasks, he had lots of activities planned for the next day and didn't want to come into a messy room.

After all was made right again, being tired, the soldier patients trudged off quietly to bed. Blinky escorted Mr. Flack to Room 423, and when the administrator asked, his secret serviceman was kind enough to tuck him in.

The staff members of the psyche ward were amazed. There were no bad dreams that night. For the first time that they could remember all the soldier patients slept soundly.

At the Rustic Lodge, Julie was thrilled to be near Wally. Vowing to never let him out of her sight again, she took her drink, pulled up a chair and parked herself where the big guy could see her when he woke.

Sally parked Wally's truck in back of the funeral parlor. Blue's hometown was only four hours away, and being it was late, there was no traffic to speak of. Making good use of the time on the road, he spent it in self-contemplation about the positive karma he was racking up with each mile on the speedometer.

Not wanting to disturb Mrs. Morgan at such a late hour, Sally went to a local bar and inquired on the proceedings that were to be held in Blue's honor. Ascertaining the name of the funeral parlor, he had a hunch that in a small town such as this one it would not be overly secured. He went directly from the bar to the funeral parlor's back door to see what exactly he was dealing with. His hunch was right. Slipping a credit card into the space between lock and door frame, Sally gained entrance into the building.

He was quick to scout out a gurney using it to transfer Blue from his uncle's truck to the room that was waiting for him. Seeing Blue's dress uniform laid out on a chair, the attendant took it upon himself to change the private into it.

"Well guy, we've had some time of it, haven't we? Looks like your momma got some good money from the army; she picked you out a right nice place to stay. Try to think of it as a smaller than usual kind of apartment. Don't forget to put in a good word with the Big Guy for me."

The job done, Sally looked down at Blue and saluted the fallen soldier. Having never served his country, he didn't think anyone would mind much.

All at once, Sally found he was tired. Having spent the previous night listening to Rhonda Blisnick's travails for what seemed an eternity and with no empty bed to nap in while he was working, the attendant was in sore need of some zzz's.

"Think I'll keep you company for a while," he said to Blue.

He laid down on a row of chairs and with all the good karma he would need for some time to come, fell fast asleep.

When they returned home from the rifle range, the kids locked themselves in their respective rooms. Caroline packed, Michael Jr. fell asleep, and Jeremy stayed in his clothes as he sat up in bed wondering when his time was coming. The head of the family was leaving in eight hours, not wanting to be taken by surprise the middle student was prepared to stay up all night if he had to. It was about one in the morning before he finally fell asleep.

The Sergeant stuck to his pledge to keep Rory awake till ten. Using methods that worked on the soldiers in his unit, the youngest Delaquot was, without a doubt, put to the test. The boy's screaming didn't bother his mother at all. She had left the rifle range without returning the ear protectors.

Promptly at ten, Rosie opened Rory's bedroom door and the Sergeant laid his screaming child down. Before they could shut the door the tyke was out like a light.

"Tomorrow you wake him up no later than 0700."

"Yes Sir."

"If you don't you'll undo what I did."

"Yes Sir."

"Then you'll have to start all over without me."

"Yes Sir."

"Does your yes mean yes?" he asked with a roguish smile.

"Yes Sir."

Standing in the hallway, the Sergeant picked up his wife and held her in his arms.

"What about Jeremy?" Rosie asked.

"You'll find out soon enough."

"And Caroline?"

"Don't worry about her."

The Sergeant carried his wife to the doorway of their bedroom.

"When we cross this threshold I don't want to hear another word about the kids."

"Yes Sir."

"Not a thing."

"No Sir. Not a thing."

She wrapped her arms tight around his neck. He entered their bedroom and kicked the door closed.

***

Randle woke up with a fright. It took a minute to get his bearings. The first thing he caught sight of was Julie draped over Wally. Turning sideways to see that he had been sleeping on Nathanial, a thought flashed through his inebriated mind that they were in a hotel doing some kinky stuff.

The startled man who was married and engaged couldn't deal with the idea of having a third intimate relationship, especially with someone of his own sex. He tried his best to jump up, but his body was unable to as it was stiff from sleeping in a cramped diagonal position. The motion he made was more like a spasm. Unable to straighten, his knees buckled and he landed on the floor. From that angle, Randle had a blurry vision of a moose head. He let out a relieved breath. They were still at the lodge.

Realizing his masculinity hadn't been compromised after all, Randle crawled to the bathroom and when he came out he crawled to the bar and ordered a house special.

"You're cut off," said Tom as he looked down.

"Says who?"

"Sally."

Not wanting to argue with someone who was bigger than he was, Randle let this sift through his mind. Why would Sally cut him off? He looked down at his surgeon's scrubs and remembered.

"I've got to get my uncle out from underneath Julie. Can you help me?"

The former soldier helped Randle off the floor. The lodge employees had plenty of practice removing smothering women from atop the bodies of men, especially husbands who had to get home to their wives. Tom called Matt over and the three went to the booth in the back and reviewed the technical difficulties.

"When I lift Julie, you slide Wally out," said Matt.

The former soldiers lifted and slid. Randle assisted by catching his uncle's head before it hit the ground. Julie was gently placed back in the booth. Nathanial continued to sleep soundly.

Being in a hurry, Randle held his uncle's nose. Wally thrashed around like a shark with a grapple hook in its mouth. Satisfied that the man was awake, his nephew let go.

While Wally caught his breath, Randle expressed the urgency of getting on with the business they came for. They begged for a drink before setting out. Sally was nowhere to be found so Tom relented.

Russ would want to make his goodbyes known to Blue's relatives; Matt went to the back room and woke him up. The former soldiers bid them a safe journey. Wally and Randle took their leave only to come back a few minutes later after they made a thorough search of the lodge and medical facility parking lots.

"Our truck is gone!" they declared.

Another dilemma to be solved called for some drink and Russ went behind the bar to make a pitcher of house specials.

"We don't have time," said Wally.

He was more in fear of facing Julie than he was in facing his sister. The two men told how they messed up Sally's plan to get Blue home in time for the funeral, which also explained why they were dressed in surgeon's scrubs.

The former soldiers saw need of another covert operation, and due to the temperaments of both the sleeping operator and Mrs. Morgan, they quickly agreed on a name. Operation Code Blue was put into motion.

With the clock running, Russ' men chose to forgo the mandatory choosing procedures of drawing straws, picking names out of a hat, and rock, paper, scissors.

199

Russ volunteered the commandeered ambulance as their vehicle, with only the promise that after the funeral Randle and Wally would take it back to Forkship Township. To seal the deal, they spit on their hands and shook hands with Russ.

Tom and Matt volunteered their services. One would drive the ambulance over to the facility while the other would go in with the two men and help get Blue out.

Louie volunteered his services. He would make himself a direct target if Julie woke up before Tom and Matt got back.

With synchronized watches that weren't really necessary to the operation, but done for the fun of it, the men got started.

The first problem arose when they found the back doors to the facility were on an automatically timed lock system and couldn't be opened from the outside till morning.

They couldn't drive the ambulance to the emergency room as there were two guards and they would more than likely ask questions. Tom and Matt wanted to go back to the lodge and confer with Russ, but Wally would have none of it. They would go through the front door, he declared. Warned that Donna was on duty, the big man, who women couldn't seem to resist, assured the fellows this was not going to be a problem.

Donna was sleeping as usual, so her interfering in this part of the covert operation was a moot point. Wally, Randle and Tom walked right through the lobby, past the elevators, down the hallway and past the kitchen, grabbing a gurney along the way.

The operation hit another snag when the team members reached the morgue. They saw a woman sitting at the desk. Actually she was slumped over. In a rush, and as this was the morgue, the three men assumed she was dead and that whoever worked the day shift did not do their job properly.

Keeping to the plan, they looked for Blue. They looked and they looked.

"Alicia's gonna kill me," cried Wally.

"Who's Alicia?" asked Tom.

"Blue's mother. She's a hellcat. If I go home without him, she'll cut me one, big time."

Randle, who had seen his aunt cut his own mother one big time, nodded his head in agreement. The men of Operation Code Blue were stuck. There was no going backward and yet how were they to go forward.

Tom took over the covert operation reigns.

"You need a body – right?"

Blue's relatives nodded in the affirmative.

"It's only a few hours till the funeral – right?"

Wally and Randle nodded. Tom paced as a bright idea came through his brain to his lips.

"If you leave now, can you get to the funeral parlor, break in, put a body in the casket, seal it tight, and greet everyone at the door with an explanation of why it's closed?"

Wally and Randle looked at each other.

"Can you do it or not?"

Randle being young and impetuous piped up, "We can do it!"

Wally slapped his nephew on the head.

"Remember what happened when Uncle Silas died and gone missing? Aunt Shirley's still got the limp from jumping down into open graves and prying their boxes open."

"I forgot all about that." Randle remembered as he rubbed his sore head.

They eventually came to an agreement that Blue had to be somewhere. Tom promised that the former soldiers would search the facility and its perimeter. When they found him the Operation Code Blue team would call right away for further deliberation on what to do next.

This wasn't good enough for Wally. He wouldn't agree until the former soldier swore that when the operatives that were left behind did find Blue, they would come and help dig up whoever was buried in his place. Tom agreed and the three men looked around for a replacement.

There was none. Well, actually the only replacement they could see in the room was the lady at the desk. Thinking she was probably too old to have family and that they would only need her help for a short amount of time, they placed Bridget on the gurney and covered her with a blanket.

They pushed her past the kitchen, down the hallway, past the elevators, through the lobby, past the switchboard office and through the sliding doors.

"What took you so long?" Matt questioned.

"Hit a bit of a snag," answered Tom.

They loaded the elderly volunteer into the back of the ambulance. Wally took the driver's seat, Randle not wanting to be alone with the old dead lady, rode up front with his uncle.

The two Morgan's said their goodbyes and thanks and drove out of the facility parking lot.

***

As Wally and Randle got on the Witchitauki Highway, the Sergeant got off his wife. Along with seeing to the various needs of his children, before returning to the duty of his country he felt it was his duty to leave Rosie a satisfied woman.

He tried several times to wake her during the night. She pushed him away each time saying she'd gladly settle for some good old fashion snuggling. He claimed he only wanted to leave her with a good memory of the man she married.

Rosie was having none of that. She sat up in bed and asked her husband what the heck was going on. He confessed he heard the twenty to thirty year old soldiers under his care talking. They said on the last night of leave they'd make love all night long. It would prevent some lothario preying on their lonely women while they were gone.

"Garlic hanging around their women's neck would do the same thing."

After she made this remark, Rosie looked at her husband who had seen the better side of twenty more than nineteen years ago. Seeing he was serious, she laughed and got out of bed. It never failed; she always got the biggest kick out of the way of thinking her husband took to on these occasions.

"For a secure man, you are the most insecure man I've ever known."

With a hangdog look he asked, "Any funnel cake left?"

"I saved you one."

The two left the bedroom, he to check on the kids, she to get the cake.

1800 hrs
MAY 18th

It was daybreak and Betty Lu's apartment smelled of cake and roses. The afternoon before, after showing off her bridal gown and making a lay-away payment, Arnold bought her a bouquet of flowers and they went to a nearby bakery that specialized in wedding cakes.

He had readily agreed with her choice of yellow roses as they brought out the color of her eyes, but they couldn't agree on what cream her wedding cake should have.

After much taste testing and haggling, they narrowed the choices down to whip cream with strawberry filling or chocolate mousse with mocha cherry cream filling. Buying both sample cakes, they went to Betty Lu's place. She put the teakettle on and he put the roses in a vase.

The hour grew late and all this talk of weddings made the patient coordinator more than a bit frisky. The two medical facility employees soon tired of feeding each other cake. Filled to the brim, Betty Lu forgot all about her fiancé and invited Arnold to stay over.

Though tired from a night spent listening to his snoring, Holly awoke early to make breakfast for Bryan. When he finally dragged himself into the kitchen, she gave her personal opinion on why he should see a doctor for sleep apnea while he came up with his best arguments on why she should take the day off.

The dedicated nurse was having none of it. She told the doctor she missed too much time the day before while fooling with the various medical facility and Rustic Lodge employees and was determined to get back to work.

Dr. Sorenson, a bona fide member of team Operation AWOL Soldier, was looking to prevent Nurse Shipley from going on a rampage in front of the staff and patients in the psyche ward. There came a point when he knew he'd have to take the brunt of it.

"Sit down Holly. I have something to tell you."

She sat down and Bryan told her all about the former soldiers and how they wanted to help out the AWOL soldier and how Blinky got the long straw and that they wrapped his head in bandages, commandeered an ambulance, etc., etc., etc.

Drinking her coffee, she listened with wonderment at the things soldiers would do for one another.

Finished with the tale, he waited for her response.

"I knew it was Blinky. I couldn't let Russ and his men get away with it so easily. With the crowd they handle, they'd be sneaking all kinds of crazy people up to my ward. I'm going to take my shower and get to work."

Leaving the doctor with a feeling of acute admiration, the nurse left the room.

***

The Sergeant placed Caroline's bags into the trunk of Nathanial's car and wiped a tear from his eye. He had looked in on the boys who were still sleeping. Rosie came out to see her husband and daughter off.

She had tried her best to get her husband to let her in on his plan. It was the first time she heard the term – plausible deniability. He explained the need for her to be able to maintain an appearance of complete surprise and the ability to answer truthfully when Caroline accused her of being involved in whatever it was that was going to take place.

Rosie gave her daughter a heartfelt goodbye and dozens of motherly warnings to be careful. As her mother went on and on Caroline struggled to be released from her death grip.

The head of the family finally pulled the two apart.

The convertible backed down the driveway. Caroline stood up and shouted she would miss her mother and bid her not to worry as she'd be back in a month or two, maybe three.

The father and daughter had a good talk during their ride to the airport. He did his duty in speaking about the rules of travel, how she was to keep identification documents and money with her always.

Since she was going with the man of her dreams, when the Sergeant tried to warn her about falling in love with the romantic young men she would meet during her travels who were seeking to meet a future green card providing wife, Caroline laughed at him and broke the news she was expecting to be engaged by the time she landed back home.

Her dad mumbled something under his breath when he heard that bit of news.

They arrived at the airport and a porter helped with the bags while the Sergeant protectively placed his arm around Caroline's shoulder as they walked into the terminal. Her professor who instigated the trip was waiting for them.

The Sergeant shook his hand, told him it was good to finally meet and how happy he was to know his daughter was traveling with a mature and experienced man of the world.

Caroline's professor turned travel companion had done this trip with a few of his female students and was even socked in the nose by one irate dad. He was extremely happy to be setting out on this journey with the blessing of his protégé's father.

With nothing more to say, father and daughter kissed a final time. The Sergeant wiped a tear from his eye, which touched her heart. He turned to go and didn't look back.

Walking toward the sliding doors, several men and women were on their way in. The Sergeant made an almost undetectable nod of the head as they passed each other.

Caroline was helping her traveling companion with his bags as they walked toward the airline counter. Suddenly, one of the women who entered the door moments before grabbed the girl's arm. She held up an id that described her as a member of Homeland Security. A man from the same office grabbed the professor's arm. Two National Guardsmen and two police officers aimed their weapons at the couple in case they tried to escape.

As they put him in handcuffs, the professor was alarmed to see the chancellor of the college walk through the airport sliding doors.

As they placed handcuffs on her, Caroline shouted for her dad, but he was already on the highway headed back to the medical facility in Nathanial's red convertible.

***

Wally and Randle entered the Eternal Rest Funeral Parlor. It only took them two short hours to get from the medical facility to their hometown. The two men had a fun time speeding along the highway with the ambulance siren and lights blazing. Passing many a police car on patrol, they swore when they got money enough they would purchase a vehicle of this type to have for their very own.

As it was still before hours, the funeral parlor wasn't open yet. With more than enough time to take care of the situation, they entered through the front door, which was never locked, and rolled the dead woman through to the room where the family would gather to pay their respects.

They lifted Bridget off the gurney and were about to place her in the casket.

"I wouldn't do that," said a voice.

The two men being of a superstitious nature, thought it was a ghost and almost dropped the elderly volunteer.

Sally walked up to them.

"Blue's here."

Thinking he was a ghost, they almost dropped Bridget again. Putting her back on the gurney, Wally made sure the attendant was real by socking him in the jaw. As Sally lay on the floor, the two men took at peek at their relative.

"Look how fine he looks," said Blue's cousin.

"We have to get ourselves some fancy duds like that," said Wally with a tear in his eye. "Good to have you home, boy."

With everything in hand, Wally picked Sally up from the floor, Randle latched onto his nose until he woke up. When the attendant came to, he slapped the nose holding hand away. Catching his breath, Sally took a swing at Wally and the three men proceeded to duke it out right then and there. Knocking over several chairs, they were tussling on the ground when they heard a rather loud snort.

That stopped them.

In a bear-hug threesome, they looked around. There was the sound of another snort. It was coming from the woman on the gurney. Her arm moved. The men scrambled to the farthest corner of the room.

They watched as the dead woman rolled off the gurney and onto several of the flower arrangements which broke her fall. Randle being fond of science fiction and creature features was the first to creep over. He touched the woman's arm. She smacked it. He crawled back to his uncle and hid behind him.

A faint hint of recognition came over Sally. He got closer.

"Bridget?"

She opened her eyes.

"She ain't dead," noted Randle who was a keen observer.

"Where am I?"

They helped her into a chair. Sally introduced the two men, which wasn't necessary as she recognized Blue's relatives. After a few demands to know how she came to be where she was, they offered to tell her over breakfast at a nearby eatery.

Being she hadn't eaten since lunchtime yesterday, the elderly volunteer took them up on the offer.

***

The Sergeant was heading towards Rte. 28, just about the time his family, minus Caroline, was getting ready for the day.

Michael Jr. was already on his way to school. When the girl who was giving him a ride, gave him a hello kiss, she took one whiff and told him he smelled just like her dad. He hesitated a moment before asking if that was a good thing. She answered in the affirmative, gave him another kiss, and took off for school.

Rosie was preparing for what awaited her. Wearing ear protectors, she stood on the hallway side of her youngest son's door. Hand on the knob she stood tall.

"You're the staff sergeant of your household. You can do this."

Saying a short prayer like the sports teams do before a big game, she gained her fortitude and opened the door. To her surprise Rory was already up. Actually, he was dressed.

"I'm hungry," said her youngest as he put the right shoe on the wrong foot.

He ran out the room to the kitchen. Rosie took off the ear protectors.

In the next bedroom, Jeremy was tearing the place apart. Opening his underwear drawer, he found not the stylish array of boxes and briefs a rap artist or prison inmate would be proud of, but a belt. His father's belt.

He searched under his bed for the usual stray and found nothing. He looked in the dirty laundry hamper - nothing. He looked in the closet - nothing.

209

Rosie was on her way to the kitchen to make her youngest breakfast when her middle son came charging out of his room screaming at the top of his lungs. Knowing it was her husband's hand at work she put the ear protectors back on.

Jeremy came out of the laundry room, "Where's my drawers?"

No answer.

He yelled at the top of his lungs with a voice that was in the process of changing. It was a high-pitched yell that even rifle range ear protectors could not silence completely.

"What's the matter?" Rosie asked.

"I have no underwear."

Thinking back to her husband's explanation of plausible denial, Rosie questioned her son on just what the heck he was talking about. Jeremy showed her the belt. She went on about remembering the belt and how she bought it for Michael on his thirty-third birthday. She even pointed out the extra notches he made when he had gained a little weight that year.

Jeremy was not interested in how his dad lost the extra pounds by his thirty-fourth birthday and how his mother had to buy him another belt. He was not interested.

"How am I going to school without underwear?"

"Try your brothers," was the mother's simple solution.

Jeremy ran into his room, opened his brother's drawer and put on a pair of his boxers. They fell to the ground.

"Aaaaahhhhhh!"

Seeing how she had to drive him to school, Rosie kept the ear protectors on and poured milk into Rory's cereal bowl.

***

The night shift staff greeted Nurse Shipley with nods of hello and glad to see you's. The soldier patients, who were taking their early morning exercise by walking the hallways, were smiling and greeted the nurse, too.

"What's going on, Constance," Nurse Shipley asked the night nurse.

"It's all Sergeant Delaquot's doing. He's wonderful with the men. I've never seen anything like it."

The day nurse walked the night nurse to the elevator, receiving an update on all that had taken place since she left the ward the afternoon before.

Out in the parking lot, the morgue employee was opening the passenger side door of his car and offered his hand to Betty Lu.

"Thank you, Arnold."

The two walked into the facility hand in hand. They parted ways with a kiss as the patient coordinator had a little business she needed to speak to Donna about.

"Where's Julie?" Betty Lu questioned as she shook the sleeping night operator.

Having slept her shift away, Donna didn't have a clue. They tried calling Julie's home, but there was no answer. As they pondered where she could be, Arnold came back.

"I need to speak to you." He took the patient coordinator aside.

"What's the matter?"

"Blue Morgan's gone."

"I'll be right back," said Betty Lu and she went out the sliding doors.

Louie wasn't at the door when Betty Lu got there, so she let herself in. Russ wasn't behind the bar. The patient coordinator, who never knew the place to be unattended, became suspicious. She looked around and saw Julie and Nathanial. They were tied to chairs.

Betty Lu took the gag out of Julie's mouth and the operator shouted, "Get me loose."

"What happened? Did Russ get robbed? Did killers kill him? Where are Tom, Matt, Blinky and Louie? Did the killers kill them too?" Betty Lu questioned as she undid the ropes.

"It was no robbery and they weren't killed, you old fool."

"Who are you calling an old fool?" Betty Lu shot back.

The two women would have gone hand to hand if it wasn't for Nathanial's moaning. Betty Lu untied the PR while Julie went for the rifle that was kept behind the bar.

Just then, Russ, Louie, Tom and Matt walked in.

After Randle and Wally took off in the ambulance with the dead woman, Tom and Matt reported back to Russ that Blue was gone. They explained how they got a replacement, but in the meantime they would search the hospital and find the wayward Morgan family member, hopefully in time for his funeral.

With Operation Code Blue hitting the biggest snag possible, Russ had shooed all his customers out of the lodge and wanting no interference from the PR and the operator, his men had tied them up.

When they got to the medical facility, the team members walked past Donna who was snoring and went directly to the laundry room. They changed into hospital scrubs, divided the facility floors and began their search.

Tom took the lower level, Louie took the main floor, Russ the second and Matt the third. During the search, Russ called Blinky on his cell phone. The Sergeant's stand-in assured Russ he would do a sweep of the psyche ward and if the missing dead private was found, he would obtain a key from one of the staff and leave him by the elevator.

When Russ was done with his floor, he went to the fourth floor to check. There was no body waiting by the elevator. He gave a thumbs up to Blinky who was looking through the door's window.

The four former soldiers met back at the laundry. It was so early in the morning the staff that did the wash couldn't care less about the four men who were changing back into their clothes. The kitchen staff was just as disinterested as they took that way out of the facility.

The members of Operation Code Blue walked back to the lodge with the intention of planning their next step. Entering the lodge's threshold they realized this was not going to be necessary as Julie Binder was taking charge.

"I want to know where Wally is and I want to know right now," said the operator as she held the gun on them.

***

Rosie was under the gun to get her son to school on time. Jeremy had spent the last hour throwing a tantrum. As his mother yelled at him to get moving, he was kicking and screaming that he couldn't go to school without underwear. He begged his mother to take him to the store to buy some. She hated her son going around with his pants hanging off his butt and stood staff sergeant firm.

He refused to go to school and locked himself in his room. Hearing him smash up the furniture, she decided enough was enough.

Taking the unloaded rifle out of the closet, Rosie screamed, "Open that door!"

"No!"

"I said open that door, boy!"

"No!"

"If I have to shoot you and the lock, so be it."

All went quiet. She cocked the gun. The door opened.

"Don't shoot me!"

His mother lowered the gun, "I'll be waiting in the car."

Later, Jeremy came out the door wearing no gothic make-up, no baseball cap, no pocket protector and no plaid shirt. Just a t-shirt and pants held up with his father's belt.

"I hate you."

"I know."

"I hate dad, too."

"I know son," and she started the car.

After they left the Eternal Rest Funeral Home, Randle, Wally and Sally crossed the street to a local eatery. Being Bridget was weak from hunger, they pushed her on the ambulance gurney. The patrons who were eating their breakfast didn't think much when they wheeled the old woman to a table, picked her up and sat her down.

Bridget, whose last remembrance was rummaging around in the morgue, thoroughly enjoyed the men's story of mistaking her for dead and becoming a stand-in for their relative. Mind you she didn't take to the idea of being buried alive, but seeing how it was their plan to dig her up again when they found the missing private, she saw no reason to get upset about the whole thing.

It was a few short hours before Blue's funeral was to take place. Wally and Randle wanted to do right by the woman they almost buried alive. They invited Bridget and Sally to the affair as the Morgan's always threw a bang-up good time for one of their own and with Blue's mother winning her case against the army, there was sure to be tons of fun things to do.

Being they were there anyway and had no transportation to get home, Sally and Bridget decided to stay and Wally agreed to take them back in the truck after he and Randle returned the ambulance.

***

With his husbandly and fatherly duties done to perfection, the Sergeant was enjoying the countryside at its sunshiny morning best. He had walked out the airport doors and into Nathanial's red convertible knowing his daughter was in the capable hands of various departments of the government whose salary were paid by his tax dollars. Thinking it was money well spent, he enjoyed the breeze that blew his crew cut hair this way and that. His left arm dangled as he maneuvered the steering wheel with his right.

The open road lay before him. Having spent the preceding day yelling at Rory and after a few hours spent bellowing renditions of God Bless America, America the Beautiful, The Star Spangled Banner and The Army Goes Rolling Along, his throat became hoarse and he switched on the radio.

Being a man who liked to stick to his word, the Sergeant was thrilled the straightening out of family matters had gone so smoothly. Promising to be back on the nineteenth, give or take a day or two, and as this was the eighteenth, he had it in his heart to get back by at least 2200 hrs. This would allow him to deliver Nathanial's car, partake of a few house specials and question Russ on the matter of his lower extremity wounds and their connection to his brain's lack of memory, before once again returning to the cradling arms of the medical facility and the US Army.

He figured what had been a forty-eight hour or thereabouts ride to Tuscaloosa would be shortened considerably if there were no over-turned trucks and county fairs along the way and the only stops he made were for lunch, gas and the occasional bladder-emptying stop by the side of the road.

At the medical facility, Dr. Sorenson was making rounds. He checked on his hernia patient and Bobby Wallington's 'not so little Bobby'. Between patients, he got a page from the day nurses who practiced their life saving skills in the ICU.

It seems that the resident physician, after he had been unnecessarily shocked back to life, decided it was time to end the marathon he was on and get some rest. The services of Dr. Sorenson were enlisted to check on the resident physician as the staff was in need of the bed he slept in, and even though they tried several times, they couldn't convince him to give it up.

Nurse Shipley was in the common room with the soldier patients and the entire fourth floor staff including social worker Penny Carlough. They were enjoying the sock puppet show Blinky was presenting.

Mr. Flack insisted his secret serviceman act out the tale of his travails at the lobster and shrimp shipping company, only this time with a better ending. Blinky borrowed two socks and made them up to look like the president and the former vice-president.

All parts to the story were played out and in the newly written end, the vice-president sock puppet took a baseball bat, represented by a toothpick, and he beat the cheating husband with it.

"This is for what you did to your three wives!" said the lobster and shrimp vice-president puppet as he hit the president puppet. "And this if for getting me fired!"

At the end of the show, the social worker was amazed at the administrator's breakthrough. She hugged Mr. Flack who was crying and confessing that that was the way he should have handled things.

Grabbing onto the opportunity, Penny handed him a tissue with the reminder that vengeance is the Lord's work and affirmed he really did the best he could under the circumstances.

***

For the entire ride to the middle school Jeremy grilled his mother on the whereabouts of his underwear and what exactly was her role in what could only be her husband's doing. Rosie was grateful that she could answer honestly. What with dealing with Rory's screaming for most of the previous day, she didn't have a clue what the father of her children had spent his time doing.

Jeremy, without his underwear, was as relentless as Rory without his sleep. The middle Delaquot son wouldn't give up his questioning till his mother swore on the life of all her children that she was innocent of any wrong doing.

Arriving at their destination, the conversation changed to whether there was school at all. Pulling up to the building, they saw the entire student body, faculty, band and some of the parents surrounding the flagpole.

The frazzled mom, who had all the school holidays marked in bright red on the calendar at home so she wouldn't have to get up early on those mornings, thought she might have missed a national holiday. Her son, who had a special pair of red, white and blue underwear, to be worn only on occasions of national importance, started to rant again about his father and the lack of privacy in the Delaquot household.

Embarrassed to face his peers with his pants up, Jeremy would only get out of the car when his mother promised to take him shopping for underwear on the way home. She knew taking her son for underwear would undo the work her husband started, so staying staff sergeant strong she kept her fingers crossed when the promise was given. The student got out of the car and went in search of a group to stand with. Rosie wanted to know what the assembly was observing and took Rory out of the car to find out.

"What's going on Lionel?" she asked of the principal.

"Seeing it's such a fine day, we've decided to hold the school's opening ceremony outdoors. Go ahead Arthur!"

The custodian pulled on the ropes. The band began to play the National Anthem. The old red, white and blue began to rise. At mid-point in the flag raising the crowd began to twitter and then they began to outright laugh.

Pair after pair of boy's underwear, boxes and briefs of all colors and sizes, was lifted into the air. As there was some wind to speak of, they even flapped a bit wildly.

Jeremy turned beet red when he saw his patriotic red, white and blue shorts rising higher than the school building.

He looked around at the group he was standing with. They were all the boys in the dropped drawers group and they were also wearing pants held up by their father's belts with not one pair of exposed underwear among them.

The middle Delaquot son knew it was his dad's hand at work. He had stayed up half the night and still hadn't seen it coming. It was humiliating to see his mother standing with the other moms. They were all laughing and having a good time at their expense.

The student body knew the group that owned these garments; they were snickering and pointing their fingers at the boys. To further make the administration's point, Arthur threw a match into a metal trash barrel. The rest of the boxers and briefs, designer or not, were burned in infamy.

Using a bullhorn to ensure he was heard loud and clear, Principal Thornapple announced to one and all that he had received written permission from the parents that the next time there was a sighting of underwear walking the halls of his school Mad Arthur would confiscate said briefs right then and there and they too would be burned. The custodian then took a fire extinguisher, doused the flames and the principal dismissed the students.

The Sergeant's middle son walked into the building red faced and practically naked as he saw it. Jeremy now knew his dad had an in with the principal, he vowed from that day forward to never be caught with his pants down again.

1200 hrs
MAY 18th

A car was speeding down the Witchitauki highway and Julie Binder was holding a firearm to its driver.

Earlier, after Betty Lu loosened her ropes, the operator was overcome with a fury that caused her to make a beeline for Russ' rifle that he kept behind the bar. She saw the owner and his cohorts walk into the lodge and demanded to know where her true love was. They didn't answer quickly enough, so she fired a bullet into the lodge's ceiling.

Being they were still in the middle of Operation Code Blue and that it had recently taken a seriously wrong turn when they replaced Blue with the dead elderly woman, the former soldiers admitted everything they knew that would not incriminate them. In other words – they circumvented the truth as they filled the explanation with lies.

Having spoken to Mrs. Morgan and finding her to be a hysterical woman, Julie accepted the explanation that Wally and Randle had to get Blue home for the funeral as his grieving mother was going to read them the riot act. They let her know that Wally was sincerely troubled that he had to leave in such a hurried way.

What Julie couldn't accept, and this is where the former soldiers went a little over the line, was when they told the newly engaged Betty Lu not to worry that her fiancé was without a doubt returning to her. Julie jumped on this bit of information and questioned if Wally left word that he was coming back. The former soldiers hesitated. She shot the gun off once more. They ducked in time as the bullet whizzed over their heads.

The angry switchboard operator felt the passion of a woman-scorned rise in her. She declared to one and all that it was her place to be by her new love's side as he buried his nephew. Keeping the rifle trained on Russ, Julie allowed him to make a pitcher of house specials to help her think on how she would get to Wally. She debated the need for taking them all as hostages and as Russ poured her one drink after another, he debated back with his need to keep the lodge open.

Seeing the point that the lodge had never been closed in all its years of operation and there would be medical facility staff in need of a place to go when off duty, Julie agreed to the owner's argument. Louie, Nathanial and Betty Lu would run the lodge and she would only take Russ, Matt and Tom as hostages.

Only mere moments before they got into this hostage situation, Russ was returning with his men from their search of the medical facility for the missing private. When they walked out the sliding doors the leader of former soldier's anger got the better of him. He socked Tom in the nose for coming up with the bright idea of replacing Blue with another stiff when a couple of hundred pounds of rock would do. Then he socked Matt in the nose for not stopping Tom.

As they were stemming the blood flow from their respective noses, Russ explained to the covert operation team members that they would have to close up the lodge and get to Blue's hometown as quickly as possible to stop the funeral.

Walking into the lodge to find Julie behind the bar and holding his rifle wasn't an expected part of the plan, but actually worked out the best for all involved.

Good customer that she was the former soldiers were fond of the switchboard operator and decided to let her have a bit of fun. Before starting out on their journey, Julie, who was feeling no pain due to the house specials, put the rifle down to go to the bathroom. Tom wanted to hide the gun, but Russ thought better. He emptied the bullets and put them in his pocket.

Julie came out of the bathroom, picked up the rifle and ordered the three men to get going. Russ sped along the Witchitauki Highway with the weapon pointed at his head.

Tom and Matt were sitting in the backseat playing eye spy. With several beer and whiskeys spurring them on, the former soldiers were feeling young again and exuberant about partaking in something bigger than the usual every day happenings. They were at the helm of something big. Wanting to play up the hostage scenario, when Julie threatened to shoot their brains out if they made one wrong move, they yelled back that they'd have no problem overtaking her.

Dopes that they were they didn't figure on the scorned operator knowing how to do what she did next. Julie took the butt of the rifle and smacked Tom in the head with it. Matt was so shocked with the unexpected hit his buddy took, he didn't see it coming when she smacked him. The two men slept the rest of the trip. Russ, who knew better than to mess with a woman when her heart was busted, tossed it up to another lesson his men needed to learn and put a heavier foot to the gas pedal.

***

With a remembrance of times recently gone by, and being the place was on his way, the Sergeant made it a point to stop at Grandma Wimpole's Restaurant for lunch. He pulled into the parking lot and saw sitting on the side of the building the Framer's RV. Going inside he was surprised to see the couple working behind the counter.

"Why Sergeant Delaquot, you're back!" said Pansy.

"Good to see you," declared Fred.

The two good-natured vacationers explained the change in their travel schedule while they served up a pulled pork sandwich with a heaping pile of fries and extra pickles to the military man.

"After you left, it took two days for the party to wind down and as we liked this area so much, we chose to extend our visit," related Fred.

Between swallows of one of the best sandwiches he had ever eaten, the Sergeant questioned how they got to be behind the counter.

"Thought we'd be of some help as everyone's gone to a funeral for one of the local boys," explained Fred.

"Poor thing died under tragic circumstances," added Pansy.

"He was one of yours," said Fred.

"Army?" asked the Sergeant.

"Private as I understand it," said Fred.

***

Thanks to the money won in the lawsuit, Mrs. Morgan had the wherewithal to throw a big send off for her son and she was especially happy that the entire community had turned out for the occasion.

Not wanting to take any chances with the mourner's safety, outside the Eternal Rest Funeral Parlor was a row of portable toilets she had delivered especially for the occasion. On the opposite side of the road, bagpipers in kilts were playing alongside a country western band.

Filling the atmosphere with good smells, barbeques were lined up with smoking meat of all kinds. The bar that was Blue's favorite had a table set up where they could serve soft drinks, assorted whiskeys and beer from a keg.

On several tables there was an over abundance of pies and cakes that were supplied by the local ladies. The pies had the added benefit of all sorts of flavors of ice cream provided by the local grocery where Blue had worked during summers off from school.

Besides the townsfolk, the entire Morgan family, all seventy-nine of them, was in attendance. They greeted Wally and Randle with slaps on the back for bringing their tragic relative home at last. When it was explained that Sally and Bridget worked at the medical facility and had taken part in Blue's care during the last six months and that they had made the trip especially to see him off, they were welcomed by the family with open arms.

The same couldn't be said for Julie when she showed up.

With only one thing on her mind, when she and the former soldiers got into town and saw the goings on, the operator forgetting she was holding the rifle, got out of the car, and before the men could stop her, she was walking in the midst of the crowd outside the funeral parlor pointing the gun at one and all and shouting her new love's name.

The big guy was standing at the barbeque trying out some of the ribs and when he heard his name called with that familiar tone, he stopped in mid-bite. Turning around, Wally saw the crowd had parted to let the crazy woman holding a gun through.

Mrs. Morgan, who was downing a beer, stopped when she recognized the loud voice calling for her brother. It was the same irritating sound that answered the phone every time she called the medical facility to inquire about her son.

Blue's mother being a feisty woman, and big like her brother, saw Julie coming. Gun or no gun, she was out to stop the operator from turning her son's funeral into a circus. Mrs. Morgan put down her beer, came out of the crowd, and blocked Julie's path.

The two women looked at each other. Julie didn't need anyone to tell her who was standing before her; the face was a female version of the man she came for.

"Out of my way."

"You want my brother; you'll have to go through me first."

Word got around fast and the crowd who were in the funeral parlor paying their last respects came flowing out. Among them was Randle. His wife was by his side and he was actively trying to avoid his girlfriend who showed up with her husband.

The crowd stepped back to make room as the two women began to circle each other.

"You ain't getting nowhere near my brother."

"Who says so?"

"Put down that gun and I'll show you who."

Julie put the gun down and her dukes up.

"That crazy woman's gonna fight Alicia for you," stated Millard, the town's only barber.

"Ain't that something?" responded Wally as he resumed eating the smoked rib.

"That woman's dynamite," admired Phil, owner of Phil's Rodent Extermination Emporium.

"Pretty too," added Spencer, a Morgan second cousin.

"She a keeper all right," determined Waldo, who was an automotive mechanic and local garage owner.

Seeing it was Julie who had yelled for his uncle, and knowing the power he had over women like her, and as it wasn't the first time he had to help out in a situation such as this, Randle took a place behind the operator. He made eye contact with his uncle, who tossed the rib bone, wiped his hands on his pants and stepped up behind his sister.

Watching on the sidelines was a member of the Morgan clan, a distant relative who lived in Ridleyville and was considered the black sheep of the family. Willie wanted to place odds and get the betting started, but the idea was quickly shot down by the surrounding Morgan's as they were convinced there would be no takers on the stranger as their relation was never beat in hand-to-hand combat.

Russ and Matt took a temporary break from Operation Code Blue. Having never seen this side of the medical facility employee before, they went over and helped themselves to a beer. Being it was his fault they were there, Tom was made designated driver, so he got a soda, which he livened up with three scoops of ice cream.

***

Always having time for those who serve the country he loves, the Sergeant made it a point to pay his respects to the fallen soldier. Finishing with lunch, he changed into his dress uniform which he always carried for times such as this and gave his home address and phone number to Pansy and Fred before saying his goodbyes. Leaving the convertible in Grandma Wimpole's parking lot he walked over to the cemetery, which was across the street and down a ways. Seeing there was no one there yet, he took a seat under a tree and promptly fell asleep.

He was awakened about a quarter hour later by the sound of a rifle shot.

As it was looking to be a long fight, after finishing their drinks, Russ, Tom and Matt took up Operation Code Blue once more. Everyone's eyes were on the two tussling women and no one noticed Tom picking up the rifle. The former soldiers went back to the car. Russ loaded the gun while Tom and Matt looked for the crowbar that was stowed in the trunk.

Skirting the crowd, they proceeded into the funeral parlor. They were prepared to force open a closed casket and were more than shocked to see the fallen member of the armed forces right where he was supposed to be. Tom was about to ask where the old woman was, but the sound of a loud snort beat him to it. They turned around and saw Bridget slumped alongside the Reverend. The pair had their eyes closed.

Tom, recognizing the woman as the one from the morgue that they had put into the back of the ambulance, stepped up close. She snorted again and he jumped back.

"She's alive!" Tom exclaimed.

Russ slapped his employee's head.

"You were going to bury that poor old thing alive?" He slapped Tom a second time.

The former soldiers didn't care how Private Blue Morgan got to be where he was. They were just glad Operation Code Blue was successful in its outcome and officially over. The smell of burning meat wet their appetites and they agreed to attend the festivities before returning home.

To get the ball rolling, Tom woke the Reverend, Matt woke Bridget and Russ stepped outside. The Rustic Lodge owner enjoyed a good fight between two of the opposite sex as much as the next guy, but he had a business to run. When he got clear of the building and the crowd he fired a shot into the air.

"Blue's waited long enough!" he shouted.

"Who is that handsome man with the rifle?" questioned Mrs. Morgan who had her opponent in a headlock.

"That's Russ," answered Julie.

"Is he married?"

"Nope."

"Employed?"

"Owns a bar."

"Would you introduce me?"

"It'd be my pleasure."

Wally and Randle picked the women up off the ground and Mrs. Morgan, who appreciated an even match, escorted Julie to the refreshment table.

***

One and all of the townsfolk said Blue's funeral was the best they ever attended. Mrs. Morgan was congratulated on doing her son proud and many said if Blue had been able to attend, he would have thoroughly enjoyed himself.

There was a good turnout at the cemetery, including Julie, Sally and Bridget representing the medical facility and Russ, Tom, and Matt, the Rustic Lodge.

Besides the Honor Guard, the Sergeant was the only one in uniform in attendance. All the guys the private had a chance to make friends with in his short time in the service were overseas. Mrs. Morgan spotted the soldier in the back of the crowd. Thinking he was a special friend of Blue's she went over personally to escort him to a seat in front.

When the Reverend asked if anyone wanted to say a few words, Mrs. Morgan nudged the Sergeant not to be shy. The AWOL soldier was one to quickly partake of the opportunity to speak when it was called for. He knew he could do justice to the occasion as Fred and Pansy Framer filled him in on the details about Blue and how he came to an untimely demise while in the service of his country.

"Damn," said Russ when he saw Delaquot stand up.

"Damn," said Sally when he saw the escaped psyche ward soldier patient Bed No. 42.

"Damn the army!" shouted the Sergeant and he got the attention of the entire crowd. "If only they had kept their toilet training practices to themselves until Blue had a chance to acclimate himself."

"Amen!" shouted Mrs. Morgan.

"Of course, he got himself killed peeing in the street while on leave. Who was watching out for him and his buddies? I'm asking you?"

The crowd couldn't answer.

"I for one warn my fresh off the bus men and women about the evils of re-toilet training and their need to be aware when they go out in the world again."

"Amen!" yelled Blue's mother.

227

"A mother's training is sacred and should never be taken for granted."

Mrs. Morgan sobbed into a handkerchief.

"I feel very close to this young man, heck, I'm gonna take the chance and say that beyond a doubt, one way or another, he has done me a good turn."

"Truer words were never spoken," said Sally before he shouted, "Amen!"

"And I want to say to all of you young men and women out there who are thinking of serving their country. For safeties sake, when you and your buddies go out on leave make it your business to visit the establishment of former soldiers. They'll watch out for you."

There was not a dry eye between the Rustic Lodge owner and employees.

"That's all I have to say," and the Sergeant sat down.

After a few more words from the Reverend, the 21-gun salute from the Honor Guard and another 15-gun salute from the hunting members of the Morgan family, one and all let Blue get down to the business of being buried and they got down to the business of partying in his honor.

When the cemetery proceedings were over and the crowd was walking away, Russ, Tom, Matt and Sally made their way over to the Sergeant who was glad to see them. The fellows hugged and Russ knowing what day it was, let the others know that Operation AWOL Soldier would be taken up again after they respectfully enjoyed the Morgan family's hospitality.

The Sergeant thoroughly enjoyed watching those he protected during his military career partaking of the soldier's send-off festivities. He couldn't have been more surprised to see Conrad Haney, his wife, plus the five little Haney's serving up one after another of the sugared fried dough to the attending mourners who waited on line. When he stepped up,

Conrad remembered the Sergeant and was kind enough to pack him a bagful of funnel cakes for the road.

While enjoying the circus acrobats as they performed, the Sergeant remembered his momma's words about knowing when to leave and the matter of returning to the medical facility by the promised day of the nineteenth.

He took Russ aside and the leader of the former soldiers got his crew together.

Over beer and ribs, they discussed the next steps of Operation AWOL Soldier. Sneaking Delaquot back into the medical facility so he could change places with Blinky was one. His head would have to be bandaged. As he did a good job with their man who was sent inside, Matt was given that assignment.

The timeline was discussed. With the ambulance siren's blasting and lights blaring and including the time it would take to give the stolen vehicle back, they'd make the facility in just about two and a half hours, three tops.

As he had maintained soberness, Tom was given the assignment to drive the ambulance while Matt would be in back doing his bandaging best. Russ would drive his own car, and seeing the necessity, they made Sally a member of the team. He would have the job of driving Nathanial's car and Bridget back to the lodge.

With the final details set, they synchronized their watches. The operation team members wanted to say their goodbyes to the Morgans and give thanks for a good time before hitting the road. Russ put the nix on that idea as he was a keen observer of women in love and had earlier noticed Mrs. Morgan had her eye set on him.

***

What happened next during Operation AWOL Soldier would be the topic of discussion and fierce debate at the Rustic

Lodge for many years to come. Those who were participants in the covert action and those customers who were made privy while downing their house specials would argue the key points and come to their own conclusions.

Maybe the operation going the way it did was due to not having a former soldier with the rank of captain or major among the team. Maybe it was due to the army never letting those of a lower rank have the experience of sitting in on the planning stages of major covert operations.

Many future customers enjoying house specials would argue these maybes on why the two major components of any stealth operation – planning for the unknown - and the unexpected – were never discussed.

Much like the three wives of the president of the lobster and shrimp shipping company, those who were party to Operation AWOL Soldier, would for years after, ask themselves, "How could we have not known?"

Doing their best to keep from being noticed, especially by Mrs. Morgan and Julie, the members of the operation, as per plan, collected Bridget and Sally. They put the volunteer in the passenger seat of the convertible and instructed Sally to drive like the wind. Russ got into his vehicle. Tom took the driver's seat of the ambulance while Matt and the Sergeant got in back.

In order not to attract attention, the caravan quietly made their way to the nearest highway. As they entered the on-ramp Tom cranked up the siren and the ambulance warning lights blazed. With topped off speeds of ninety miles per hour for the medical vehicle and top speeds of eighty and seventy five miles per hour for the vehicles following, they made the trip to the garage from whence the ambulance was confiscated in about one hour forty-five minutes.

Waiting for the others to show up, Tom, Matt and the Sergeant picked the lock on the gated fence and parked the ambulance in the spot from where it was taken. They were relocking the fence when the two vehicles arrived. Time for a pit stop was taken as those who partook of the keg had bladders that were full to overflowing.

Happy the operation was going smoothly and with the relief that came from relieving themselves, they were ready to make the last leg of their journey. That's when they heard the banging coming from Russ' car. He got the rifle from the back seat and held it on his vehicle as Tom opened the trunk.

"Don't shoot," shouted Randle.

Russ lowered his gun and Tom and Matt helped him out.

"Whatcha doing back there?" was the main question asked by all.

The sound of banging coming from the convertible delayed the answer. Russ had his rifle pointed again as Tom opened the trunk. The men couldn't be more surprised when Wally popped out.

The ambulance returned to its rightful place, the members of the caravan and the two stowaways shifted seats and the automobiles took to the Witchitauki Highway for the final stretch. Riding in the convertible with Sally, the Sergeant and Bridget, Randle explained why he was on the run.

"My girlfriend came to the funeral due to her husband being a childhood friend of Blue's. Wish my cousin had told me that bit of news," Randle sighed. "When my girlfriend saw me kissing my wife, she came over and introduced herself. My wife started yelling at my girlfriend. My girlfriend's husband yelled at my wife saying she was married to an idiot. That didn't set well with my Hazel."

Sally and the Sergeant could see the woman's point. Bridget was of the opinion that all men are dogs, married men eventually cheat, and as this was the best result of thousands of years of evolvement, Randle's wife should have sucked it up.

Blue's cousin continued, "After we pulled my wife off my girlfriend's husband, she lit into me about my cheating ways. I faked being sick to my stomach, which for the most part I

231

was, and made a beeline for one of those deluxe on the street toilets. I hid out there until I saw my wife helping herself to some smoked ribs, my girlfriend helping herself to pie, and her husband arm wrestling with Cousin Nero. Figuring I'd better leave town till things cooled down and not wanting to make use of my uncle's truck, I jumped into the vehicle closest to the merry-go-round my aunt rented for the funeral."

One car lane over, Wally was telling his tale to the former soldiers.

"Julie told my sister we were a match made in heaven. As she could hold her own in a fight, Alicia agreed that marriage was the way to go, and being the Reverend was handy, all the relatives gathered and there was plenty of food and drink, now was as good a time as any. That's when I knew it was time to hightail it out of there. I don't know whether it was my sister or Julie who slashed the tires on my truck. I figured it'd be better to jump in on someone else's ride. I chose this car cause red's my favorite color."

Being they only bought used cars made in America, Russ, Tom and Matt agreed on his choice.

***

It was about the time Julie was enjoying her fourth beer that she realized her big man was gone and that Russ, his employees and his car were nowhere to be found. She went back and told Wally's sister that she had been left standing at the altar.

Alicia Morgan was having none of that. One look at Russ firing his rifle and taking charge of the funeral, she had set her sights on him.

Not one to have her time wasted while a man came to the same conclusion, Blue's mother had already made up her mind that there was going to be a double wedding. Her husband-to-be had made his escape while she was changing from the sequined gold dress she reserved for funerals for something more suitable for a bride.

Grabbing Julie by the hair, Alicia dragged her over to the table where members of the Honor Guard were enjoying refreshments. Wanting to be of service to the kin of a fallen soldier, they agreed to take the two by helicopter to the destination of their choice.

Hazel, who was done fighting with her husband's girlfriend and her husband, couldn't find Randle and knew that wherever Wally was he was. Cooling down with a whiskey and soda, the bartender told her Julie and Alicia were going in search of their future husbands.

The helicopter was taking off; Hazel jumped onto one of its landing skids. A member of the honor guard who had been bumped from his seat by the two ladies in search of their men, signaled to the pilot and a member of the honor guard who hadn't lost his place in the helicopter pulled her in.

0000 hrs
MAY 19th

Three hours and forty-six minutes into the ending of Operation AWOL Soldier is when the unexpected took place.

At precisely 0000 on the day he promised to be back, give or take a day or two, the Sergeant walked through the Rustic Lodge doors accompanied by Russ, Tom, Matt, Bridget, Sally, Randle and Wally.

Alicia Morgan, Julie, Hazel Morgan, Betty Lu, Nathanial, and Louie Dombrowski were waiting for them.

That's when all hell broke loose.

All parties to the recent events were arguing and some were throwing punches when Russ walked silently behind the bar. He methodically made up two large pitchers of house specials, set up a row of glasses and poured the contents into them.

When he was ready, Russ fired one shot into the air. He downed his drink and saw to it that everyone finished theirs before he gave marching orders.

"Mrs. Morgan…"

"Call me Alicia."

"Alicia, you are the best woman wrestler I have ever seen in my entire life. Now that your boy is settled in the hereafter, why don't you come work for me?"

"I'd like to marry you."

"We'll talk about that at a later time."

She agreed on both matters.

"Betty Lu," Russ continued. "I want you to meet Randle's better half."

As his wife and fiancé shook hands, Randle backtracked towards the door and into the body of Arnold Manheim, the medical facility morgue employee, who was walking in.

"Oh, there you are honey," cooed Betty Lu.

She walked towards the two men. Randle held his breath. When Betty Lu latched onto the arm of the recent arrival, he exhaled.

"Randle I can't marry you," declared Betty Lu.

"What do you mean you can't marry me?"

Before Randle's wife could fully grasp the situation, and before Betty Lu could answer her hurt ex-fiancé's question, Arnold spoke up.

"You're hurting me."

The patient coordinator let up on her grip. She gave Randle a goodbye kiss and the two walked out the door.

"Of all the fickle women in the world, I had to get engaged to her," said the jilted man.

Tom and Matt held his wife back while Russ poured Blue's cousin another house special and got back to the business at hand.

"Randle, your engagement is over. Take my car, go home and settle things with your wife and your girlfriend."

Blue's cousin took the keys from Russ and as he led his wife to the door, she clocked him.

"Wally...," said Russ.

"Yes."

"You won't find a better woman than Julie Binder."

The operator smiled up at the big man.

"I agree," he said and kissed her.

Julie invited her future husband and his sister to stay at her place and they left.

"Sally, it's time for you to take Bridget home," said Russ.

The attendant walked the elderly volunteer out the door.

"Nathanial, the keys to your car fell out of your pocket." Russ tossed them to the PR. "You're got work in the morning, time to go home and get some shuteye."

235

Nathanial said his goodnights. Russ turned to the register. He hit a key that opened the drawer, took something out, and turned back to those who were left waiting.

"How'd the family business go?" Russ asked the Sergeant.

"My girl was arrested by Homeland Security. She should be home in bed by now. My oldest boy has all the makings of becoming a fine man. My middle son is done flying by the seat of his pants. And my youngest has seen the light of day."

"And your wife?"

"I believe I left her with more than a fond memory," smiled the Sergeant.

"May I see your arm, Delaquot?"

The Sergeant placed his right elbow on the bar. Russ placed a brand new identification bracelet made especially by Mac Treeter around the AWOL soldier's wrist. The Rustic Lodge owner made another pitcher of house specials and served them to Matt, Tom, Louie and the Sergeant.

He poured one for himself and raised his glass, "Good to have you back."

The team members and the Sergeant clinked glasses. As they discussed the day's events, Russ took the pitcher, came out from behind the bar and walked to the booth in the back, in the corner, in the dark where Nurse Shipley was enjoying the attentions of Dr. Sorenson.

He poured the doctor another drink. "Your soldier patient Bed No. 42 is here."

"Thank you, Russ. Bryan, I have a little business to take care of."

"I'll be waiting, doll."

Russ went behind the bar. Nurse Shipley went up to her patient.

"Can I escort you back, Michael?"

"That would be my pleasure."

She took his arm.

"Would you like some funnel cake?" inquired the Sergeant as they walked out the door.

***

As the nurse and her patient walked to the medical facility, Russ called his man inside. After hanging up, Blinky made sure his roommate was sleeping peacefully.

"I'm going to miss you, buddy."

He went into the bathroom to wait.

The locked ward was quiet. Nurse Shipley escorted the Sergeant into Room 423. He got out of his clothes and back into Bed No. 42. She knocked gently on the bathroom door and Blinky, no longer covered in bandages, came out.

The former soldier and the soldier patient exchanged a thumbs up. Then Blinky escorted the nurse out the locked door, down the elevator, through the lobby, past Donna who was sleeping at the switchboard, across the parking lot to the lodge and back to her date.

The sun rose on the morning of the nineteenth on a back to business as usual sort of day. Penny Carlough spoke to the attending psychiatrist about Mr. Flack's amazing breakthrough. Upon awakening, the administrator was feeling more chipper than he had felt in a very long time and after meeting with the social worker, he was released. He said goodbye to his roommate and got back to his office.

Dr. Sorenson came up to the fourth floor to personally remove the bandages from Michael A. Delaquot's head. Nurse Shipley was standing by.

"Now that things have gotten back to normal, why don't you and I take a much needed vacation," said the doctor as he worked.

"Hawaii?"

"I always wanted to get married under a waterfall."

"You're a terrible romantic," said the nurse.

"Don't I know it," replied the doctor as the final bandage fell to the wayside. "There you go; you're free to get back to the military machine."

"Actually my enlistment is up in two months. Mind if I wait them out here?" questioned the Sergeant.

"I don't see why not. Do you have a problem with that, Nurse Shipley?"

"None at all," she replied.

EPILOGUE

While the Sergeant waited out his final days in the military, there were changes in the medical facility and Rustic Lodge staffs.

Betty Lu and Arnold resigned their positions. They married and opened a wedding planning/funeral arrangement business of their very own.

When Blinky heard about the opening, he applied for the position of patient coordinator. During his interview with Mr. Flack, the administrator recognized something familiar about Blinky's blinking eyes, which gave him a great amount of security that he was hiring the right man for the job.

The former soldier and now former Rustic Lodge employee had found the career he always wanted and quickly became a favorite among the staff. Blinky took it upon himself to enlarge his position and when he wasn't seeing to new arrivals, he could be found on the fourth floor working with the soldier patients.

After marrying Wally, Julie stayed at her switchboard. Her husband took Blinky's old position and Russ, still unable to commit to marriage, gave his sister a job serving behind the bar and as bouncer when the former soldiers and Wally wanted time off. Alicia Morgan was happy with the arrangement.

These two recent additions to the lodge's employee roster upped the business tenfold. Having relatives that worked in a bar was a coup the Morgan clan could appreciate. They made the Rustic Lodge a favorite spot to stop while on vacation. Seeing how well their aunt had made out with her former soldier boyfriend, the numerous Morgan nieces made it a point to visit often. It didn't take long for Tom, Matt and Louie to wed into the family.

Randle and his wife reconciled their problems. Glad that her husband was cheating with a woman whose husband wouldn't let the two get carried away, she agreed to his seeing his girlfriend once a week instead of the two he had previously partook of.

Holly and Bryan took their vacation to Hawaii. While standing under a waterfall the two were wed. When they came back to work, the medical facility staff threw a reception for them. The party was thrown at the Rustic Lodge and Betty Lu and Arnold's new company was hired to do the catering honors.

The male nurse eventually felt well enough to get back to work. Upon his return he met with Mr. Flack, who went over his record and suggested a change in his position.

Due to his own recent breakdown and breakthrough, the administrator had a keen awareness of his employee's nervous system and the toll it had recently taken. The male nurse was promoted to Arnold's position and from the first day found working in the morgue soothing to the nerves.

Sally joined the ranks of those men who only had one date with Rhonda Blisnick. Though she had a beautiful body, it wasn't worth that much listening to get to it. He also gave up his secret meetings with Mildred Harrington as the strain of always looking out for her husband Stan was wearing thin.

The attendant made it a point to reform and kept his wandering eye directed mainly at Nurse Happenstance from the second floor, Constance Blake, night nurse on the fourth floor, Nurse Honoria Cantone, who delivered meds and Nurse Cheryl Chelswick who continued to seek out soldiers with those excrement-inducing tools of hers.

Nathanial hooked up with Mac Treeter. When Mac's book – If You Love My Computer So Much, How Come You Can't Love Me - became a bestseller, Hollywood came calling about a screenplay.

Mac was busy on the road promoting the book, so he hired the PR to collaborate on the script. Nathanial kept his medical facility position, but now instead of spending his working hours drinking he could be seen at the lodge typing away on a laptop as he sat at a table.

When the last two months of the Sergeant's duty to his country were up, Russ threw him a little going away party. Michael had made himself useful during his final days in service, and all the medical facility staff that weren't on duty showed up to wish him well.

The former soldier's return home was a surprise to the Delaquot family as he kept his plans not to re-enlist top secret.

"The school district offered me a job," he explained to his brood when he appeared at the door.

Rosie cried over the return of her husband to civilian life and as she wiped the tears from her eyes she broke the news that she was pregnant.

All and all, the former soldier was happy to see that his previous trip to straighten out the lives of his children had not been a waste. It also did his middle-aged male ego good to know that even though he was losing his hair, at least his 'little Michael' wasn't shooting blanks.

As for his children, Caroline, while being held by homeland security, had to spend several hours listening to the pitiful tears of her ex-professor after the chancellor told him he no longer had a position with the university.

She was eventually released to Lion and Mad Arthur who were waiting outside. On the ride home, as secretly instructed by her father, they gave a talk about the points of getting a good education. The next day she went back to college and signed up for the next semester.

Sticking to only one kind of deodorant whose scent reminded them of their fathers, Michael Jr. received phone calls from girls at all hours of the day and night, which eventually drove his family crazy.

Needing a place for Rory so the new baby could have its own room, when Michael Jr. graduated high school they encouraged him to get a place of his own. To his parent's surprise he had already enlisted in the Navy, as it was his secret life goal to see the world from a whale's point of view. He found basic training to be a lot like home, and passing through with flying colors, was quickly assigned to duty on a submarine.

Jeremy never did drop his draws again for the sake of fashion. To his parent's delight, he found a click they could relate to - the kids who just went about the business of going to school and getting an education.

Rory stayed up all day every day and when he went off to school in the fall, his mother who was getting larger by the day, was exceedingly grateful.

Michael A. Delaquot became chief of security for the Tuscaloosa school district. His presence was felt as he walked the hallways using the same tactics he used on service men and women. Lion received national attention and high honors for his student's enforced dress codes, attendance and jump in student grades.

The former soldier was especially proud of helping to put the fear of Mad Arthur back in the children and on mac and cheese days, the three former students enjoyed a lunch together in the school cafeteria.

Lastly, regarding the question of Mr. Flack's sexuality.

Being they had men of their own, Betty Lu and Julie let the matter drop. Donna didn't give it a second thought as she was consumed with the mystery of whether or not the hot dogs served by the kitchen were kosher.

One day, not long after being mistaken for dead, Bridget went to see the administrator about working fewer hours. When she knocked on the door there was no answer. With the intention of leaving a note, she let herself in.

To her surprise, Mr. Flack and social worker, Penny Carlough, were getting up close and personal on a new leather couch. The entangled couple was about to get into an upright position when the elderly volunteer told them not to bother.

She stated why she had come, the administrator agreed. On her way out, Bridget picked up the picture of the woman and children from his desk.

"I don't think you'll be in need of this anymore" and she dropped the picture, frame and all, into the trashcan.

"Thanks Mom," said the administrator and he got back to business.